Cheers for AJ Pearce and DEAR MRS. BIRD

"A joy from start to finish. *Dear Mrs. Bird* is as funny as it is heart-warming."

—John Boyne, author of *The Heart's Invisible Furies*

"I relished every moment of *Dear Mrs. Bird.* What a joy! Hilarious, heartwarming, and unutterably charming."

—Jennifer Ryan, author of *The Chilbury Ladies' Choir*

"Charming and funny."

—*New York Post*

"Vividly evocative of wartime life . . . A very English tribute to the women of the home front."

—*Kirkus Reviews*

"Fans of Jojo Moyes will enjoy Pearce's debut, with its plucky female characters and fresh portrait of women's lives in wartime Britain."

—*Library Journal*

"Set against a backdrop of war-torn London, this is a charming and heartfelt novel. Pearce brings to life a tale of true friendship, and how love will outlast even the most challenging times."

—*Booklist*

"Full of as much pluck and grit as its protagonist."

—*BookPage*

"Clever . . . The novel has a wonderfully droll tone, a reminder of the exuberance of youth even under dire circumstances. Headlined by its winning lead character, who always keeps carrying on, Pearce's novel is a delight."

—*Publishers Weekly*

"Emmeline Lake is the most endearing character to emerge from the world of British fiction since Bridget Jones. She's funny, she's indefatigable, and she faces the worst of circumstances with the pluckiest of resolves. You cannot help but love her."

—Kimmery Martin, author of *The Queen of Hearts*

"The sweetest, most uplifting, lovely book about courage, friendship, love."

—Marian Keyes, author of *The Break*

"Books that make you shake with laughter and sob with tears are rare. I gulped this one down but didn't stop thinking about it for a long time."

—Katie Fforde, author of *A Secret Garden*

"Utterly charming and helplessly funny."

—Jenny Colgan, author of *The Bookshop on the Corner*

DEAR MRS. BIRD

– A Novel –

AJ PEARCE

SCRIBNER
New York London Toronto Sydney New Delhi

For Mum and Dad.

Scribner
An Imprint of Simon & Schuster, Inc.
1230 Avenue of the Americas
New York, NY 10020

Originally published in Great Britain in 2018 by Picador

First Scribner trade paperback edition May 2019

Interior design by Jill Putorti

Manufactured in the United States of America

10 9 8 7 6 5 4 3

Library of Congress Cataloging-in-Publication Data

Names: Pearce, A. J . (Amanda-Jane) author.
Title: Dear Mrs. Bird : a novel / A J Pearce.
Description: New York : Scribner, 2018.
Identifiers: LCCN 2018010911 (print) | LCCN 2018014770 (ebook) | ISBN 9781501170089 (eBook) | ISBN 9781501170065 (hardback) | ISBN 9781501170072 (trade paperback)
Subjects: LCSH: Advice columnists—Fiction. | Female friendship—Fiction. | World War, 1939–1945—England—London—Fiction. | BISAC: FICTION / Historical. | FICTION / Coming of Age. | FICTION / Humorous. | GSAFD: Historical fiction | War stories
Classification: LCC PR6116.E675 (ebook) | LCC PR6116.E675 D33 2018 (print) | DDC 823/.92—dc23
LC record available at https://lccn.loc.gov/2018010911

ISBN 978-1-5011-7006-5
ISBN 978-1-5011-7007-2 (pbk)
ISBN 978-1-5011-7008-9 (ebook)

LONDON

December 1940

Chapter 1

AN ADVERTISEMENT IN THE NEWSPAPER

When I first saw the advertisement in the newspaper I thought I might actually burst. I'd had rather a cheerful day so far despite the Luftwaffe annoying everyone by making us all late for work, and then I'd managed to get hold of an onion, which was very good news for a stew. But when I saw the announcement, I could not have been more cock-a-hoop.

It was a quarter past three on one of those wretched December afternoons when the day seemed to start getting dark before it had quite made up its mind to be light, and even with two vests and a greatcoat on, it was impossible to get warm. Sitting on the top deck of the number 24 bus, I could see my breath if I huffed.

I was on my way home from my job as a secretary at Strawman's Solicitors and looking forward to a sit-down before my overnight shift on the fire-station telephones. I had already read every word of *The Evening Chronicle*'s news pages and was now looking at the horoscopes, which I didn't believe in but thought worth a go just in case. For my best friend Bunty it said, "You will be in the money soon enough. Lucky animal: polecat," which was promising, and for me, "Things may pick up eventually. Lucky fish: cod," which in comparison was rather a dud.

And then I saw it, under "Situations Vacant," squeezed between a position for Jam Boilers (no experience necessary) and a Mature Supervisor at an overalls factory (references preferred).

JUNIOR WANTED
Part-time Junior required at
Launceston Press Ltd., publishers of
The London Evening Chronicle.
Must be capable, enthusiastic hard worker
with 60 wpm typing/110 wpm shorthand.
Letters soonest to Mrs. H. Bird,
Launceston Press Ltd., Launceston House,
London EC4.

It was the best job I had ever seen in my life.

If there was anything I wanted most in the world (other, of course, than for the war to end and Hitler to die a quite grisly death), it was to be a journalist. Or to be precise, what people in the know referred to as a Lady War Correspondent.

For the last ten years—ever since I'd won a trip to the local newspaper as my prize for writing a quite dreadful poem when I was twelve—I had dreamt of a journalistic career.

Now my heart beat like anything, thumping through the vests and the greatcoat and threatening to leap right out and onto the lady in the next seat. I was jolly grateful for the job at Strawman's, but I was desperate to learn how to be a reporter. The sort of person who always had a notebook in hand, ready to sniff out Political Intrigue, launch Difficult Questions at Governmental Representatives, or, best of all, leap onto the last plane to a far-off country in order to send back Vital Reports of resistance and war.

At school my teachers had told me to simmer down and not have such excitable aspirations, even if English was my best subject. They stopped me writing to the Prime Minister about his Foreign Policy for the school magazine as well. It had been a dispiriting start.

Since then I had persevered, but finding a job when I had almost no experience had proved tricky, especially as I had set my heart on working for a newspaper in London's Fleet Street. Although in general an optimist, even I didn't think three summer holidays writing for *The Little Whitfield Gazette* was going to get me to Berlin.

But now here was my chance.

I examined the advert again, wondering if I might make the grade.

Capable

That was me, even if I wasn't sure what they wanted me to be capable of.

Enthusiastic

I'd say. I was very nearly shouting like a mad person on the bus.

Hard worker

I would sleep on the office floor if that's what it took.

I couldn't wait to apply.

I rang the bell to get off at the next stop and at the jaunty ping the bus began to slow down. I grabbed my handbag, gas mask, and the onion, shoved the newspaper under my arm, and hurried downstairs double quick, managing to leave one of my gloves behind in the rush.

"Thank you," I shouted at the conductress, narrowly avoiding flattening her as I leapt off the back of the bus.

It hadn't quite come to a halt next to where Boots the Chemist was still open despite having had all its windows blown out the week before last, but I jumped onto what remained of the pavement and began to head towards home.

Boots wasn't the only shop to have taken a biff during the raids. The whole street had had a rotten time of it. The grocer's was now little more than half a wall and some rubble, four of the flats next door had been completely bombed out, and there was just a big gap where Mr. Parsons' wool shop had been. Pimlico may still have had its chin up, but it hadn't been without loss.

Hurdling craters, I ran across the street, slowing down as I called a hello to Mr. Bone the newsagent ("With my name you'd think I'd be a butcher!"), who was rearranging a stack of papers outside his shop. He had his warden's overalls on already and blew on his fingers to keep warm.

"Afternoon, Emmy," he said between puffs. "Have you got the early edition? Lovely picture of Their Majesties on the front page." He smiled brightly. Despite everything the war had done to him, Mr. Bone was the most cheery man I knew. It didn't matter how horrible the news was, he always pointed out something nice. "No, don't stop—I can see you're in a bit of a rush."

Usually I would stay to chat about the day's news. Mr. Bone sometimes gave me back issues of newspapers or *Picture Post* if someone had reserved one but forgotten to collect it, even if he was meant to send them back to the publisher, but today I just had to get home.

"Page two, Mr. Bone," I shouted gratefully. "*The Chronicle* needs a Junior. I think this might be the one!"

Mr. Bone was terrifically supportive of my dream to become a Lady War Correspondent, even if he did worry about my wanting to go behind enemy lines, and now he broke into an even bigger smile and waved a copy of the evening paper in triumph.

"That's the spirit, Emmy," he shouted. "Best of luck. I'll save you today's *Times*."

I yelled a thank-you and waved my free hand wildly as I ran on to the end of the road. A few minutes more and then a sharp right, avoiding two elderly ladies who were showing great interest in Walter the hot potato man, most probably because of the warmth, and then past the tearooms to home.

Bunty and I shared a flat on the top floor of her granny's house in Braybon Street. If there was an air raid, it could be a mad dash downstairs to the Anderson shelter in the garden, but we were used to it by now so it didn't worry us unduly, and we were awfully lucky to live there for free.

I threw open the front door, rushed across the tiled hallway and up the stairs.

"BUNTY," I shouted, hoping she might hear me from three floors up. "You'll never guess what. I've got the best ever news."

By the time I made it to the top of the stairs, Bunty had appeared from her bedroom, wearing her dressing gown and wiping sleep out of her eyes. She was working nights as a secretary at the War Office but of course had to be very tight-lipped about exactly what that involved.

"Have we won the war?" she said. "They didn't say anything at work."

"Only a matter of time," I said. "No, but look, next best thing."

I shoved the newspaper into her hand.

"Jam Boiler?"

"No, you idiot. Underneath."

Bunty grinned and scanned the page again, her eyes widening as she saw the advertisement.

"Oh my LORD." Her voice got louder with every word. "EMMY, THIS IS YOUR JOB."

I nodded violently.

"Do you think so? Really? It is, isn't it?" I said, not making any sense.

"Of course it is. You're going to be marvellous."

Bunty was the most loyal friend in the world. She was also tremendously practical, and leapt into action with immediate effect.

"You need to write to them today. Be the first in line. Mr. Strawman will give you a reference, won't he? And Captain Davies at the station. Oh goodness—will you still be able to do your shifts there?"

As well as my day-time position at the solicitors, I had joined the Auxiliary Fire Service as a volunteer before the start of the Blitz. My brother, Jack, had been flying and fighting like mad and it was high time I pulled my weight too. Bunty's boyfriend, William, was a full-time fireman on B Watch and when he suggested volunteering as a telephone operator at Carlton Street fire station, it sounded ideal. I would work three nights a week and fit it in around my secretarial job. An interview with the station's Captain Davies, a medical to make sure I wasn't about to conk out, and there I was. Smart navy blue uniform with gleaming buttons, stout black shoes, and as proud as punch in my cap with its AFS badge.

Bunty and I had known William since we were children, and when I joined the Service our village newspaper had come up to London and taken a picture of the three of us. They printed it with the headline "Little Whitfield to the Rescue" and made it sound as if William and Bunty and I were responsible for keeping the entire city safe and the War Office going, all on our own. They'd mentioned my fiancé, Edmund, too, which was lovely, as he was from Little Whitfield as well, even if they did slightly imply he was in charge of half the Royal Artillery, which Edmund said was rather a stretch. I'd sent him the cutting and it had given him a good laugh. It was nice that the paper had talked about us all. It made it feel like old times, before the war got in the way and Edmund got sent halfway round the world.

Within two weeks of my joining the Fire Service, the Germans had started having a go at London and I was pleased to be useful in some way. My friend Thelma on B Watch said that even if I couldn't be a Lady War Correspondent just yet, at least I was doing my bit.

"Oh good, it's part-time," said Bunty, reading the advert again and answering her own question. She had stopped shouting now and become deadly earnest. "Honestly, Emmy," she said. "This could be your big chance."

We looked at each other for a moment, considering its enormity.

"I bet you're right up to date on Current Affairs," she said. "They'll be ever so impressed."

"I don't know, Bunts," I said, suddenly nervy. "They'll have awfully high standards, even for a Junior. Could you test me?"

We headed into the living room, where two piles of magazines and three scrapbooks of news cuttings were balancing precariously on the coffee table. I took off my hat and reached into my bag, pulling out the notebook I always carried Just In Case and then flicking through to the back where I had written APPENDIX in large red letters and then MEMBERS OF THE WAR CABINET on the next line.

I handed it to Bunty, who had plonked herself on the sofa.

"I'll pretend to interview you," she said, pointing at the least comfortable chair in the room. "And I shall be very stern. First off, who's Chancellor of the Exchequer?"

"Sir Kingsley Wood," I said as I unbuttoned my coat and sat down. "That's easy."

"Well done," said Bunty. "All right then, Lord President of the Council? Do you know, I can't wait for you to start. Your parents are going to be so pleased."

"Sir John Anderson," I said, answering the question. "Steady on though, I haven't got the job yet. I hope Mother and Father will be happy about it. They'll probably worry about my having to do dangerous things."

"But they'll pretend they're absolutely fine," said Bunty. We both grinned. Bunty knew my parents almost as well as I did. Our fathers had been friends in the Great War and she was very much part of the family.

"Ask me a really hard one," I said.

"Righto," said Bunty, and then stopped. "Oh, I've just thought. What do you think Edmund will say? I reckon he'll have a blue fit," she added, before I could answer.

I wanted to jump to his defence, but Bunty did have a point. Edmund and I had been seeing each other for ages and been engaged for the last eighteen months. He was wonderful—clever and thoughtful and caring—but he didn't exactly applaud my hopes of a career in newspapers. Sometimes he could be a bit of a stick-in-the-mud.

"He's not that bad," I said, being loyal. "I'm sure he'll be pleased."

"And you'll take the job even if he isn't," added Bunty with confidence.

"Crikey, yes," I said. "If I'm offered it." I loved Edmund but I wasn't going to be a doormat about things.

"I do so hope they'll give you the job," said Bunty, crossing her fingers. "They have to."

"Can you imagine? A Junior at *The Evening Chronicle*." I stared into space, seeing myself tearing around London in a taxi, poised for a scoop. "The start of a Journalistic Career."

"Good for you!" said Bunty earnestly. "Will you specialise as a Lady War Correspondent, do you think?"

"Oh yes, I hope so. I shall wear trousers, and after we've won the war I will save up for my own car and Edmund and I can rent a flat in Westminster, and I shall probably smoke and spend my evenings at the theatre or saying droll things at the Café de Paris."

Bunty looked enthusiastic. "I can't wait," she said, as if we were booking it in for the week after next. "If Bill doesn't ask me to marry him, I might pursue a career in politics."

Before war broke out Bunty's boyfriend had been studying to become an architect. He'd planned to qualify and start earning some money before they got engaged.

"Oh, Bunts, that's a splendid idea," I said, impressed. "I didn't realise you were interested in that sort of thing."

"Well, I'm not terribly, not yet anyway. But I'm sure lots of MPs will want a rest after we've won, and I've always liked the idea of being on the wireless."

"Good thinking. And people will respect you as you've worked at the War Office."

"But I shall never speak of it."

"Of course."

Things had really perked up. I was going to be a journalist and Bunty was going to be on the BBC.

"Right," I said, getting up. "I'm going to write my application letter and then go down to the station and try and see Captain Davies. I'm not sure how being a volunteer telephone operator is going to get me a job at *The Evening Chronicle*, but it can't do any harm."

"Rubbish," said Bunty. "It's perfect. If you can keep answering phones in the middle of Hitler trying to blow us all up, you'll be absolutely top-notch when you're a Lady War Correspondent under fire. William says you're the pluckiest girl on the watch and you didn't even turn a hair when Derek Hobson came back in from a job really bashed up."

"Well, I am first-aid monitor," I said. I didn't really want to think about it. You didn't make a fuss about that sort of thing, but it had been a horrible night and Derek was still off on leave.

Bunty picked up the newspaper again. "You're jolly plucky," she said. "And you're going to be smashing at your new job. Now, you'd better get on," she said, handing the paper to me. "It says 'letters soonest' . . ."

"Honestly," I said, taking it from her and going a bit glassy-eyed. "I can't believe this might actually come true."

Bunty grinned and said, "You just wait."

I picked up my bag, took out my best fountain pen, and started to write.

Chapter 2

MR. COLLINS, FEATURES AND EDITOR AT LARGE

A week after the newspaper advertisement, I was trying terrifically hard to remain calm. Having taken Being Up To Date With The News to an unprecedented level of mania since writing my letter to Mrs. H. Bird, I was actually on my way to an interview at *The London Evening Chronicle*.

Bunty had continued to test me to a point of interrogation, and when I told my family and the B Watch girls, everyone had become both enormously excited and quite worryingly overconfident about the prospect of my getting the job. I had written to tell Edmund about the interview, and while it was far too soon to have heard back from him, I had lots of other support. The previous day I'd finished my shift at the fire station to cries of Good Luck from the girls and shouts of Hold The Front Page and Go Get 'Em, Kid, from William and the boys in a spirited attempt to sound like newspaper people you see in the films. It was lovely of them all and I felt as if half of London—and all of Little Whitfield—were behind me.

Today, London was operating under a low and dreary grey sky, the sort that looked like a giant boy had flung off his school jumper and accidentally covered up the West End. Braving the cold, I was wearing a smart blue single-breasted serge suit, my very best shoes, and a little black tilt hat I had borrowed from Bunty. I hoped I might look both businesslike and alert. The sort of person who could sniff out a scoop and get the measure of it in a moment. The sort of person who was not feeling as if her heart might positively explode.

I had the day off work and even though it would have taken less than an hour to walk, I had caught two buses so that I wouldn't get all windblown and turn up looking a scruff. Having arrived horribly early, I stood outside Launceston House, feeling nervous as I stared up at the huge art deco building in front of me.

That I might work *here*? It was a dizzying thought.

As I tipped my head back, holding onto Bunty's hat with one hand and clutching my handbag in the other, I was already slightly unbalanced when a very cross voice boomed, "Quick sticks there, no one likes a slow coach."

A substantial lady had come out of the building and was heading towards me in what looked like a man's fedora hat. A short pheasant's feather on the brim gave it a country air unusual for town, while another part of the dead bird had joined forces with a piece of rabbit to make a smart brooch on the lapel of her coat. She reminded me of my Aunty Tiny, who had gone on her first grouse shoot at three and been blasting things out of a hedgerow ever since.

"I'm so sorry," I said. "I was just . . ."

The lady grimaced and swept past in a cloud of carbolic soap.

". . . looking."

As I watched her head purposefully across the road, I had the oddest feeling of being at school. Any minute now a bell would ring for PE.

I shook the feeling off. I was here for a job working on Serious News about Vitally Important Things so I should jolly well buck up and go in. Taking a deep breath, I looked at my watch for the hundredth time, then walked up the wide marble steps and through the revolving door.

Inside, the entrance hall was very grand and almost as cold as outside in the street. The walls were covered with huge portraits of grim-faced men as two hundred years of publishers looked with oil-painted disdain at a young woman in a borrowed hat dreaming of becoming a Correspondent. Any second now one of them would tut.

Hoping I didn't slip on the polished floor, I walked over to the walnut reception desk.

"Good morning. Emmeline Lake, here to see Mrs. Bird, please. It's for an interview."

The young woman on the desk gave me a sympathetic smile.

"Fifth floor, Miss Lake. Take the lift to the third, go left down the corridor, up the stairs for two flights, and along to the double doors when you get there. Just go straight through. There won't be anyone to let you in."

"Thank you," I said, smiling back. I hoped everyone here was this nice.

"Fifth floor," she said again. "Jolly good luck."

Bolstered by her helpfulness and almost forgetting the disconcerting lady on the steps, I joined two middle-aged gentlemen in large coats who were waiting for the lift and arguing about the Prime Minister's radio broadcast last night. One of them was getting hot under the collar about Allied activity in Africa and kept waving his hands around until the ash flew off the end of his cigarette, narrowly missing his friend. The other one didn't seem to be listening to him but was still making loud exclamations of "Pah!"

I eavesdropped as the brass arrow above the door stayed at the fourth floor and the men continued to argue.

"It's a ridiculous move. They haven't a chance. And anyway, Selassie doesn't know what he's doing."

"Total rot. You're blowing hot air."

"Pah! Five shillings says you're wrong."

"I'd be embarrassed to take it off you."

I hadn't realised I was staring until the one with the cigarette glanced in my direction.

"So what do you think then, sweetheart? Is Eritrea a goner? Should we even bother while we're about it?"

Crikey. I was being asked for a political opinion and I hadn't even got to the interview yet.

"Well," I said, feeling prepared. "I'm not entirely sure, but if Mr. Churchill thinks it's a good idea, I'd say going at them from the Sudan is the best bet."

The man nearly swallowed his cigarette. His friend hesitated for a second and then let out a guffaw.

"That told you, Henry! They're not all as dim as they look."

The other one sneered. "Anyone can repeat a line they've heard on the wireless."

"Actually I read about it in *The Times*," I offered, which was true. Neither responded, but started to argue again as the lift finally arrived.

I followed them in and politely asked the attendant for the third floor. Then I lifted up my chin and felt uppity from under my hat. Becoming a Lady War Correspondent would hardly be a walk in the park, but I wasn't surprised. My mother always said that a lot of men think that having bosoms means you're a nitwit. She said the cleverest thing is to let them assume you're an idiot, so you can crack on and prove them all wrong.

I loved my mother, not least as every time she said something like *bosom* in front of people, Father rolled his eyes and pretended to clutch his heart for effect.

The thought of my parents cheered me as I got out at the third floor and headed up the stairs. At the top, I stopped for a second to powder my nose and poke a stray bit of hair behind my ear, and tried not to feel self-conscious in front of a large framed picture of a rather stern gentleman with white hair and somewhat forceful eyebrows. I recognised him at once. It was Lord Overton, millionaire philanthropist and owner of Launceston Press. He and his wife were always in the news for their charitable work and I hugely admired them both.

For a moment my nerve nearly failed. I hesitated at the double swing doors that led to Mrs. Bird and my interview.

Deep breath, shoulders back.

I pushed open the doors and walked into a thin, dark corridor. It was a far cry from the imposing entrance hall downstairs. As warned, there was no receptionist. Ahead of me was a line of doors, all but two of them shut, and apart from the muffled sound of typing, barely a sound from anywhere. If I'd expected a bustling newsroom full of chaps like the two in the lift, I was mistaken. Perhaps everyone was out reporting.

Clutching my handbag in front of me, I noticed a half-open door a little way down on the right-hand side and wondered whether a measured call of "Hello there" would be too forward a way to start things off.

I dismissed the idea and decided to knock on one of the doors. If I were to get this job, I might have to telephone America and ask to be put through to the White House. This was no place for faint hearts.

The office on my right had "Miss Knighton" written in a careful hand on a card taped to the door. On the wall next to it was a framed fashion print of a woman walking a poodle and looking immeasurably gay about it. I couldn't see what that had to do with Significant World Events, but each to their own. There was a similar print on the wall opposite, only in this one the woman was in a summer frock and laughing like anything at a kitten.

I frowned. I was keen on animals but didn't see what a major newspaper was doing putting up pictures of them during these Challenging Times. Surely a portrait of The King or someone out of the War Cabinet would be a more fitting use for the wall?

Perhaps it meant the people here were cheerful types. But cheerful or not, it was most awfully quiet.

"MISS KNIGHTON . . ." a man bellowed from behind the other half-open door. "MISS KNIGHTON! Oh, for God's sake . . . MISS KNIGHTON. Where the hell is she? I might as well talk to the deaf. DON'T WORRY, I'LL DO IT MYSELF . . ."

There were rumbles and then a crash.

"Oh, for God's . . . Idiot."

"Hello?" I called, heading in the direction of the noise. "Are you all right? Might I help?"

"Of course I'm all right. Kathleen, is that you? Hang on."

There was more scuffling, and then a slim gentleman in his mid-forties stumbled into the corridor. He was dressed nicely in tweed trousers and matching waistcoat but had got himself in rather a state. His shirtsleeves were rolled up, his brown hair was in need of a cut, and his hands were covered in black ink.

He was surely a journalist. It was very exciting, even if he did look quite murderous.

The journalist, who didn't introduce himself but glared at me for not being Miss Knighton, pushed the hair out of his eyes and smeared ink all over his forehead. For form's sake I pretended not to notice.

"HOW DO YOU DO," I said in a loud voice, as when nervous I have a tendency to shout. "I'm Emmeline Lake. I have an interview with Mrs. Bird."

"Oh God." He looked at me with some alarm. "Already?"

I smiled in what I hoped was a keen but intelligent manner. At least he seemed to know about me coming.

"It's at two o'clock," I said, trying to be helpful.

"Right then. Well, I'm afraid she's not here. Of course, she's never here, which is a plus. Small mercies and all that. Probably organizing some poor charity or another into submission, but there you have it."

He stopped. My face had dropped into my boots.

"Right," I said, trying to remain positive.

"So you're here for the interview, Miss . . ."

"Lake. Yes. But I can wait if that helps?" I looked around for somewhere to sit but the corridor was empty.

"Oh, don't worry about that," he said, not unkindly. "I'm afraid you've got me instead. But my hands are covered in this bloody ink . . ."

I decided not to mention it was all over his face too, in case it prompted even more of a swear, but instead scrabbled in my bag and offered him my handkerchief. My mother had embroidered a flower and my initials on it for Christmas.

"Thank you. Disaster averted." He started to obliterate her handiwork. "Good. Well, come in then."

I followed him into his office, noting the worn name on the door.

MR. COLLINS

FEATURES AND EDITOR AT LARGE

"Watch out. It's gone everywhere," said Mr. Collins, and I made my way into the messiest room I had ever seen.

He squeezed himself behind a desk piled high with books and papers, together with an over-flowing ashtray and the unhappily upturned inkpot. The whole scene was given a dramatic edge by the only light in the room, an industrial Anglepoise lamp that looked as if it had been requisitioned from a condemned medical-supplies factory.

I spotted a pale blue blotter on the floor by the desk and bent to pick it up, then handed it to him, as if it were my credentials.

"Ah, good. Yes." He dabbed at the spilt ink, looking dispirited.

After a few seconds, during which I glanced around and wondered if it was general practice for journalists to use a half-empty bottle of brandy as a bookend, he sighed heavily, gave up on the mess, and stared at me.

"Right," he said. "Let's get this over with. Now, Miss Emmeline Lake, here promptly at two o'clock to be interviewed by Mrs. Bird and owner of a small but currently appreciated handkerchief . . ."

For all his floundering, the Features and Editor At Large had not missed a thing.

"Tell me," he said. "What on God's earth possessed you to apply for a job working here?"

This was not how I thought the interview would start.

"Well," I said, remembering how Bunty and I had practised at home. "I am very hardworking and I can type sixty-five words per minute and take shorthand at one hundred and twenty-five words . . ."

Mr. Collins stifled a yawn, which put me off my stride, but I pressed on.

"My references say I am very capable and . . ."

He closed his eyes for a moment. I tried to add some more weight.

"I've worked in a solicitors' office for the past two and a half years, so . . ."

"Don't worry about that," he said. "Let's get to the point."

I braced myself, ready to be quizzed on the most effective members of the Government.

"Are you easily scared?"

He was cutting right to the chase. I tried not to look over-excited as I pictured myself charging around London in an air raid interviewing people.

"I don't think so," I said, underplaying what I hoped would be my immeasurable bravery if required.

"Hmm. We'll see. Good at taking dictation?"

Or shadowing a Top Correspondent, jotting down his every word as we tracked down Information of National Importance.

"Absolutely. One hundred and twenty—"

"Five words a minute, yes, you said."

Mr. Collins appeared distinctly underwhelmed. I reasoned that perhaps I should also find interviewing Juniors very dull if I were a Features and Editor At Large working against the clock to meet brutal deadlines. No wonder his office was a mess. It couldn't be easy keeping it under control, especially with Miss Knighton so unreliable. He was probably exhausted.

My mind wandered. Perhaps this would be my job? Helping Mr. Collins meet his deadlines. Taking dictation from People In The Know as he ruthlessly grilled them to get the very best news. Reminding him that he had an off-the-record meeting with a Parliamentary Secretary at three.

"Which essentially means, are you any good with cantankerous old women . . . in fact utter old boots?"

I realised I had accidentally stopped listening.

I couldn't quite see what utter old boots had to do with *The Evening Chronicle*. I thought of my grandmother, who Father said hadn't smiled since before the last war.

"Oh yes," I said with confidence. "I'm very good with utter old, um . . . them."

Mr. Collins raised an eyebrow and nearly smiled but clearly thought better of it as he felt inside his waistcoat pocket and fished out a cigarette case.

"Right," he said, leaning on his elbow as he lit a cigarette. He took a long drag and grimaced. "Now look here, Miss Lake. You seem pleasant enough."

I tried not to look thrilled.

"Are you sure about this? The previous Junior lasted a week. And the one before that didn't make it to tea. Mind you, that was partly my fault." He paused. "I am told that on occasion I shout," he added for clarification.

"I'm sure that's not true," I lied, thinking of the foghorn calls for Miss Knighton. "And anyway, sticks and stones."

"Hmm?"

"Might break my bones," I ventured. "But words will never hurt me."

Mr. Collins looked at me again, and I had the feeling he was thinking something he wouldn't tell me. Finally he pursed his lips and nodded.

"I think you might do," he said. "I think you might actually do. When can you start?"

If I had heard him correctly, this was the best day of my life. I didn't mind for a moment that he hadn't asked me about any of the topics I had been revising for days, and all the insightful questions I had planned to ask flew out of my brain as soon as he said the word *start*.

"Gosh," I said, failing to make the sort of sophisticated impression I had been aiming for. I tried again.

"Thank you, sir. Thank you very much indeed. I can hand in my notice straightaway, if that is all right?"

Now I saw a tiny hint of a smile. "I dare say it is," he said. "Though you might not thank me once you're here, you know."

I absolutely bet I will, I thought, but didn't say so, as being very nearly a member of staff at a famous newspaper was all that mattered. Mr. Collins seemed an ironic type and I felt sure his warnings were just part of his ways.

"Thank you, Mr. Collins," I said as we shook hands. "I promise I won't let you down."

Chapter 3

YOURS SINCERELY, MRS. H. BIRD

With the benefit of hindsight, my failure to ask Mr. Collins a single question about the job was something of a mistake.

But what with the Is That You Miss Knighton business and the Good With Old Boots questions, and the whole thrill of being in a publisher's office in the first place, it had quite slipped my mind. Which is why, when I arrived three weeks later to start work, feeling slightly nervy in a new brown check suit I had remade from one of my mother's old ones, and with my favourite fountain pen, three new pencils, and a spare hanky in my bag, some confusion arose.

I had left my job at Strawman's with their good wishes and instructions not to forget them, and gone home to Little Whitfield for Christmas with my parents. With my new job to look forward to and the shops managing to put up a good display despite everything, it had been merry, even though my brother, Jack, had not been able to get leave. Because it was Christmas we all pretended we weren't sad about that, or worried about him either, even though we were, and then Bunty and her granny had visited on Boxing Day, which gave everybody a boost. I still hadn't heard from Edmund but wasn't dispirited as sometimes one didn't hear anything for weeks and then four letters might arrive all at the same time. I was quite sure I would receive a message soon—probably with a drawing of a Christmas tree or a snow scene as Edmund very much liked to draw. I had written to him about my new job of course, and even if he had pooh-poohed my dream of becoming a War Correspondent in the past, I was sure he would be pleased for me. I tried not to worry that he might want me to give up working when we were married, but as we hadn't actually set a date for the wedding yet, I pushed the thought to the back of my mind.

Back in London, the start of January had been bitterly cold. We could have done without it, but the girls at the fire station reckoned that after the dreadful pounding the Luftwaffe had given the city after Christmas, the weather was now putting them off. Thelma was sure it was A Very Good Sign and Joan was convinced that if a bit of a cold snap was all it took to dampen their spirits, things would be over before very long.

Whatever happened, nothing could stop me feeling on top of the world as I arrived at Launceston Press clutching quite the most wonderful letter in the world.

Launceston Press Ltd.
Launceston House
London EC4
Monday 16th December 1940

Dear Miss Lake:

Further to your interview with Mr. Collins, I confirm your appointment as part-time Junior commencing Monday 6th January 1941.

You will work each day from nine o'clock to one o'clock. This includes a tea break of ten minutes but no break for luncheon.

Your salary shall be nineteen shillings per week and you will receive seven days of paid leave as holiday each year.

You should report to me, Mrs. Bird, at nine o'clock sharp on the day your employment commences.

Yours sincerely,

Mrs H. Bird

Mrs. H. Bird

Acting Editress

Acting Editress! I had no idea Mrs. Bird was the Acting Editress and that the position meant working for someone so important. And a lady at that. I was hugely impressed. Even if most of their young men had been called up, it was still very forward thinking of *The Chronicle* to have a woman in charge.

This time I was more excited than nervous when I arrived at Launceston House. I would have raced up the stairs two at a time if I could in my work shoes but sensibly took the lift as far as it went and attempted to arrive with decorum and in full puff.

I knew that as a Junior I was starting at the bottom, but I didn't mind in the least. I pictured myself becoming chums with Lively Types, discussing the news of the day in between admirable amounts of hard work, typing like billy-o or taking down impossibly fast dictation. Perhaps—given time—suggesting an idea for a news feature or, should someone very unfortunately be taken ill, stepping up to the mark and filling in for them at the scene of a terrible crime or during a raid in the middle of the night.

I arrived at the fifth floor, gung-ho but ready for them to send me straight back down to the bigger, brighter floors in the building where Mrs. Bird's office must be. I didn't mind if I had to sit in a broom cupboard, but the Acting Editress was bound to have a very important office, or perhaps even a suite.

Pushing through the double doors, I was greeted by an empty corridor. I had expected the offices to be busy on a Monday morning; after all there was no shortage of news to report. I tried not to think that I would probably have to type up some pretty grim copy as part of my job. It was the least I could do really. I was cheered to see that Miss Knighton appeared to be in as her office door was ajar and I could hear her typewriter—she was awfully fast.

I risked interrupting something vital and tapped on the door.

"Hello," I said, peeking into the tiny space. "I'm sorry to trouble you but I'm the new Junior. Could you tell me which floor Mrs. Bird is on, please?"

Miss Knighton, a freckly girl of about my age with pretty green eyes and unfortunate hair, looked at me blankly.

"Floor?"

"Yes, which floor is her office on, please?"

"Well"—she paused, as if it were a trick question—"this one."

Miss Knighton struck me as quite young to be An Eccentric, but I said Righto as I was new and you don't make friends if you're standoffish.

"Just across the corridor," she continued. "The door without a name. It fell off last week and no one's been up to fix it." Miss Knighton's voice dropped to a whisper, as if this was the most terrible crime.

The sudden noise of a door opening violently made her nearly jump out of her chair and then start typing even faster than before. Taking this as a hint, I shot out of the little room and straight into the door-opener herself.

"Oh gosh," I said, stepping back again and looking up at the looming figure. "I'm terribly sorry."

"I should say," the woman said. "That was my foot."

I looked down at a perfectly polished stout shoe with my footprint on it and tried not to wince. I had recognised her straightaway. She was the notable lady I had bumped into outside the office building on the day of my interview. Decked out in the same feathered hat, she wore the sort of expression that Mr. Churchill sported in newsreels when Hitler had really mucked him around.

She appeared to recognise me too, which gave even less grounds for optimism. I looked at her shoe again and considered a bout of hysteria.

"I really am dreadfully sorry," I said. "My name is Emmeline Lake. I'm here to see Mrs. Bird."

Throwing caution to the wind, I smiled in an encouraging way. There was a strong likelihood I was coming across as a simpleton.

"I am Mrs. Bird," the woman announced.

"How do you do," I said in a small voice, trying to exhibit surprise, excitement and terrific respect all at the same time.

Mrs. Bird stared at me as if I had arrived from the moon. She was a striking woman in her late sixties, with an oblong head, formidably square jaw, and dark grey waved hair. She had the look of a later-life Queen Victoria, only even crosser. It was hard not to feel scared.

"Miss Lake, do you always introduce yourself by hurtling into people? Wait there," she added, before I could come up with an answer. "I am too hot in this coat."

With impressive mobility for a woman of large stature and certain age, she turned on her heels and marched into the office opposite, smartly shutting the door behind her.

I stood in the freezing corridor, my heart thumping.

After a very long moment, a shout of "You can come in" thundered through the door in the manner of someone who sees loudhailers as an indication of weakness.

I took a deep breath, imagining a room with a vast mahogany desk and a manly sideboard full of silver salvers and crystal decanters for toasting the journalists when someone got a big scoop.

But I had pictured it entirely wrong. The room was the same size as Mr. Collins' office, although with a window and without the anarchic mess. Rather than presiding from an enormous leather chair at the head of a magnificent desk, Mrs. Bird was sitting behind an ordinary wooden affair.

The window, which took up half of the back wall, was wide open, despite the fact it was January, and blasts of freezing air were gusting in. This did not appear to bother Mrs. Bird in the least. She had already removed her coat and hat and they were now overwhelming a coat stand in the corner of the room.

Other than a large steel filing cabinet and two secretaries' shorthand chairs, the room was wildly austere, with little evidence of a woman at the helm of a busy newspaper. The desk was almost entirely bare, apart from an untouched ink blotter edged with green leather, a telephone, and a large framed photograph of Mrs. Bird in front of an ornamental lake. Dressed informally in a thick woollen get-up and leather gloves, she was surrounded by a large group of gun dogs, all of whom were gazing up at her with quite fanatical devotion.

"Aha," said Mrs. Bird. "You've spotted The Chaps. Brains like pudding, of course."

It was clear from Mrs. Bird's face that she would kill with her bare hands anyone who so much as thought of touching them. "Complete idiots," she added. Her chest inflated with pride.

"Are they all yours, Mrs. Bird?" I asked, keen to make up some ground.

"They are," she said. "Some advice, Miss Lake." She leant forward, which was alarming. "Dogs are like children. Noisy, trainable, but dim and likely to smell disagreeable on the arrival of guests." She frowned. "I have eight."

I glanced back at the photograph.

"*Dogs*," Mrs. Bird snapped for clarification. "In terms of children, four is ample. More than that and one veers into the working classes or Catholicism."

I nodded, unsure of the appropriate response. But Mrs. Bird had moved on.

"Of course if we were in Germany, The Chaps would all be dead. Twenty-one inches to the shoulder. Any taller and unless they're an Alsatian: killed." She banged her fist on the desk.

"How awful," I said, thinking of Brian, my Aunty Tiny's Great Dane who we all loved. I wondered if he would mind learning to crouch.

"That's Nazis for you," said Mrs. Bird darkly.

I nodded again. The Führer had no idea what he was up against here.

"Now." Mrs. Bird cleared her throat. "This chitchat won't do, Miss Lake. I understand you have experience in periodicals?"

Calling *The Little Whitfield Gazette* "periodicals" would be a bit steep.

"Not exactly," I said. "But I've wanted to work for a newspaper for ages. I hope to become a War Correspondent one day."

My cards were on the table. I felt rather bold.

"War?" boomed Mrs. Bird as if it had come out of the blue despite the whole of London permanently bracing up to the sound of enemy guns. "We don't want to bang on about that. You do know you'll just be typing letters, don't you?"

I looked blank.

"Mr. Collins did tell you about the role?" Mrs. Bird frowned and tapped her right index finger on the desk in an irritated fashion.

I hesitated. Now I thought about it, he hadn't.

"Typing letters," I said, thinking out loud rather than answering the question.

"That's right. And of course any other typing I may need you to do."

"Typing," I said again.

Mrs. Bird looked at me as though I was an idiot, which I had a horrible feeling might be about right.

"Just that. Not, um, helping the reporters?"

Another icy gust of wind blew in.

"Reporters? Don't be ridiculous," barked Mrs. Bird. "You're a Junior Typist, Miss Lake. I fail to see the confusion."

I tried to think on my toes. Something was wrong. I had nothing against typing; in fact I had expected to be doing a lot of it. And taking notes in shorthand. Helping the reporters out. Learning on the job.

I took a deep breath. I wasn't going to let Mr. Collins down on day one. He was the man I had to thank for getting me here. And anyway, it was my own fault for not listening.

I pulled myself together. If the job was a little less exciting than I'd hoped, that was all right. I was still at *The London Evening Chronicle*. I was still entering the world of journalism. It might take a bit longer than anticipated, but I would just have to work harder.

"Yes, Mrs. Bird," I said, trying to be spirited. "No. Yes. Absolutely."

I didn't feel very spirited at all.

Mrs. Bird kept tapping her finger. "Hmm," she said. "We'll see how you get on. Miss Knighton will show you the ropes. You must sign the Confidentiality Agreement today, and no loitering about reading the letters. Not a word outside this office, and at the first sign of Unpleasantness it's into the wastepaper bin. Is that clear?"

"Righto," I said forcefully, though I hadn't the foggiest clue. I perked up at *Unpleasantness* and *Confidentiality*, though. That sounded exciting. They might not like banging on about the war here but clearly they dealt with some pretty stiff news.

"Good. Whenever you aren't working for me, you will help Mr. Collins. Miss Knighton will know when you can be spared." Mrs. Bird adopted a stern look. "You will find I am very busy. This is not my only commitment."

"Of course," I said with reverence. "Thank you."

She glanced at her wristwatch. "I am late. Good morning, Miss Lake."

I very nearly dropped into a curtsey but remembered in time that Mrs. Bird was not my headmistress and retreated to the corridor.

Things had taken a bit of a turn. But even so.

Confidentiality Agreement. Not a word outside this office. We'll see how you get on.

It was still the most exciting day of my life.

"My name's Kathleen," said Miss Knighton shyly as I stood in her tiny office. "I hope we'll be friends."

Kathleen was friendly and keen, though she spoke in nearly a whisper and it was hard to imagine her coping with the thundering Mrs. Bird. Her curly red hair boinged around as she spoke, sticking out at all angles and giving the impression that her hand had been stuck in a socket.

"Thank you," I said. "I hope so too. Please call me Emmy. Your cardigan is lovely."

"I made it at the weekend," she said, beaming, and then glanced nervously at the door. "Has Mrs. Bird gone out? Only, she doesn't like chatting." She pulled a worried face. "I always fill in when people don't stay, so I can show you the ropes. That's your desk there."

Kathleen's battered oak desk faced the door and mine was tucked right behind it. Wedged beside each desk so you had to squeeze into your seat was a tall wooden cabinet with filing drawers. Kathleen had a pot plant on top of hers, which partially obscured my view of a pinboard on which there was a monthly calendar with a ring around every Thursday, several pictures of woollies from magazines, and a list of names with telephone extension numbers. Both desks had three wooden in-trays in a stack, and a typewriter. Mine was huge, old, and green, with "Corona" printed on the front in gold. It only had three rows of keys and looked as if it would take a battering ram to get it to type. I was quite sure it was into its second war so I reckoned it must be robust. I sat down and got out my pencils.

"Kathleen, what sort of articles does Mrs. Bird write?" I asked.

Kathleen looked confused.

"What sort of articles?" she repeated. "It's *Mrs. Bird*," she added, as if I had been behind the door when brains were given out.

"Well," I said, "she mentioned *not saying a word outside this office*." I lowered my voice. "Is her work Terrifically Hush Hush?"

You could tell that Kathleen was used to people asking questions about sensitive information. Her expression remained resolutely blank.

"What?"

The girl was a professional. The cloak of secrecy did not fall.

"Of course," I said, warming to my new job like anything, "I understand we probably shouldn't say. Walls have ears, even here."

Kathleen frowned and scrunched up her nose. She had the look of someone who had been given a particularly hard sum to work out in her head. I was all for secrecy but did hope we wouldn't have to keep this up permanently as it was quite hard to make any progress with the conversation.

"Crikey," she said at last. "I can see why they gave you the job. You're very good on confidentiality."

I felt my face go a little warm at the compliment.

"Well," I said heroically. "I try."

"You'll still need to sign the Agreement, of course." She rooted around in a drawer. "Here you are."

Quick as a flash I took my new pen from my bag and signed my name. Then I began to read what it said on the sheet.

> I . . . . [enter name] hereby agree that as an employee of Launceston Press Ltd., all correspondence from readers of *Woman's Friend* shall be treated in the strictest confidence. I agree that I will not repeat the contents of letters to any persons other than permanent members of the *Woman's Friend* staff . . .

This was unfortunate. Kathleen had given me the wrong agreement.

"Oh dear," I said. "I'm so sorry, but this appears to be something about a *Woman's Friend*?"

"Yes." She gave me a wide, encouraging smile. "Don't worry, it's really just that you mustn't go around telling people what the readers write in about. Mrs. Bird is very strict on this." She paused. "Some of it is awfully *personal* as you can imagine."

I smiled back, but I couldn't imagine at all.

Kathleen took my silence for concern. "Don't worry, Emmy," she said. "Mrs. Bird won't answer anything Racy so you won't find yourself in a difficult spot."

I glanced at a bookshelf to Kathleen's right. It was stacked with periodicals. It dawned on me that one of us might have the wrong end of the stick.

"Kathleen," I said. "What exactly does Mrs. Bird do?"

She laughed and grabbed a colour magazine from a shelf piled high with them.

"Surely you've heard of Henrietta Bird Helps? She was famous at *Woman's Friend* before you and I were even born." She leant over and handed it to me. "Page before last."

"I'm sorry," I said, still blank. "What has Henrietta Bird Helps got to do with *The Evening Chronicle*?"

Kathleen laughed again, but then stopped suddenly and took an intake of breath.

"Oh no. You didn't think this was a job for *The Chronicle*? Oh my goodness, you did!"

"But this IS *The Evening Chronicle*," I said, now more in hope than certainty.

"No, it's not. They're downstairs. In the swanky bit. We're both owned by Launceston Press, but they never speak to us. We're the wretched poor cousin." She appeared remarkably upbeat about it. "Oh, grief. I typed up the advertisement for Mrs. Bird. It didn't actually say, did it?"

I turned to the front of the magazine. Proud as punch, there it was, in horrid old-fashioned letters:

WOMAN'S FRIEND
For the Modern Lady
Crochet your own dressing table doily.
Adorable pattern inside!

Underneath the headline was an ornate drawing of something lacy. The rest of the cover was given to a photograph of a woman holding a terrifically large baby and some writing in a circle that said, "Nurse McClay says: 'Open That Window And Give Baby Some Air!' "

It was a keen approach for January, but I wasn't an expert. I tried to take everything in.

"Mrs. Bird was *Woman's Friend*'s Most Loved Advice Writer for over twenty years," explained Kathleen helpfully. "She retired in 1932 but Lord Overton personally asked her to come back when our editor was called up last year."

Lord Overton. Launceston Press' owner. *The Evening Chronicle*'s owner. Personally asked Mrs. Bird.

I stared at the gigantic baby.

"Emmy," continued Kathleen in a voice you use for people who aren't the full ticket, "*Woman's Friend* is a weekly women's magazine. Your job is typing up the letters for the Problem Page."

I nodded but couldn't speak. Kathleen waited as it sank in.

Finally I gave what I hoped was a plucky Everything Is Absolutely Tip Top smile.

But things weren't even remotely tip top. My morale went into a terminal decline.

As Kathleen offered to show me around, I tried to think straight. This couldn't be further from the first rung of a journalistic career. A million miles from running around after reporters or putting phone calls through to the White House.

I had taken entirely the wrong job.

Chapter 4

MRS. BIRD WILL HELP

Kathleen's whirlwind tour of the *Woman's Friend* editorial offices kept up a pace as I followed her down the thin, dreary corridor, thinking frantically. What kind of an idiot left a perfectly decent position at a solicitors' office to type silly letters for a ladies' magazine? Especially one which, from what my new colleague was saying, appeared to be on its last legs.

"Back when *Woman's Friend* sold masses of copies, we used to have lots more journalists and everyone sat in here, only we don't now, so it's empty," Kathleen said as we walked past Mr. Collins' office, which she said was locked. She opened the next door on our right. "The typists had the room on the other side of the corridor. But it's just me and you now."

I looked into the journalists' long, narrow room, which had two rows of vacant desks. The nearest one to the door had cardboard boxes stacked on it, which was a definite fire hazard, but all the others were vacant, with no hint of typewriters, inkwells, or paper trays. Lines of pinboards ran along on the walls, some still with articles ripped out of magazines, hinting at what had once been a hive of activity. Some of the papers were beginning to curl at the edges and the room smelt musty, a funny combination of tobacco, and cheese and pickle sandwiches.

"How long is it since anyone worked in here?" I asked.

Kathleen crossed her arms and gazed into thin air, thinking. "Ages." She lowered her voice. "*Woman's Friend* hasn't really kept up with the times. It's a bit old-fashioned, I suppose. Although I always read it," she added.

I nodded, feeling even gloomier than before, as Kathleen chatted on.

"Pretty much everyone has joined up and they've never been replaced. Mr. Collins writes all the fiction and he's ever so good. They get people to send the other things in as it saves money. Anyway, come and meet everyone."

She marched off down the corridor as I glanced at my watch. At twenty past nine Mr. Collins was nowhere to be seen. I felt as if I were in a museum after it had closed for the night.

"Across the corridor is the advertising team. Which is just Mr. Newton." Kathleen lowered her voice as she continued to the next door. "He isn't in today. He hasn't much to do as there aren't that many advertisers. And this is the Art Department. They do the illustrations and pictures of frocks." She knocked on the next door and went in without waiting for a reply.

"Morning, Mr. Brand. How are you? This is Miss Lake, our new Junior."

I followed her into the office, which, like all the others, was a rather gloomy affair but at least looked as if something was going on. An elderly man with thick tortoiseshell glasses and heavily brilliantined hair was drawing a dashing scene of a man in naval uniform holding up a woman who looked rather faint.

"How do you do?" said Mr. Brand. "*We laughed only yesterday.*"

It was an unusual hello, but he was obviously a creative type.

"How do you do," I replied. "I'm so sorry . . . you laughed only . . . ?"

"*Yesterday.* It's next week's lead story. I'm working on it at the moment."

"I see," I said, trying to look In The Know. "It's lovely."

Mr. Brand beamed.

"And this is Mrs. Mahoney," Kathleen said as a plump, middle-aged woman with a comforting face waved at me from behind a stack of huge sheets of paper.

"Hello, Miss Lake," she said. "I'm Production. I'm very nice but please don't miss your deadlines." She gave me an encouraging smile as I said Hello and then Kathleen led me out of their office.

Apart from the terrifying Mrs. Bird, everyone had seemed very friendly. I tried to buck up, but the truth was horribly disheartening. While the rest of the country was standing up to Hitler and putting every possible effort into the war, I'd be typing up readers' problems and frivolous, made-up stories. It couldn't be less like working at a newspaper. I wished I hadn't written to Edmund about it. He would think me such a fool. So would Bunty. And the girls at the fire station, especially Horrible Vera on A Watch. She'd have a field day. It served me right for thinking I was on my way to a dramatically exciting career.

Back in our little office Kathleen started to explain the intercom system and I tried hard to look agog. My short experience of Mrs. Bird's vocal strength suggested the need for an intercom was minimal.

"First thing," said Kathleen, "is to open the post and put the letters on Mrs. Bird's desk. But only the *acceptable* ones. Absolutely nothing off-colour." Her expression became deadly serious.

I looked at the issue I had left open on my desk. Alongside a photograph of a determined Mrs. Bird taken around 1915 in which she appeared about to punch someone, a short piece of copy explained all.

MRS. HENRIETTA BIRD WILL HELP

There's nothing that can't be sorted with common sense and a strong will.

Mrs. Bird is here to answer your worries. For a postal reply in confidence, send a stamped addressed envelope but please note that Mrs. Bird's postbag is a full one, so there may be a temporary delay.

I thought of Bunty typing up correspondence in the War Office. This didn't exactly cut the mustard in comparison.

"I shall be jolly busy, I'm sure," I said, brightly. "How big is Mrs. Bird's postbag exactly?"

Kathleen shrugged. "Not very."

"But it says *full postbag*?"

"Oh, we put that because all the other magazines do. We don't get that many letters."

"Right," I said, looking at the magazine, where someone called Self-Conscious had written in about a struggle with fat arms. Mrs. Bird's advice was brisk.

> Pretend they are the blades of an aeroplane propeller and wave them around your head with some vigour.

I felt hopelessly glum. Britain was twenty-one miles away from a Europe in tatters and *Woman's Friend* gave its few remaining readers advice about fat arms. I'd thought I'd be typing up news about Mussolini by now.

"The main thing," said Kathleen, still very serious, "is that Mrs. Bird won't answer any letters that involve Unpleasantness. She is *absolutely* clear on this." Kathleen stopped and glanced at the door. "Mrs. Bird says our generation has Badly Let Things Slip." She paused before adding, "Mrs. Bird is keen to pull them back up. Whatever you do, as soon as you see anything that's on the Unacceptable Topics List, you must throw it away."

She opened a drawer in her desk and rummaged around while I looked at a letter from a teenager wrestling with poor gums. Mrs. Bird had replied that it was the girl's own fault for eating sweets and she should just have to press on. It was not a sympathetic reply.

"So if people send in an Unacceptable problem, their letter gets cut up, and if they've sent in a stamp for a reply, we give it to one of Mrs. Bird's Good Works. That means her charities." Kathleen pointed to a large cardboard box with "POSTAGE STAMPS" written on it and then delved back into the drawer again.

I read the next letter, which was from a lady who had taken on three evacuees, and while they were very dear kiddies she was concerned that her own children had now started to swear. Unsurprisingly Mrs. Bird was not keen on Vulgarities and her answer was very much to the point.

I wondered what she should make of me.

Dear Mrs. Bird,

I have accidentally taken an unfortunate job, due to not listening during my interview.

I now appear to be working on a sinking ship, typing letters for a lady who can shout through solid walls.

Have I been a terrible idiot? Please tell me what I should do.

Yours,

Not Usually This Gormless

I pictured the reply.

Dear Gormless,

This is entirely your own fault. I suggest you stop moaning and crack on.

Yours,

Henrietta Bird

"Eureka," said Kathleen and handed me a sheet of paper entitled MRS. BIRD'S UACCEPTABLE TOPICS. Someone had stamped HIGHLY CONFIDENTIAL across the top in red ink.

Topics That Will Not Be Published Or Responded To By Mrs. Bird

(NB: list is not exclusive and will be added to when required)

Marital relations

Premarital relations

Extramarital relations
Physical relations
Sexual relations in general (all issues, mentions, suggestion, or results of)
Illegal activities
Political activities and opinions
Religious activities and opinions (excl. queries regarding church groups and services)
The war (excl. queries regarding rationing, voluntary services, clubs, and practicalities)
Cookery

"Cookery?"

Unless I had missed something threatening in Home Economics at school, it seemed a dull bedfellow alongside extramarital relations and illegal activities.

"Forward to Mrs. Croft," said Kathleen. "She writes What's In The Hot Pot? It's mostly about rationing. Here you are." She handed me a small pile of letters. "Careful as you go. You might find some of them shocking." Kathleen bit her lip. "Usually they try to recruit an older, married lady to type these. You look even younger than me."

"I'm nearly twenty-three," I said, hoping it sounded mature.

Kathleen grinned and told me to ask her about anything if I wasn't quite sure.

I turned back to the sheet with unladylike enthusiasm. I was not the sort that runs with a fast crowd, but having a list of Racy Elements to avoid did sound rather good fun.

Words and Phrases That Will Not Be Published Or Responded To By Mrs. Bird

For further references see *Girlhood To Wife: Practical Advice By A Doctor* (1921)

A–C

Affair
Amorous
Ardent
Bed
Bedroom
Bed jacket
Berlin . . .

The list went on for pages.

Based on Mrs. Bird's idea of degeneracy, Sodom and Gomorrah would not lose much sleep. Naturally, before you were married, Going Too Far was off the menu. Getting Carried Away was strictly not on, and if you Got Into Trouble, it was nobody's fault but your own.

In fact, if you veered towards relationships in even the most innocent way, you would have to simmer right down again because Mrs. Bird ("Here to answer your worries") was highly unlikely to write back.

My wings feeling somewhat clipped, I knuckled down and started opening the letters.

Some were carefully handwritten in ink, with a proper name at the bottom, while others were in pencil and unsigned or with a made-up name such as Worried Fiancée or A Sailor's Girl. Others had included a stamped addressed envelope, clearly hoping for a direct reply. Almost all of them were from women and girls, apart from one or two from men who had written in about their wives.

I opened a letter from a lady called Florence whose calcium tablets hadn't helped her chilblains even a bit. "Walking is now such a trial," she reported. I felt confident this wouldn't be off-limits for Mrs. Bird and perked up a bit. Then an optimistic lady called Mrs. Ditton helped out with "My daughter has passed her first aid test, do you think she could take up army nursing as a career?"

I hoped it would count as a service to the war effort and put the letter with Florence's in my Acceptable file.

But as I opened more, it became harder to find anything else to add. One reader had fallen in love with a chap who was divorced, which according to Mrs. Bird's list was an absolute no-go, while another liked a young man but had been told that "he shows affection in an embarrassing way." I didn't need to check the list to know they would go on the Unpleasantness pile. I found some scissors in my desk, diligently cut the letters into pieces, and put them in the bin.

For others it wasn't so clear. Even if they were on Mrs. Bird's List Of Unacceptable Topics, some of them didn't seem unreasonable at all.

Dear Mrs. Bird,

I am fifteen and my friends say they let boys give them a goodnight kiss. Am I right to refuse? And is kissing any different before and after people get married? I am worried that if I let boys kiss me, it will make me look cheap.

Yours,

Shy Marion

At fifteen it seemed a perfectly decent question to me. I turned to the J–L section on Mrs. Bird's list. *Kiss*, *Kisses*, and *Kissing* were all a definite not-on. I reluctantly added Shy Marion to the letters to be cut up and put in the bin. It was hardly a topic of outrage and I felt rotten that she wouldn't be helped.

As more letters failed to meet the standards of Mrs. Bird's list, I started to read them to Kathleen in the hope she might be of some help.

" 'Dear Mrs. Bird,' " I ventured. " 'My husband tells me I am unsympathetic and cold.' "

"Ooh no," Kathleen said before I could get to the crux.

I tore it in half and tried another.

" 'Dear Mrs. Bird, I am going to marry my fiancé when he comes home on leave from the army . . .' "

Kathleen looked encouragingly upbeat.

" 'But I feel I am rather ignorant about Married Life.'

" 'Married Life' is in capitals," I said as Kathleen looked into space in a ferocious manner, which must have been her thinking face.

"I'm pretty certain Married Life is a no," she said.

" 'Most specifically, the intimate side . . .' " I added helpfully.

"Oh dear me no," gasped Kathleen, glancing at the door as if Mrs. Bird might be about to crash through in a terrible rage. "*Intimate* won't do at all." She lowered her voice. "Mrs. Bird says that she didn't have to answer that sort of horridness in 1911 and she has no intention of doing so now."

Kathleen reported the diktat with such sincerity that I couldn't bring myself to argue. I tried another one.

" 'Dear Mrs. Bird, Might you have any advice on how to get burnt dripping out of the pan?' Oh, that's one for Mrs. Croft, isn't it?" I answered myself and continued to sift through the remaining post.

"What's In The Hot Pot?" said Kathleen faintly, with a look of relief on her face.

I unfolded a letter written in an elegant hand and headed "Lack-lustre Relations," from a nice lady who referred to herself only as Disappointed from the North East.

Disappointed was married to a good man but he was showing very little interest in Getting The Hang Of Things after lights-out. The letter was written in a delicate way so I thought we were in with a chance.

"No, of course not," said Kathleen, fiddling with a strand of hair as it abandoned ship from an inadequate bun. "It says *Relations*. Mrs. Bird doesn't like *Relations*."

"But they're married," I argued.

"That's not the point."

"And he's not showing an interest."

"Emmeline."

"Which can't be much fun."

"Now hold on," said Kathleen. "You're not supposed to read the details. You should have stopped after the third line."

"I did," I lied.

"Are you sure?"

"Well all right then, perhaps a bit later. But it sounds rotten. They've been married a year and she hasn't seen him without his pyjamas."

"Emmeline!" Kathleen went bright red and I decided not to mention the next sentence in case it brought on a turn. "Honestly. You aren't supposed to read anything Mrs. Bird has put on the list. You're very young."

She stood up and looked concerned.

I thought that was a bit rich seeing as Kathleen didn't seem to be any older than me, but I didn't want to make another blunder on day one, so I apologised again and said I would know better in future.

But I felt uneasy about it all. Not just for the lady in this letter, but for Shy Marion and the other readers whose problems were considered a no-go.

I could see people were ever so frank when they wrote in, which I thought really quite brave. Mrs. Bird was just a stranger at a magazine, but readers told her their secrets all the same. Some of them sounded in a real fix—lonely while their husbands were away fighting, or having their heads turned, or even just young and wanting a bit of guidance. Things were difficult for everyone at the moment and I did think it was poor of Mrs. Bird not to write back. The magazine was called *Woman's Friend* after all. Some friend Mrs. Bird was. Almost all the letters I had read would be cut into pieces and thrown in the bin.

I opened the last envelope on my desk. The reader had drawn faint lines with a pencil and ruler and while it was in a very neat hand, I could tell it had taken ages to write.

Dear Mrs. Bird,

I am seventeen and in love with a young man in the navy who is kind and generous and says he loves me back. He takes me out and to dances and now I have repaid him in a way I know is very wrong. My friend Annie is the same with her young man and we are both worried and Annie is scared if her dad was to find out. Please can you help? We don't want to lose our boyfriends.

I have enclosed a stamped addressed envelope and a postal order for the overcoat pattern from last week so my mum thinks it is for that.

Yours truly,

In A Muddle

Kathleen was checking a tricky double-page spread of patterns for early spring frocks so I quietly read In A Muddle's letter again. If I had felt sympathy for the other readers, I was especially concerned for her and her friend. They were heading for deep water.

Bunty and I had talked about similar things ourselves, sitting in the air-raid shelter and chatting into the night as you do with your best friend. Bunty was smitten with William, and while Edmund might have been stuffy about my career dreams, he had always been attentive and kind. Handsome in his uniform as well.

I almost sounded like poor In A Muddle.

But the difference was we knew where the line was, and whether we wanted to or not, we wouldn't cross it. It was probably awfully provincial to be determined to Remain Firm, war on or not. But Bunty and I had seen things go horribly wrong on this front, and it had been wretched all round.

I sat at my desk and pretended to read In A Muddle's letter again, but actually I was miles away.

All through school, Bunty and I had been in our own little gang. Bunty and me and Olive and Kitty. The four of us did everything together: joined the same school clubs, belonged to the same teams, got crushes on the same film stars, showed off around the same boys. Nothing special, just all the normal things everyone did.

But when we were sixteen and the four of us had just passed our School Cert., Kitty started seeing a chap who was older than us. He was called Doug and he was twenty. Kitty said he was very mature and thought we were all rather childish, which was probably true. But anyway, while we were all falling in love with Gary Cooper and Errol Flynn, Kitty went and fell in love with Doug. She said he loved her too. Then she got pregnant. And when Doug found out he just disappeared into thin air.

I chewed my lip and stared at In A Muddle's letter. Kathleen was right, I was young. But it didn't mean I had spent my entire life in a cave.

Kitty had been sent to stay in Edinburgh with an aunt she'd never met. We weren't allowed to visit her, so she was all on her own. She was desperate to somehow keep her baby, but four days after he was born, someone took him away. I had made Bunty come to Kitty's parents with me to beg them to rethink. But they were embarrassed and furious, and said no.

Kitty named her little boy Peter. He would be nearly six now.

I put my elbows on the desk and leant my chin on my hands, forgetting I was in a new job and should be trying to make a good impression.

"Are you all right, Emmeline?" Kathleen's face was friendly again. "Don't worry. You'll get the hang of things."

"Absolutely," I said. "It's all just a bit new."

Kathleen looked sympathetic. "Is that another Unacceptable?" she asked, seeing In A Muddle's stamped addressed envelope. "Do you want me to put the stamp in the box?"

"No, no thank you," I said, thinking on my toes. "It's from Worried About A Cat. I think Mrs. Bird will like this one."

Kathleen hesitated for a moment and then smiled. "Well done. Pets always go down a storm." She paused again. "Emmy, I know it seems harsh to ignore some of them, but Mrs. Bird says if people get themselves into a silly pickle, they've only themselves to blame."

I didn't think In A Muddle was the one who should get the blame. She believed somebody loved her, that's all. The only difference between her and me was that I knew my own mind, and Edmund wasn't a smooth operator like Doug had been. If no one helped In A Muddle, she might end up like Kitty.

"Of course, Kathleen," I said. "I'll cut it up with the rest."

Kathleen smiled warmly and returned to her typing. I waited for a moment, pretending to tidy the papers spread across my desk.

Then I put In A Muddle's letter into my drawer.

Chapter 5

DEAR IN A MUDDLE

Over the next weeks I threw myself into the swing of things and tried to make the best of it. Bunty had been terrifically supportive when I told her about *The Evening Chronicle* actually being *Woman's Friend* and said she thought it sounded wonderful all the same. Thelma and Joan and young Mary at the fire station were smashing as well and said it could lead to Great Things, which gave me a boost. I'd written to Edmund, turning it into a madcap story and a bit of a wheeze, and hoped he would see the funny side of it, but he hadn't replied. Actually, other than a short Christmas note, which had arrived in mid-January, I hadn't heard anything from him in ages and was beginning to worry that he'd been in some sort of scrape. I didn't want to appear a fusspot so only mentioned it once, when I was out having baked prune roll with Bunty and William, but I could tell they had been thinking the same thing. Bunty said rather too quickly that the army always let you know if something awful had happened so No News Is Good News and then Bill took up the baton and said Don't You Worry, Emmy, Edmund Is Made Of Very Stern Stuff. Then they gave each other a look when they thought I couldn't see.

I took them at their word, however, and decided to keep my end up and say I wasn't worried at all. It was the least I could do as poor Bunty was always having to put on a brave face about William's job as a fireman, which we both knew was as dangerous as anything. When his funny ears (the bits inside—from the outside you couldn't tell) meant the army wouldn't take him, Bill had joined the Fire Brigade instead. It had been pretty rotten for him when Edmund and my brother, Jack, joined up and left, but he had made a real go of it. I wasn't going to start flapping about Edmund when Bunty could look out of her window almost every night and see the bombs and fires and awful things that her boy was having to deal with.

At the magazine, Mrs. Bird's standard approach was to be rather cross about almost everything and in particular the readers, most of whom were a sad disappointment to her. I looked forward to the post, when a handful of problems would trickle in, and my optimism remained firm for interesting yet acceptable material, but it was hardly a stampede. There were only so many times the publication could suggest joining a Youth Club for morale.

In A Muddle's letter was still in my desk drawer. I desperately wanted to help her, but Kathleen had been very clear about the rules and I knew there was no chance that Mrs. Bird would consider it. I even thought of writing back myself, as a friend might, but that was out of the question. For a start, In A Muddle would wonder who on earth I was, and anyway, what if Mrs. Bird ever found out? *Woman's Friend* may not have been my dream job at a newspaper, but it was at least in the same building as *The Evening Chronicle*. One day an opportunity to join the paper could arise and a good reference from Mrs. Bird might make all the difference. Kathleen said Lord Overton was a personal friend, so you never knew.

I still wished I could do something, though. In A Muddle wasn't the only reader having a difficult time and Mrs. Bird's List Of Unacceptable Topics ruled almost all of them out for help.

Dear Mrs. Bird,

I am twenty-one and very much in love with a boy who is the same age. I know that he loves me too and he has asked me to marry him before he is sent overseas, but I am unsure if I should. You see, he has told me he has been very close with another girl and even though this was some time before we met, is it right to forgive him for being intimate with somebody else?

Please can you tell me what to do?

Thank you very much,

D. Watson (Miss)

Miss Watson sounded a decent sort and so did her chap. It did not seem such a terrible crime to me, after all it was well in the past and he had told her the truth when he could easily have kept quiet. I had tried my luck and given it to Mrs. Bird, but she would not have it. The letter had come back to me in four pieces and with a large "NO" and a circle around "intimate" in furious red ink.

Dear Mrs. Bird,

I have been married for five years to a man I thought loved me. Now he tells me he has fallen for a girl he met while he was away in the Services. He says he won't leave me, but I know they go away together for weekends and now I have found out she is pregnant. I can't bear the thought of living with him. What should I do?

Could you print my letter please? I daren't ask you to write back to my house in case he sees it.

Yours,

Unhappy Wife

It was the saddest letter. I couldn't begin to think how she might be advised, but as Unhappy Wife had done absolutely nothing wrong, surely even Mrs. Bird would feel sympathetic? I put it in with two very bland letters and crossed my fingers, but it didn't stand a chance. As well as a huge red line through the entire letter, Mrs. Bird had written "NO" so firmly that a blot of ink had burst onto the paper. Then she had written "AFFAIRS" and underlined it three times.

It was hard not to feel frustrated. From what I had seen in my short time at *Woman's Friend*, Unhappy Wife was hardly alone. I wasn't naive enough to think that there hadn't always been problems like this, but it didn't take a brainbox to see that the war had made things even harder. I didn't know the answer to lots of the problems, but I did know that a kind response was better than nothing. I hated having to throw the letters away.

Kathleen started giving me lots of Mr. Collins' work to do. She much preferred typing up the patterns and Mrs. Bird's beauty advice, which was unsurprisingly vigorous and based almost exclusively on not wearing make-up and applying something alarming you mixed into a paste. Mr. Collins wrote the features and fiction and I had to admit that even if it wasn't the same as typing up how the RAF were walloping Axis bombers close to Tobruk, it did make a nice change from the legal documents of my last job.

Mrs. Bird spent more time out of the office than in as she was in charge of an enormous number of Good Works. Whenever she left for her meetings, we would hear a mighty roar from the corridor as she announced both her destination and estimated time of return. It took some getting used to, as a hearty bellow of "Tube Station Bunk Beds—a quarter past three" did rather give you a start.

One morning, a few weeks into my new job, there was a mild bang from the corridor and a sound of trundling.

"That'll be Clarence," said Kathleen as a high-pitched voice squeaked out, "Second post," and then a very deep voice added, "Delivery, Miss Knighton."

"Come in, Clarence," called Kathleen.

"All right then," said the voice, which, sounding panicked, shot back up to soprano.

Clarence was Launceston's most dedicated and easily embarrassed post boy. Fifteen years old and already a good five foot ten with unpredictable skin that was a torment, he did his rounds several times a day. He balanced a keen interest in the war with the tragedy of almost total paralysis brought about by an uncontrollable crush on Kathleen.

As Clarence was rendered speechless if she even glanced at him, he directed everything he should like to say to her at me.

"Morning, Miss Lake," he said, covering three octaves. "Miss Knighton," he added, which came out very nearly high enough to start a conversation with a bat.

"Good morning, Clarence," I said.

"Hello, Clarence," said Kathleen.

Clarence looked as if he wished he were dead.

"Parcel for you, Miss Lake," he said and, turning his back on Kathleen so he could cope, added, "We've got them on thc run in Abyssinia," as if the two were connected.

"They can't beat our boys," I said, knowing it would make Clarence beam.

"Better crack on, Clarence," said Kath gently. "Or you'll have Mrs. Bird about you."

Clarence glanced in her direction but was struck dumb by the result and with an awkward wave hurried off.

I set to the day's correspondence at once and was rewarded when the first letter asked for Mrs. Bird's advice on War Savings stamps. That was nice and safe so I was off to a good start. The second was from a lady who was a recent martyr to a thyroid goitre. It did not make for a relaxed read even though I wasn't the squeamish type. I double-checked it against the list and decided that if we could cut out some of the more medical elements, it might just about do.

Of course, the letter after that was about a lady who wanted to get a divorce, which I reluctantly cut up and put in the bin. It was all down to the final postcard, which was written in bold hand and wasted no time.

Dear Mrs. Bird,

Do you know of an exercise for ankles? Things are acceptable presently as I have fur boots for the day and only attend events if in evening dress, but the summer is a torture I can hardly bear. Please might you advise?

Yours,

Unfortunate Legs

I felt for Unfortunate Legs as life seemed challenging enough at present, without limiting enjoyment to a long frock, but she had certainly got me out of a fix. There would be enough letters for that issue's problem page.

Putting them all into a buff cardboard file for Mrs. Bird, I squeezed past Kathleen's desk and into the corridor, which as usual was deserted and had a faint smell of boiled cabbage and soap. It was a dispiriting mix, which I put down to poor pipes.

Mrs. Bird was out at a Cats Evacuation meeting so I put the file on her desk and then called in on the Art Department to tell Mrs. Mahoney that so far I was on time for this week's deadline. She was explaining to Mr. Brand how to make an Easy Sausage Savoury and I happily joined in. I liked them both and thought it was a pity we didn't all share the journalists' old office as it would have been tons more jolly than being cooped up in our dingy little rooms.

Mrs. Mahoney asked me to give Mr. Collins a chivvy on his film-review column so I reluctantly left the conversation and knocked on his door. I was still wary of his mercurial ways but today, rather than sitting on his own looking deep and brooding, it appeared he was in a jovial mood.

"Miss Lake, is that you?" he said without looking up from his desk. "Come in then."

He was working in a half gloom surrounded by chaos, which, as I had quickly learnt, was his way. I was already used to his handwritten scripts, messy and crumpled, and occasionally torn in two and then taped back together. On one manuscript he had scribbled out an entire half page and started again. Despite his cynical air, I rather thought he cared about what he wrote and didn't just dash off any old thing.

"So," he said. "How are things going? You've already outlasted the two previous Juniors. Is Henrietta behaving herself?"

Mr. Collins was the only person who ever referred to Mrs. Bird by her first name.

"Everyone's lovely," I said, being diplomatic. "I'm learning lots about readers' Problems."

"I see," said Mr. Collins. "Kathleen informs me it's a challenge to fill up the page."

I nodded. I wondered if he knew about all the people whose letters were ignored.

"There are enough letters," I said. "But Mrs. Bird won't answer most of them. Some people are in a real pickle, but she says they're just Unpleasantnesses."

"She would," said Mr. Collins. "I have to say, it's all Greek to me. That's why I stick to fiction. Making things up is somewhat easier than sorting out real life."

I glanced over at the bookshelves. The brandy bottle was still there.

"I feel sorry for people," I said sadly, thinking of In A Muddle. "It seems such a shame not to help them all."

Mr. Collins sat back in his chair and rubbed his chin thoughtfully. It didn't look as if he had shaved. Then he leant forward again.

"Don't be downhearted, Emmeline. Henrietta was doing this advice business when I was virtually still a boy and I'm afraid you won't change her. To be fair to our beloved Acting Editress, she leaves me to get on with the stories and features because she knows that's what I do, and I try to make a decent job of it. Believe it or not, I do actually hope people like them."

He said it almost to himself as an aside. I nodded and started to say how much I enjoyed his work, but he interrupted me with a wave of his hand.

"It's not exactly literature," he said. "And goodness knows, the competition is beating us hollow and the poor old magazine is slipping away. But the few of us left are doing what we can. Look at Mr. Brand's illustrations. Beautiful stuff, really. Emmeline, stop worrying about Henrietta. Just do what you can, as well as you can. I promise you one day it will be worthwhile."

He scratched the back of his neck and then stretched out his arms as if he might yawn. "Good Lord, I'm in danger of boring us both. Lecture over. Find out what *you're* good at, Miss Lake, and then get even better. That's the key."

He looked down at the disarray on his desk, which I took as a sign he wanted to get back to work, so I gave him the message from Mrs. Mahoney and headed back to my office. Oddly, I felt a tiny bit perked up—encouraged even.

Find out what you're good at, Miss Lake, and then get even better.

It was an odd thing to be inspired by a brandy-drinking cynic of indeterminate middle age who sometimes seemed even less happy to be at *Woman's Friend* than me, but I was. Mr. Collins was right about the stories—he never let the *Woman's Friend* readers down. Their heroes were brave, their heroines plucky, and there was always a happy ending. It was a far sight more than Mrs. Bird did with the problems.

Kathleen had left a note on my desk saying she was out on an errand, so I sat on my own chewing the end of a pencil and thinking.

I didn't really know what I was good at, not yet. I only knew that I had wanted to become a War Correspondent to tell people important news and somehow make a difference. Now here I was, stuck at *Woman's Friend* ignoring even the small number of people whose lives Mrs. Bird had the power to change.

Do what you can, as well as you can.

And then I decided. With my heart speeding up, and wondering just how quickly I could type, I fed a new piece of paper into my typewriter and then took out In A Muddle's letter from the drawer. Readers like Unhappy Wife had problems I couldn't begin to understand, but I knew what to say to In A Muddle. I'd seen my friend Kitty in the same situation, and when it had gone awfully wrong for her, I hadn't done nearly enough to help.

I read through In A Muddle's letter again, biting my lip and trying to think like the sort of experienced person one would turn to in a crisis. A version of Mrs. Bird if she were friendly and actually cared. I would be for the absolute high jump if I was ever found out, but I had to at least try. I started to type using a style similar to Mrs. Bird's no-nonsense way, but far less savage. It was easier than I thought—I told In A Muddle that cinema trips and presents or not, she absolutely didn't have to "repay" her young man in any kind of a way. She should stick to her guns and if he went off her, then it was his loss.

I almost felt Mrs. Bird would approve.

But at the end of the letter I stopped. How on earth should I sign it?

I heard the door in the corridor bang open. It would be Kathleen back from her errand. I couldn't risk her seeing what I had done. I ripped the paper out of the typewriter and, grabbing my fountain pen, hastily wrote:

The very best of luck,
Mrs. Henrietta Bird

Chapter 6

PEOPLE ARE NOT ALWAYS GOOD SORTS

By the time Kathleen came in chattering about having nearly left her gas mask on the Tube, I had put the letter into my bag and was casually typing up a feature as if nothing out of the ordinary had happened. If it hadn't been for the fact I had signed In A Muddle's letter "Mrs. Henrietta Bird," it could almost have been as if it really was just me writing to a friend.

But it wasn't. I had forged her signature.

And used *Woman's Friend* headed notepaper. And written the letter on *Woman's Friend*'s time.

So, actually, it wasn't anything like me writing to a friend.

As I made a pantomime about leaving the office that afternoon, I could hardly look Kathleen in the eye.

"IS THAT THE TIME I AM SO LATE I MUST GO HOME SEE YOU TOMORROW GOODBYE," I said overloudly, without pausing for breath.

Then I hurtled out of the office with my hat and coat in my hand before she could see I had gone crimson with guilt.

Leaving the building was interminable. I stood in the lift and sweated profusely as it stopped at every floor, and then I lolloped across the foyer in a wonky combination of half walk, half trot while all the time expecting a heavy hand on my shoulder and instant arrest.

By the time I was outside in the sleet-soaked street, I could hardly wait to deposit the evidence in the post box before leaping onto the wrong bus, which took me nowhere near the direction of home.

I could never do this again. It was terribly wrong. Even though I felt confident Mrs. Bird would never find out, it had still been a crazy thing to do.

I wondered what Bunty would say. I had a feeling she would tell me I hadn't an ounce of brain and would get the sack if anyone found out. She'd be right too. I was hopeful I might have been able to help In A Muddle, but pretending the advice was from Mrs. Bird? Bunty really would think I had gone mad. As for Edmund—I dreaded to think.

I decided it was better to not tell a soul.

For the rest of the week, I worked like fury, trying to be the very essence of a good sort. The disappointment of making a hash of things and ending up at *Woman's Friend* still stung badly, but I had kept up my shifts at the fire station so was still trying to do my bit. I continued reading all the newspapers as well, keen to be poised with thoughtful political insight should even the smallest opportunity to move into *The Evening Chronicle* crop up. I continued to write to Edmund every day, making my letters breezy and light.

At the office I typed up the problems for Mrs. Bird's page double-quick, socked out two romantic stories by Mr. Collins on the ancient typewriter, and volunteered to do every job that Kathleen or any of the others said they didn't much fancy themselves. Things ticked along and when Mrs. Mahoney, who I liked very much, called me A Treasure, life at *Woman's Friend* started to feel better.

And then the following week, things became tricky again.

I honestly did try to weed out Unpleasantness from Mrs. Bird's letters, but with the paltry amount of correspondence and the bar for immorality set awfully low, it was hard to make up the numbers. I would begin every letter with optimism, encouraged by a mild opening, only to have my hopes cruelly dashed when a "has stopped making love to me" or "and now I am having a baby" put its hand up halfway through the second line. While Mrs. Bird was convinced that a hearty outlook and a brisk walk would invariably solve one's problems, most of the *Woman's Friend* readers had tribulations that an absolute busload of fresh air was not going to sort out.

I still couldn't bear to cut up some of the Unacceptable letters. I secretly kept them in my desk, even though there was nothing I could do about them.

On Monday I was soundly told off by Mrs. Bird for giving her a letter from a lady whose husband had had an affair. I had felt so sorry for her. "My heart is broken," she wrote, "as I have just found out that my husband, who I still love after twenty years, has gone off with a friend of mine at work . . ."

But Mrs. Bird didn't care.

"Miss Lake," she snapped. "Affairs. Have you gone entirely mad?"

Two days later I was in hot water over a young woman worried about her wedding night. "My friend said hers was nothing to write home about but I'm worried about what to expect" brought on another decisive response.

"Might I ask you, Miss Lake, is *Pleasurable* on the list or is it not?"

I did have the odd success. A maverick query asking if Mrs. Beeton was real and was it true she'd died young ("Of course she was real, Miss Lake, twenty-nine") and an overseas reader who found living in Canada rather lonely ("Dreariness won't win anything, Miss Lake, we must tell them to buck up") went over quite well, but very few letters were free from Unpleasantness to the acceptable degree.

"Honestly, Kathleen," I said one morning when I was struggling to find enough post to give to Mrs. Bird, "if we won't answer proper problems, it's no wonder no one writes in."

"Some still do," said Kathleen. She was wearing a complicated double-knit cardigan and looking perturbed.

"Not many," I said. "If you look at other weeklies, they're full of advice about rotten husbands, and having babies or not having babies, and what to do when your boyfriend's been away fighting for a year and you wonder if you'll ever see him again." I thought of Edmund and how most of the time I didn't even know where he was. "That's what people are worried about, not whether ants are likely to be a problem this June. Who cares about that?"

Kathleen glanced nervously at the door.

"For goodness' sake, Kathleen, she's out," I said.

It wasn't fair to snap just because I was tired. The previous night's raid had been heavy, and while I had worked another long shift at the fire station, half of London probably hadn't slept either. We were all in the same boat. But ignoring the readers still struck me as wrong.

"We should be helping people like this lady," I said, and I began to read a letter out from someone who had signed it Confused.

" 'Dear Mrs. Bird,

I am very much in love with my fiancé, but he has suddenly become very cold to me. He says he is fond of me but not passionately.' "

"Emmeline," whispered Kathleen, going pale. "Don't."

I ploughed on.

" 'Should I marry him and hope that he comes round?' "

I glared at her, which was entirely unfair as she wasn't the one I was cross with.

"Why can't Mrs. Bird help?" I asked. "This girl is going to have a wretched time if he doesn't actually love her. We'd only have to say there are plenty more fish in the sea. Or, or, this one." I opened the drawer where I had put a desperately sad letter I couldn't bear to throw out.

" 'Dear Mrs. Bird,

I am a mother of three and was widowed before the war. I don't have many friends and when a very kindly soldier was billeted with us, we became close. Now, to my horror, I find I am going to have his baby. I have written to him but he hasn't replied. I am desperate—please tell me, what should I do?' "

"Emmeline, stop it," said Kathleen, now getting impatient. "You know these are the type of people Mrs. Bird won't entertain."

"Type of people?" I said, thinking of Kitty and her little boy. "For heaven's sake, Kathleen, it could happen to you or me. It's not just a Type Of People. Listen to this one:

" 'Dear Mrs. Bird,

When they first evacuated the kiddies from London, I couldn't bear to let my little boy go. Two months ago we were bombed out and now my boy has been crippled for life.' "

I stopped. I was not a crybaby, but I felt my voice catch in my throat. I had shown this letter to Mrs. Bird. She'd said the woman had only herself to blame.

"Honestly, Kathleen," I said. "What's the point of *Woman's Friend* having a problem page if we don't help anyone out?"

I knew I was speaking to the wrong person. I should be trying to persuade Mrs. Bird.

Kathleen sighed.

"Emmy, look," she said in her quiet voice. "I know it can be awful. Sometimes I feel terrifically glum about it as well. But there's nothing you can do. If Mrs. Bird says to ignore someone who has, um, you know, is having . . . a baby, then that's what we have to do." She shook her head and her hair joined in sympathetically. "Even if we don't like it."

I bent down to pick up an envelope that had fallen under the desk.

"If I was having a baby," I said to the dark wooden floor, "I'd like to think someone would help."

I heard Kathleen's chair scrape against the floor. Then a different, decidedly chilly voice, said, "And is that a possibility, Miss Lake?"

The wall clock behind Kathleen's desk chimed, a useful reminder that Mrs. Bird was due to return to the office at eleven, having been sorting out an unfortunate dipsomaniac who had been run over outside in the street.

I kept my head under the desk as the clock continued to strike. I wondered if I could stay down for the entire eleven chimes.

"Miss Lake?"

"Yes, Mrs. Bird?" I said, finally emerging. Kathleen was standing to attention. She had gone the same colour as a lady I had once seen rushing out of the Dr. Crippen exhibit at Madame Tussauds.

"I trust, Miss Lake," said Mrs. Bird, calm in the face of potential depravity, "we were being hypothetical?"

"Oh yes, goodness, of course," I said, clearly a goner. "Kathleen and I were just discussing one of the readers' letters."

I saw Kathleen blanch and too late remembered that discussing the letters was strictly Off Limits.

"I see," said Mrs. Bird, who didn't look as if she did.

"Well, I say we were discussing," I said, backpedalling to first-team standard. "It was more me *saying*, really. Kathleen was stuck here having to listen."

I hoped I could at least get my friend out of the mire.

"And what was it you were *saying*, Miss Lake?" asked Mrs. Bird, managing to look apoplectic and icy at the same time. She was wearing an ancient and vast fur coat, which gave her the appearance of a large bear that had just failed to catch an especially juicy fish. "Because I was unaware that as a part-time Junior Typist, you were employed to say *anything* very much at all."

I braced myself. I had been at *Woman's Friend* for less than a month and now I was going to be given the sack.

Then again, if I did lose my job, it would mean I would have no alternative but to join up, even if it would send Mother and Father quite lunatic with concern. At least then I would have proper war experience and that might even help me get a job as a War Correspondent one day.

Perhaps I could join the Women's Auxiliary Air Force. That was a wonderful idea. I could train up to pack the parachutes and then join my brother, Jack's, squadron and make sure I did his. Or perhaps the ATA so that I could ferry around planes as a lady pilot instead, even if the rules meant they wouldn't let me shoot anyone down.

As Mrs. Bird got into the swing of telling me off, I considered more options. Perhaps I could stay with the Fire Service and do the motorcycle course to become a dispatch rider. I'd met a couple of girls who did that and they were excellent sorts—bright and hardworking, and always rushing off right into the thick of things. Jack would laugh his head off if I learnt to ride a motorcycle but it would also mean I could stay in London, which I was very keen to do. There'd be Bunty and the station girls, and William and his chums too for the cinema and dances and things, so really nothing would change. We could ask Kathleen along too.

Perhaps leaving *Woman's Friend* would be a good thing. Even if being sacked after just a few weeks would look rather grim on my record. I could say it had all been a mistake and I was just enormously keen to do more for the war effort. I would feel bad about leaving the readers that Mrs. Bird ignored, but there was nothing I could do to help them anyway.

"And I hardly think the *Woman's Friend* reader wants her afternoon spoilt by This Kind Of Thing, do you?"

Mrs. Bird had come to the end of her speech. It had been quite an innings.

"No," I said firmly. "No, she doesn't."

I steadied myself for an exit, although as it turned out, Mrs. Bird had only momentarily stopped play for tea and was now firmly back at the wicket.

"Miss Lake. You are An Innocent Abroad," she thundered, making it sound like a crime. "You will learn that PEOPLE ARE NOT ALWAYS GOOD SORTS."

Mrs. Bird put her hands behind her back as if she were inspecting the troops. "Particularly ones like these," she said, nodding at the mess of letters on my desk.

"Affairs . . . losing their heads . . . babies . . . UNPLEASANTNESSES," she boomed, pausing to let the abomination sink in. "And, even, Miss Lake . . . NERVES."

The look that accompanied this suggested we had moved on to a level of quite treasonable offence.

"These women are having The Time Of Their Lives while our men are off fighting for the future of the free world. I do not call that deserving of help, do you?"

I hardly thought this was true from what I had read, but with Mrs. Bird in full throttle there wasn't much point in arguing. And really, why should I care about the problem page anyway?

But as Mrs. Bird motored onto the second leg of her lecture about how awful people were, I realised I *did* care. I really, truly did.

I cared about the women who wrote into this old-fashioned, dead duck of a weekly magazine. Mrs. Bird received so little post that it would have been entirely possible for her to find time to answer every one. Instead, she had a lowly assistant like me cut up their letters while she charged around London on her do-gooding committees. It must be bad enough having your house bombed out, I reckoned, without Mrs. Bird turning up and insisting on a rallying speech and a reminder about backbone and stiff upper lip.

She may not have cared about those readers, but I did.

Joining *Woman's Friend* had been a mistake. But giving up on it would be worse. I might not be getting very far trying to stand up to Mrs. Bird, but if I lost my job, what if the next Junior Typist didn't even try? What if no one ever stood up for the women desperate enough to write in?

I had always thought the proper war action was reported in the newspapers. The battles and enemy casualties and important announcements by politicians and leaders. I had wanted to be part of that. Now I began to think I had been wrong. The Government was always saying everyone at home was vital to the war effort and needed to keep supporting our lads and get on with normal life as if nothing was different, so Adolf wouldn't think he was getting us down. And we should be chipper and stoic and jolly good sorts and wear lipstick and look nice for when the men were on leave and not cry or be dreary when they went off to fight again. And of course I agreed with that, *of course.*

But what about when things got difficult or went wrong? The

papers didn't mention women like the ones who wrote to Mrs. Bird. Women whose worlds had been turned upside down by the war, who missed their husbands or got lonely and fell in love with the wrong man. Or who were just young and naive and had their heads turned in a trying time. Problems that people had always had, only now, with everything so topsy-turvy, they were expected to just battle on.

Who was supporting *them*?

I still wanted to be a proper Correspondent. A lady war journalist like the ones I had read about who marched off to report on Spain's Civil War with nothing more than two fur coats and a fierce determination to find out the truth. I wanted to be part of the action and excitement.

But trying to become a news journalist could wait. Mrs. Bird was stuck in another age. Her views may have been accepted thirty years ago but they were out of date now. This wasn't just her war. It was everyone's. It was ours.

I wanted to make a go of it. I wanted to stay at *Woman's Friend* and try to help the readers out. I still didn't know exactly how I would do it, but people needed a hand.

It was time to gorge on humble pie.

"Mrs. Bird," I said with vigour, "I apologise profusely. I'm afraid I'm still getting the hang of all this." Looking soft in the head seemed the best approach. "I now understand everything far more clearly. I really am *very* sorry I have been so terribly slow on the uptake. You won't have to tell me again. Might I show you this letter from a lady who is Disappointed With France?"

I held out a letter which Mrs. Bird took, still looking ferocious. After a very long moment, she gave a short nod.

"Miss Lake, your moral standards belong in the gutter. They are quite extraordinarily low."

She made it sound as if I had been brought up by a group of exceptionally awful prostitutes or had made a habit of punching the infirm. Nevertheless, I looked as contrite as I could.

"I do not want to see that sort of letter," she said, pointing to my desk in a final declaration. "I will *not* read them, I will *not* answer them. They are not from Good Sorts."

With that she took a handful of the letters I had been reading to Kathleen and threw them all into the bin.

Then, like a galleon that has outflanked an Armada despite having an off-colour day, she made as magnificent an exit as the size of the room would allow.

Kathleen and I sat in silence, until we heard the door to Mrs. Bird's office slam shut.

"Crikey," I said, feeling heady with triumph.

"I say," said Kathleen in a whisper, her eyes like soup plates. "That was brave."

"Do you think we can call it a draw?" I said, suddenly giggly.

"I thought we were for it there," said Kathleen. "Thanks awfully for saying it wasn't me."

"Well, it wasn't," I said. "You were thc one telling me to shut up. I'm sorry about getting you involved. I won't mention the silly letters again."

"That's all right," said Kathleen. "I quite enjoyed it really. I'm going to the Post Room now." She looked hugely relieved the row was over and rushed off to the stairs.

When Kathleen had gone, I leant back in my chair and let out a breath.

I do not want to see that sort of letter. I will not *read them, I will* not *answer them.*

It all seemed quite clear. I would buckle right down. I would follow Mrs. Bird's instructions to a tee and never show her another letter that didn't exactly comply with her list.

And if Mrs. Bird didn't want to answer them, I would write to the readers myself.

It was risky, of course. Enormously risky. But I had written to In A Muddle and signed it from Mrs. Bird and nothing awful had happened about that. No one had known a thing. I bit my lip as I considered it. Yes. I could do this. If I was tremendously careful, I was sure that I could.

I took a big stack of Mr. Collins' work from my in-tray and arranged it at the front of my desk so that if Kathleen came in, she couldn't see what I was looking at. Then I fished out the letters Mrs. Bird had thrown into the wastepaper bin and read them all again.

I was horribly out of my depth with some of them. I hadn't a clue what to say. My personal experience wouldn't come anywhere near the mark. I sat back in my chair, chewing my thumbnail, and thought of Mr. Collins telling me I should do what I can, as well as I can.

I would have to bone up. Research what a decent advice columnist would say, so as not to risk making things worse for the readers. I immediately felt cheered. That's what journalists did all the time—research a big story. War Correspondents knew all about going undercover. I would approach helping the readers in exactly the same way.

Even if I didn't have the answers to the problems, lots of other, far more popular magazines did. I wouldn't copy from them, but I could learn. I felt most confident talking to girls my own age, so if nothing else, I could start by helping them.

By the time Kathleen appeared with Mrs. Bussell, the tea lady, who was in a fluster because she was late, I felt galvanised. My bin was stuffed with a satisfactory amount of shredded envelopes from readers, while three letters hid under cover of darkness in my bag to take home. I would buy all the other women's weeklies I could get my hands on and ask Bunty and the girls at the station if they could lend me theirs too. I could write letters and send them from the postbox just outside in the street, and even if someone did write back to thank Mrs. Bird for "her" advice, as I opened all the letters, I could make sure Mrs. Bird wouldn't see it.

She would never have to know a thing.

It was espionage of the highest order and I should have felt sick to my stomach if Mrs. Bussell hadn't begun her usual warning about the perils of mid-morning tea.

"You wait until you're forty," she announced. "You'll be halfway through The Change and everything will go to your hips."

I gave a suitable response to this traumatic news and took a flamboyant interest in the choice of biscuit. As the selection was limited, within a few moments I was back behind my typewriter with a cup of tea and an only slightly broken ginger nut.

I felt high as a kite with my plan. Kathleen was also in a jubilant mood as she had been able to track down a lost parcel for Mrs. Bird. She started chatting away.

"I'm glad I found it," she said, after Mrs. Bussell had left us to make another department fat. "It's a whole lot of new patterns and samples. Mrs. Bird would have gone positively barmy if we'd lost that. After this morning it's probably best if you and I keep our heads down."

I let out a shrill laugh, which wasn't like me.

"I should say!" I roared with my mouth full.

Kathleen put her finger to her lips and said Shush.

I returned to Mr. Collins' work.

Head In The Clouds. Further chapters of our dashing new romantic serial.

"*Silly young Clara,*" I typed, following his script. "*So much to look forward to in this gilded, lucky life. If only she would open her eyes and see how much the young captain might love her . . .*"

It was painful, giddy stuff. I typed on as the story became more and more dramatic. I was just a part-time Junior, diligently doing her job.

Chapter 7

A QUANDARY OVER NEXT STEPS

The only thing that really bothered me about deciding to write to the readers was not telling my best friend.

Bunty and I didn't have secrets. You can't be friends with someone your whole life and not tell them what you're up to. I was convinced she would disapprove of my plan, but I was dying to tell her about it. I hoped if I explained properly about helping people, she would understand.

At the end of my morning at *Woman's Friend*, I arrived home, a small parcel of letters hidden in my bag and a stack of women's magazines from Mr. Bone the newsagent under my arm. It had been snowing heavily again and I stamped my feet on the hall mat. I would stuff my shoes with newspaper when I got upstairs and dry them out there. As I pounded up the three flights to the flat, I called out a hello to Bunty, but she didn't respond. She had been working nights again so might well be having a nap. I carried on up to the flat and into the living room.

But rather than sleeping, Bunty was standing by the fireplace wearing a worried expression and her second best blue skirt.

"Emmy, I'm so sorry," she said, handing me an envelope before I'd even taken off my hat. It was a telegram addressed to me. We never received telegrams. I could only think of one thing.

Edmund.

I felt myself go pale. I looked at Bunty and then back at the envelope. Then I took a deep breath.

Bunty hovered as I opened it and read the five lines inside.

But it was not what I had feared.

In fact, when the contents revealed Edmund to be really quite well, I was in rather a quandary over next steps. I was enormously glad he hadn't been shot by a German, but my spirits hardly soared with regards to the rest.

"I'm so very sorry," said Bunty again. "Would you like a hankie?"

She offered me hers. It was nice and clean, with lemon edging.

"No thank you," I said, remaining polite in what was clearly A Difficult Situation.

Bunty looked distressed. "Would you like to sit down?" she said. "Perhaps *I* shall sit down. Is it Edmund? Poor, dear Edmund."

Bunty switched off the wireless, which had been playing an encouraging tune. Like everyone else, she knew that telegrams from overseas only ever contained very bad news.

"Was he tremendously brave?" she asked, clearly hoping for further information about Edmund's probable death. Bunty was always terribly good in a crisis but not noted for her patience.

"No," I said slowly. "No, I wouldn't say that. Actually, Bunts, he's gone off with a nurse."

"What?" Bunty's eyebrows became gymnastic. "I thought he was going to be dead."

I handed her the telegram and tried to think of the right thing to say. She read the contents and responded with some animation.

"What's he doing sending telegrams to you when clearly he is Perfectly Fine?"

I stared back at her with my mouth open. It didn't show much backbone on my part, but it was all I could muster.

Bunty stuffed the lemon hankie up her sleeve as if it were a nasty reminder of misinformed grief.

"A TELEGRAM?" Her voice came out as a shriek. "WHAT IS HE DOING SENDING A TELEGRAM WHEN HE'S NOT DEAD?"

She began to read it out loud, which I wasn't sure was wise as she already looked well on her way to a seizure.

"'. . . fell for Wendy. Getting married on Saturday. No hard feelings. Cheerio then Edmund. PS . . .'" Bunty stopped reading and looked up. "Emmy, he's jilted you. WHAT AN ABSOLUTE PIG."

Bunty was always good at making sure things were quite clear.

I took the telegram back before she ripped it up in a fury and then put it on the mantelpiece, which was a mistake as now it looked like a last-minute invitation to an exciting event. Which, I supposed, for Wendy, it probably was.

I tried to think calmly. It was the most enormous relief that Edmund was well. But other than that it was as if someone had whacked me in the stomach. I felt as if I might actually be sick.

"Well," I finally managed. "We must be glad that Edmund's all right. And not dead. That's really terribly good."

"Well, yes. Of course." Bunty nodded. "Yes," she said again, trying to make a good fist of joining in. Then she gave up and added, "But it's still utterly awful of him."

Bunty was right. I struggled to let it sink in. Edmund had been very quiet the past weeks, hardly writing at all, but I had told myself he was off fighting, which had been preferable to worrying that he was all right. It hadn't occurred to me he might be off falling in love with somebody else.

"How could he? You've only just sent him that vest," said Bunty, making it sound as if I'd managed to build him his own tank.

She was right again there. I could sew almost anything you might like, but I was dreadful at knitting and the vest had taken an age.

"Perhaps he hadn't received it," I said.

I sat down heavily as my knees decided to give up.

"I'll get you a drink," Bunty said. Neither of us drank much at the best of times, but as today wasn't turning into the best of anything, perhaps it was a good time to start.

She lifted the lid off the drinks cabinet, which was in the shape of a globe. It was a huge, hideous article, but Bunty's grandmother thought we would find it Modern. Bunty and I had decided that if the Germans invaded London and broke in, we would push it down the stairs at them. The full extent of the British Empire was featured in a rather confident orange and we thought that would make them quite wonderfully cross.

"I'm making you a whisky and soda," said Bunty, who was keen on American films.

It was twenty past three in the afternoon and neither of us drank whisky, let alone during the day. It was probably the sort of thing Bette Davis did all the time and would have been exciting if only it hadn't been brought on by Edmund not wanting to marry me. I'd had no idea he'd gone off me. How could I have not seen it? I put my head in my hands and tried not to cry. I felt so stupid. And hurt.

Bunty handed me my drink. I bet Bette Davis wouldn't feel hurt. Actually, I bet she wouldn't have got engaged to Edmund in the first place. He was probably a bit sensible for her, and anyway, he would have thought being a famous actress was showy. After all, he had laughed at me just for saying I wanted to become a War Correspondent.

I took a sniff of the whisky. Bunty, who was watching me anxiously, raised her glass and so did I. Then we both took what people in the know call a Big Slug.

Within a moment my lungs started to burn and we both broke into a fit of coughing. After a time, I wiped my eyes and tried to pull myself together.

"Bette Davis," I said. "What would she do? About Edmund?"

"Shoot him with a pistol and go on the run," wheezed Bunty, sitting down beside me on the sofa and smoothing her skirt. "Honestly, Em, I know the vest looked like a maniac knitted it in a blackout and it probably did put him off you a bit, but running away with someone else really does take the biscuit."

"Doesn't it?" I agreed.

The truth was I'd loved Edmund, or at least I'd thought I had, and we'd been together for ages, so it had seemed perfectly sensible to get engaged. I wondered what had happened to make him change his mind about getting married. Was it something I'd done, or had Wendy been too perfect to ignore? I didn't know what to think.

I sounded like one of the readers who wrote to Mrs. Bird.

Sitting in the winter gloom of the living room, I considered whether to risk another go at my drink. Now that the burning had calmed down, it wasn't as bad as all that and I did feel it was helping me take a certain philosophical bent.

I nodded towards the telegram on the mantel.

"I wonder what Wendy is like," I said.

"I bet she's awful," replied Bunty, loyal to the hilt and without a shred of evidence.

We both sat in silence for a moment, contemplating the enormity of the situation.

"I'm going to have to let everyone know," I said.

Bunty made a sympathetic face. "They'll understand. Honestly, everyone will just want to help out and cheer you up. I can tell people if you want. I'll tell William anyway," she said. "He'll probably want to kill Edmund on your behalf. That's if your brother doesn't get to him first."

I gave a half-hearted smile and started to list everyone. I didn't sound as plucky as I'd hoped.

"Mother and Father and Granny and Reverend Wiffle."

Reverend Wiffle was our vicar. He had gout and a funny eye but was perfectly nice once you worked out which one it was you had to speak to. He would find a broken engagement very awkward indeed.

In fact, telling everyone was going to be grim. Father would say, "Emmy, the boy's a bloody fool of the first order," and Mother would interrupt him with, "I don't think swearing will help, Alfred, but I must say Edmund's been Very Silly Indeed."

All in all it would be a bit much.

"Bunts," I said, "I am going to be a spinster."

"Steady on," countered Bunty. "You're still in with a shot."

"No, I've missed the boat. I'll crack on, on my own."

I was trying hard to take Edmund's rejection on the chin. No one liked a wallower, and even if I was utterly crushed, I would look forward. After all, I was the one who wanted to march off to war as a reporter. I couldn't sit in the corner and cry at the drop of a hat.

I pushed on, getting up from the sofa and beginning to pace around the living room as I spoke.

"I'm not going through this sort of business again, Bunts. From now on, marriage is strictly off-limits. I shall concentrate on having a career."

"Good for you!" said Bunty, blithely ignoring my recent disastrous job choice. "Who cares about Rotten Edmund anyway?"

She took another slug of the whisky and then stood up.

"I'm so sorry," she added in a gasp. "I don't think I can breathe."

I thumped her on the back, which didn't help, and then switched the wireless back on, which I hoped possibly would.

It was too early to get ready for my shift on the fire-station telephones, but after I finished my drink I went to my room to change into my uniform and try to take stock. Though I had managed to fight off tears and put on a brave front, the truth of it was I felt crushed. I sat on my bed next to the pile of magazines I'd brought home and wished I could just go to sleep for a month until everything felt better. It was pretty rich of me to think I could dish out advice to people who wrote in to *Woman's Friend*. I couldn't even keep hold of my own fiancé.

I was entirely unqualified, although if nothing else I supposed I could sympathise, let the readers know they weren't on their own. I'd just been unceremoniously dumped, but I had friends and family who I could count on, whatever happened and for as long as I needed them. As I sat in my bedroom feeling awful, Bunty was next door in the kitchen, making me a sandwich with the last of the meat paste because it was my favourite, and she hoped it might cheer me up. And while it would be difficult to tell Mother and Father about Edmund, I knew they would listen and reassure me that in the end, things would hurt less. And Thelma and the girls at the station would tell me how Edmund must be a prize idiot and they'd never liked the sound of him anyway. It might hurt like anything but I had lots of people who would listen; I wouldn't have to plough through this alone.

How awful it would be with no one to listen. What if my only choice was to write to a perfect stranger in a magazine for reassurance or advice? And then, after all that, they ignored me and didn't reply. It would make things even worse.

I wiped my eyes and had a big sniff. I couldn't just sit around feeling low. Edmund had jilted me and I felt like a washout, but he wasn't dead and he had sounded thrilled to bits in the telegram, so I was just going to have to wish him well and get on with it. I was still better off than loads of people, and anyway, as Mother always said, Granny didn't spend half her life chaining herself to railings for today's woman to moon around waiting for some chap to look after her.

Quite.

"Right," I said out loud. "Come on."

I blew my nose, and then took the readers' letters, my pen, and my notebook from my bag and reached for the first magazine on the pile. Then I turned to the problems on the second-to-last page, took the lid off my pen, and started to make notes. The advice was practical and largely sympathetic, and they answered questions about no end of things Mrs. Bird wouldn't entertain. Women who had lost their head with a man, been let down by one, or were worried about another. Scared for their children, or fed up with their parents. Some of the readers had been foolish, but none of their problems were scandalous. A few of the magazines promised to send leaflets explaining things that they couldn't put on the page.

I looked at the little pile of letters I had brought home from *Woman's Friend.* It seemed terrifically small beer trying to help out the one or two who had included a stamp and their address, while these big colour magazines were read by thousands and thousands of people.

What *Woman's Friend* really needed was to print decent advice so more readers would see it. I wished Mrs. Bird could see the other magazines.

I re read the letter from Confused, the girl whose fiancé had lost interest in her. "He says he is fond of me but not passionately." Was that how Edmund had felt about me? If I was really honest, was that how I felt about him? Suddenly I was almost relieved that we weren't going to get married. What if he hadn't met Wendy and instead, out of duty, had gone through with marrying me? It would have been dreadful. Perhaps there really was a bright side to all this.

I felt equipped to reply to Confused and decided to draft an encouraging next move, but there was no return address or envelope for a reply. My moment of triumph was deflated. Hers was a problem I could confidently understand and quite possibly help, but now I couldn't write back.

In a funk I plonked the letter down on the bed.

A combination of a rotten day and a large glass of whisky had given me a bullish view of things. Why shouldn't we try to help Confused? Or any other girl in her position who read *Woman's Friend*? It wasn't as if Mrs. Bird cared. She probably wouldn't even notice if an extra letter made its way in.

So what if it did?

No, that would be too huge a risk. Idiotically reckless. Like going behind enemy lines and sending reports from right under the adversary's nose. Only the maddest or very boldest of War Correspondents would do that.

For the first time since Edmund's telegram, I broke into a smile.

Chapter 8

A RUMOUR OF PINEAPPLE CHUNKS

Being ditched by Edmund meant that my accidental move into ladies' periodicals was now barely newsworthy as far as my family were concerned. When I told them that I was no longer engaged, my parents had suggested a trip home for the weekend, and the promise of a rare treacle pudding and the last tin of pineapple chunks was too good to turn down. Even better, my brother, Jack, had leave for the first time in ages so I would be able to see him too.

I had spent the last week at work being an absolute paragon of virtue as far as Mrs. Bird was concerned, diligently giving her a small handful of safe letters that even she couldn't contest. Far more importantly, I had also secretly sent my own replies to three readers, poring over the answers as I drafted and then typed them up at home, and trying to keep my hand steady as I signed them "Yours, Mrs. H. Bird."

Signing Mrs. Bird's name was the hardest part and it wasn't a course of action I took lightly. Had I been found out over In A Muddle I might have been able to feign innocence, but writing to more readers was a step into very dangerous territory. That said, it really wasn't like facing German tanks or gunfire, or trying to keep London from burning down every night in the Blitz. When you looked at it like that, I wasn't taking serious risks at all.

So I signed the letters as Mrs. Bird and posted every one.

I still had Confused's letter and had drafted a short reply that would easily fit into the weekly Henrietta Bird Helps page, but I hadn't had the gumption to actually hand it to Mrs. Mahoney for typesetting. I had a slight inkling Mrs. Bird didn't bother to read the final printed copies because the ones Kathleen put in her in-tray always stayed there seemingly untouched, but I couldn't be entirely sure. Further investigation was required.

I didn't mention any of this to Bunty. I hated keeping it from her but she was so concerned about me over Edmund that I felt sure she would think I was having some sort of emotional hoo-ha. And if I was honest, while I thought I would be able to convince her that sending the odd helpful reply wasn't too rash, even I knew sneaking a letter into the magazine without Mrs. Bird knowing was taking things way too far.

A week after I became A Single Career Woman, Bunty and I set off home to Little Whitfield. Although I was slightly dreading my parents' partisan apoplexy about Edmund, it was good to get away from London. The village had been lucky to avoid many raids, although a field had been blown up when a bomber had no doubt flown off course from one of the towns. All in all the thought of two nights in a nice warm bed without the likelihood of having to sleepwalk down to the shelter or stick my tin hat on at the fire station sounded better than a week in Monte Carlo to me.

Bunty and I caught a Saturday morning train from Waterloo, which was busy with troops heading to or from their billets and people visiting their families for the weekend. The train was packed with servicemen on their way down to Weymouth, and Bunty saw it as an ideal opportunity to find a replacement for Edmund, whether I wanted one or not. Crammed into a packed compartment, we enjoyed the trip out to the Hampshire countryside in the company of some very nice officers who insisted on giving us their seats together with a bar of chocolate, two cigarettes even though we didn't smoke, and several addresses to write to.

With the early February snow falling steadily, we crunched our way along the short walk from Little Whitfield station to the house. It was a route Bunty and I had taken together hundreds of times. When both of her parents died before she was even at school, although she wasn't a complete orphan as she had her granny, right from the start it was always Bunty, me, and Jack.

Entirely aware of what my family were like, Bunty was now doing sterling work as Head Of Morale in the face of an imminent avalanche of sympathy and possible wrath.

"Your parents will be thrilled about *Woman's Friend*," she said. "They'll be pleased that you're now far less likely to get hurt in the line of journalistic duty than if you were on *The Chronicle*, so things aren't all that bad."

"Hmm," I said. "I don't think they'll worry about work. They're all so livid about Edmund, we'll spend most of the time trying to talk them out of having his guts for garters."

Bunty laughed. "That's not such a bad idea." She kicked a lump of snow with her galoshes for emphasis.

Just before Vicarage Hill we turned onto the common, pleased to see the Wildhay Oaks standing tall and stoic under the heavy covering of snow. Jack, Bunty, and I had spent our childhood running among these trees, chasing each other and going full pelt until you could shout "HOME!" If you were touching a tree, you were safe and couldn't be caught. Before the war started, Jack and Edmund and William had run circuits around them, all three boys intent on being in peak fitness for when they joined up.

Sometimes in London, when the air raids were really crashing about, I would close my eyes and picture the Wildhay Oaks, calm and dependable as ever. As long as they still stood, it felt as if we would all be all right.

As we rounded the final corner onto Glebe Lane, Pennyfield House came into view. It was a dear little Georgian house, surrounded by weeping willows and with such symmetrical windows it looked as if a child had told an architect exactly how a house should be designed. I always loved that first glimpse of home. Today, though, I was interrupted as a huge snowball hit me squarely on the head, knocking off my beret and leaving me spluttering like Father's old motorcar.

"Jack Lake," I bellowed, because it didn't take an enormous brain to work out where it had come from. "Jack Lake, if you think you are—"

My brother hurled another snowball, which hit the target, straight in my face.

"He's by the side gate, Em," yelled Bunty, unperturbed by the assault and enthusiastically gathering ammunition, her suitcase abandoned. She had spent half her childhood under attack from my brother and knew what she was up against. "I'll get him."

"Unlikely, Bunts old man," shouted my brother as a missile whizzed past Bunty's head.

"Missed!" I roared, scooping up snow. "Call yourself a fighter pilot? You throw like you're in the Girl Guides."

Jack's reply consisted of a barrage of activity, all of which scored a bullseye.

"Ladies," he taunted in a very chipper voice. "I'm trying to give you a chance."

The snow was beginning to seep through my coat, and my woollen gloves were sodden.

"Swine," I shouted. "Small fry."

"How are we going to get in?" whispered Bunty, who had taken at least one direct score to the face and now resembled a Belisha beacon. "He's probably booby-trapped the back gate."

I stifled a snort. Of course he had. It was perfect. In the middle of Europe being battered by a deranged madman and Britain doing its best to keep the hope of a free world alive, the three of us were playing like children in the snow. For these moments it was as if nothing had changed from a time when everything was simple and Mother and Father could make anything horrid just go away.

"Only one thing for it, Bunts," I whispered back. "Battering ram. Scarves up."

We wrapped our dripping scarves around our faces. Bunty squashed her hat down on her head and I wished mine wasn't lying in the middle of the drive.

It was a suicide mission of the highest order, but we saw it through and ten yards later were doing our best to heave as much snow as we could into my brother's face. Safely swathed in his RAF greatcoat and leather gloves, Jack had been completely unmarked by our efforts until this point but was now laughing so much he swallowed a big lump of snow. He fought back valiantly, managing to hold us both at arm's length so that we could only flail around like two baby birds caught by a very large dog.

All three of us yelled and laughed and shouted at each other.

"Children, really! You'll catch your deaths."

Standing at the door to the house, my mother had barely raised her voice, but we all stopped brawling at once.

Trim as ever, and a vision of calm in a pale blue ribbed cardigan and pleated skirt, Mother shook her head slightly but smiled.

"You are all revolting. I have failed horribly. Jack, go and pick up your sister's hat; Emmeline, stop teasing your brother; and Bunty, come here straightaway so I can see how you are. Come on—quick march."

We let go of each other as ordered, picking up hats, cases, and bags dropped in the scuffle. As Bunty was warmly kissed by my mother, who declared her as pretty as ever, Jack placed my beret on my head at a jaunty angle and then hugged me tightly.

"Good to see you, Sis," he said. "Sorry to hear your news. Man's a bloody fool. You all right?"

"I'm fine, thanks," I said, touched by his concern.

"Was it the vest? Mother said she couldn't make out if he was supposed to wear it or use it as some sort of tarpaulin. Still, at least now you're on your way to *The Times*."

He grinned at me, blue eyes shining and the tops of his ears bright red in the cold. He looked about ten.

"You know, I'll track Edmund down and punch his lights out if you want. Really."

I shook my head. "It's all right, thanks. Actually, it's for the best, really."

"What, being an old maid?" He seemed unconvinced. "Ah well, good for you. Don't worry, though, I can always put a word out to the chaps. Jocko Carlisle might be worth a go. No, not Jocko, he just got engaged. Or Chaser's a good lad." He considered it for a moment. "Actually not Chaser . . . clue in the name." He raised his eyebrows but then brightened up. "Leave it with me, Em, I'll give it some thought."

I nodded gamely. It was easier than trying to convince him I was just fine.

"Let's go in," I suggested. "There's a strong rumour of pineapple chunks."

It was enough to distract Jack from marrying me off to half his squadron and together we went into the hallway. Mother was helping Bunty out of her coat and saying Isn't It Marvellous Emmy Is Absolutely Fine in a voice she didn't normally use.

Bunty knew of course that this was code for You Will Tell Me The Truth, My Daughter Is Heartbroken, Isn't She?

I coughed. Mother whirled around, threw Bunty's coat over her arm, and then grasped my face in her hands and beamed.

"Darling, don't you look well!" she cried.

I knew of course that she actually meant If I Ever See Edmund Jones Again, I Cannot Be Held Responsible For My Actions.

"Thanks, Mummy, I am well."

"Yes, you are!"

"I am."

"And that's good!"

"It is!"

Mother showed no sign of moving the conversation on. At this rate, we could be here until Easter.

But then she pulled me towards her and gripped my arms as if she would never let me go.

"Men are such fatheads, my darling," she whispered. Her voice was fierce, but then lightened. "Except for your father, of course. But the rest of them: *fatheads.*"

I could barely breathe. If all my family were to keep doing this, I was odds on for cracking a rib.

"And Jack too," I gasped into her hair. "Jack's all right. And Uncle Gregory we like, don't we? So not all of them . . ."

Mother squeezed me again.

"That's my girl," she said. "Quite right. Not all of them. Well done."

"Is your mother doing the Fatheads Speech?"

My father had come into the hallway.

"Hello, Bunty, how are you?" he said, kissing her hello. "Keeping the War Office going? Hope you're checking Churchill's grammar. Germans bound to be snooty on that sort of thing."

Bunty assured him that Mr. Churchill's grammar was tip top, leaving out the fact that she had absolutely nothing to do with him and had never even seen him in the War Office building.

"Walls have ears, Dr. Lake," she added for gravitas, which went down terrifically well.

"Your father would be proud," he said, and Bunty looked happy as she always did when he mentioned her parents, neither of whom she could really remember.

Then it was my turn.

"Hello, Daddy," I said as he gave me a kiss and then frowned and looked at me over his glasses.

"Never liked him," he said, which I knew perfectly well wasn't true. "Absolute dunderhead. Your mother's worried, of course, but I've told her to look on the bright side as at least now we won't have idiots for grandchildren." He gave me a wink. "I think that perked her up."

"Thanks, Daddy," I said. It was the longest speech I had ever had from my father and he gave me another hearty squeeze on the arm and said Well Done, Chicken, even though I hadn't done anything.

I took off my coat and scarf, hanging them on the tall Victorian hall stand that used to belong to my grandparents, and followed him into the living room.

I could hear him muttering under his breath.

"Dreadful business," he said. "I'll have his guts for bloody garters."

Over a slap-up lunch of shepherd's pie without very much of the shepherd element, followed by a choice of treacle pudding or pineapple chunks with a spoonful of carefully eked out custard, I was quizzed by my parents and teased by Jack about *Woman's Friend*. By the time I had enthused about how lovely everyone was and how structurally robust the offices appeared, everyone agreed that I had secured gainful employment with a trailblazer for Women In The Workplace and, more important for my mother, The Least Interesting Target For The Luftwaffe in the whole of London.

"*Woman's Friend* is helping people, which is marvellous," my mother said, as if I were giving out half crowns to the homeless. "And as we're stuck with this silly business, at least you girls might as well get careers out of it."

My mother steadfastly referred to the war as This Silly Business, which made it sound like a mild fracas over a marmalade sponge. That aside, I was lucky to have parents who took the modern view. My father agreed.

"Emmy," he said, "you are following in a long line of formidable women."

"How is Granny, Mother?" asked Jack.

My parents exchanged glances.

"Barmy," said Jack, answering himself.

"Crackers," I said, at the same time.

"Children, really," said Mother, not meaning it.

"What do you think, Bunty?" asked my father. "It's quite all right, do go ahead."

"Um. Is she still mad as a hatter, Dr. Lake?" asked Bunty, who knew my grandmother well.

Father roared with laughter. "I think that's about the sum of it," he said. "God help the good people of Exeter. I'm sure they will be most relieved when there's Peace and she goes home."

Mother looked around at us all. "Now, Jack and Bunty will clear the table and Emmy will come with me into the village as I need to return a book to the lending library." She checked her wristwatch. "They're only open until two."

Bunty began studiously collecting up pudding bowls, mainly as I knew she didn't want to catch my eye. She had bet me thruppence that Mother would want to have A Chat about Edmund.

Mother bundled me out of the dining room and into my overcoat in much the same manner she had when I was three. Soon enough, we were arm in arm and heading through the snow and off to the library, without, I noted, a book to return.

She chatted cheerfully, updating me on local news and, I was sure, doing her best to lull me into a false sense of security.

"Bother," she said as we were crossing the road by the duck pond. She stopped and put her hands on her hips, which if you asked me, was hamming it up a bit. "I seem to have forgotten that library book. Ah well, shall we just have a nice walk?"

The snow flurried around us as we made our way along the high street and Mother pulled me in closer.

"Now," she said. "I wanted to have A Quick Chat."

Bunty had won her bet. I wondered if we could hurry this up. It was furiously cold.

"Mother, I'm fine. Really. I don't mind about Edmund at all."

My mother looked unconcerned. "Yes, darling, I can tell that. And I'm very glad indeed. Such a silly boy. Now, tell me, how is dear Bunty? I've had an invitation to visit Mrs. Tavistock and I should like to give her a report."

When war broke out, Bunty's grandmother had moved to her

small country estate. Mrs. Tavistock would not stop Bunty from staying in London, but she worried about her granddaughter continually.

"Bunty is very well," I said, because she was.

"That's good. And how is her job?"

"Busy," I said. "Very hush hush."

"Of course," said my mother. "And William. How is he? Do you think they will get married?"

"I should hope so," I said, carefully sidestepping a patch of black ice on the pavement.

"They're both jolly lucky he hasn't been sent somewhere abroad," said Mother with feeling. Her friends' sons were all, by and large, overseas.

"I don't think William would agree," I replied. "He's still smarting that the army won't have him because of his ears."

My mother pulled her scarf a little more snugly around her neck as we walked on towards the Fox and Thicket, on the east side of the green.

"Being a fireman is such a dangerous job," she said, which was rather stating the obvious. I didn't need reminding. I knew the kind of calls he was sent out on. I had an idea the conversation was heading for a You Are Taking Care Of Yourselves, Aren't You? speech. I tried to play things down.

"Mother, everything is dangerous."

She stopped trudging through the snow and turned to me, taking hold of my hands.

"Darling, we're all tremendously proud of you for seeing things through in London but you will take extra care, won't you? Mrs. Tavistock worries terribly about Bunty."

"Mother, Bunty and I can look after ourselves," I said.

She smiled, knowing I had risen to the bait. "I know. I'm just not sure what Mrs. Tavistock would do if anything happened. Or any of us. No one wants to be a man down. We all love you quite madly."

She marched on, blue eyes just like Jack's trying not to look concerned from under her fur hat.

"We'll be fine," I said in a firm manner.

It didn't wash one bit. Mother pursed her lips.

"I'm serious, Emmy," she said as I rolled my eyes like a teenager. "You must look after each other. Mrs. Tavistock doesn't need an upset. And I'm not as young as I look."

She glanced at me sideways and we both burst into laughter.

"Let's change the subject," Mother said, knowing she had made her point. "You do know you'll meet someone wonderful one day, don't you?"

I began my prepared speech about Being A Spinster And Having A Career but didn't get very far.

"Don't be absurd," she said. "You can have both. Once this silly business is all sorted, you and Bunty and all your friends will be able to get on and achieve whatever you want. Or else we're wasting our time fighting That Madman in the first place." She tilted her chin up in a way I was sure had stopped policemen in their tracks during her more bohemian youth. "Honestly, Emmy, don't let Edmund put you off. That's not the right spirit at all."

I grinned, knowing when I was beaten.

"Some decent chap will come along at some point, and regardless of all that, jolly well make a go of it at this magazine of yours. You might not be rampaging around writing about the fighting, but it's a start. And it's quite a dear little magazine. I have subscribed."

"Really?" I said, surprised. My mother was more likely to be found reading Virginia Woolf than *Woman's Friend*.

"Of course I have, darling," said Mother, looking quite indignant. "This is your career. And there's lots to like. The hot-pot page is full of wonderful ideas."

She forged on, trying hard to be supportive.

"The nurse is very informative, the stories really quite gripping, and Henrietta Helps seems most . . ." She ran out of steam.

"Harsh?" I suggested.

My mother laughed. "I was going to say *robust.* But it must be terribly helpful to the people who write in."

I said Hmm. It was odd hearing praise for Mrs. Bird.

"Actually, Mother, Mrs. Bird seems to think people—young ones in particular—are mostly up to no good." I squashed a wodge of snow with my boot.

"Then you'll have to show her she's wrong, won't you?" replied my mother. "Show her what a decent young person can do." She took my arm. "A bit of the old Lake determination is in order I think, don't you?"

I smiled into my scarf. My mother never gave in. One of Father's friends had once said that if Mother had been in charge, the Great War would have been over by 1916. Father had replied that if my mother had been in charge, she would have made damn sure the bloody thing hadn't started in the first place. Mother always said it wasn't just about keeping going, but about standing up for what you believed in as well.

I nodded. She was right. A bit of the old Lake determination *was* in order.

As the snow began to fall and we turned back towards Pennyfield House, as much as it was good being home, I couldn't wait to get back to my desk.

Chapter 9

WE DON'T KNOW A HAROLD

Replying to readers was a careful business, and not just because I was worried about getting caught. Worse even than this would be giving duff advice that made things sorrier for a reader, so I kept my replies general, encouraging people to take time and think about things, not be hasty, but never to give in. The other magazines were helpful—I learnt about what they said and how they would say it, and without actually copying them, I tried to do the same.

Dear Mrs. Bird,

I am twenty-two and devoted to Mother, but she always wants to come with me when I go to the cinema or dances with my young man. She is always paying him compliments and making his favourite dinner too. I don't want to hurt her feelings, but I wonder if she is a little too friendly at times.

What should I do?

Yours,

Joyce Dickinson (Miss), Preston

"Disgusting," said Mrs. Bird. "No."

"Dear Miss Dickinson," I wrote back. "I am sure your mother means very well and you are awfully fond of each other. However,

I suggest you speak honestly to her and explain that you need your own friends . . ."

I would take the letters home and as Bunty was now working on the day shift at the War Office, in the afternoons I would sit at my typewriter in the living room and carefully draft the replies. Once I was happy with my efforts, I would type them up, sign them in Mrs. Bird's name, which was still the worst part, and the next day, I would drop them into the postbox outside the Launceston Press building.

So far it had gone without a hitch, and in rare moments I could almost forget that it wasn't actually my job and I shouldn't actually be doing it. Mrs. Bird was busier than ever, marching off to do her charity work or rushing to the railway station to sort out Dire Emergencies At Home ("Pregnant cow stuck in a ditch. Nincompoops can't get it out"). Other than roaring instructions to everyone at the weekly Editorial Meetings, she did rather leave us all to it.

This was just as well as one morning, on the day *Woman's Friend* went to press, an advertiser forgot to send in their deodorant advert on time. It was a cardinal sin to miss the final deadline and it scared Mr. Newton in Advertising almost to death.

"Oh my word, oh my word," he kept saying, as everyone congregated in the Art Department in something of a state. "If there's no Odo-Ro-No, there'll be a two-column gap on page twelve. Nothing there. Not a thing. What will Mrs. Bird say? What will she say?"

"Never mind Mrs. Bird," said Mrs. Mahoney, threatening to reveal her firm side. "It's *my* deadline they've just messed up."

"Hold hard, everyone," said Mr. Collins, the only person who was calm. "Mrs. Mahoney, might I suggest we run last week's advert for Bile Beans again? I rather think it's the same size."

Mrs. Mahoney softened a little and Mr. Newton looked slightly less green about the gills and was able to speak for us all.

"But who will tell Mrs. Bird, Mr. Collins? Who will tell Mrs. Bird?"

Mr. Collins appeared unworried. "No one," he said as we all looked aghast. "We'll put Odo-Ro-No in next week. With luck she'll never know. Oh, come off it, you lot," he added as panic seemed about to set in. "Hands up any of you who has ever actually seen our Editress look at a finished magazine?"

No one put up their hand. I wasn't sure so I looked to Kathleen. She was shaking her head.

"There you are then," said Mr. Collins. "Bile Beans it is. If anyone's worried, come and see me. Actually, don't," he added evenly. "It's all going to be fine."

Then he marched out of the room and back to his office.

"Gosh," said Kathleen.

"He has quite a way about him when he wants," said Mrs. Mahoney.

"I shall be sacked," said Mr. Newton.

But Mr. Collins was right. Mrs. Bird didn't notice a thing.

It was the proof I needed. I had wondered if our Editress read the finished issues, but it had been little more than a suspicion, a bout of wishful thinking really, and definitely not enough to act upon. But now the combination of Mr. Collins' absolute confidence and the real evidence of Mrs. Bird not noticing a large advertisement for stomach tonic in the place of underarm daintiness meant there was nothing to hold me back.

With my mouth dry and my palms sweating, I slipped Confused's letter in with the others to be printed in next week's Henrietta Helps. I'd changed the words a bit so Kathleen wouldn't recognise it and replaced *passionately* as I knew that would give the game away. But the point about your fiancé going off you was still clear and if Confused read it, I very much hoped she would feel reassured.

It was all too easy to add the letter and my response to the folder of copy that would go to Mrs. Mahoney to be typeset, but it was the most enormous thing to actually hand it over. I knew Mrs. Bird did not look at proofs before the magazine went to press so from this point onwards there would be no going back.

My contingency plan wasn't exactly top notch. If I was found out, I would claim that Mrs. Bird had forgotten she'd written the advice. It was worse than feeble, but it was all I had. If Mr. Collins was confident Mrs. Bird would not notice a switched advertisement that took up half a page, surely one small letter would be safe?

I decided to take the risk.

It was high time I told Bunty about my secret activities. I had been putting it off long enough. Bunty was miles from being a killjoy but she was terribly keen on honesty and might not be entirely bowled over by the idea, at first anyway. I felt sure she would be sympathetic when I told her everything so decided to take my chance the following Saturday.

The sun had pulled its socks up and was making a good effort in the almost cloudless winter sky, so Bunty and I set off for a stroll through Hyde Park. She had suggested a brisk march around the Serpentine before heading to Kensington to look at the latest bomb damage before tea and then on to the cinema for a film. After a big raid it was always sad to see flattened buildings and burnt-out churches which had stood for hundreds of years, but there was something rather triumphant about the monuments and statues, even the parks and big department stores that were still there, getting on with things. The Luftwaffe may have been trying to blast us to pieces, but everyone just kept getting back up. And when you saw that they hadn't even managed to dent Big Ben and we'd stopped them from burning down St. Paul's, it did put a smile back on your face.

Bunty had been terrifically keen to get going, so we left without having lunch and had to chew on a piece of bread we'd brought for the ducks.

"Do you think Mrs. Bird is beginning to like you?" asked Bunty, throwing a crust which hit a duck and bounced off into the lake. The fat little chap bravely paddled off to rescue it.

"I shouldn't think so," I said, huffing on my gloves. "Puts up with, perhaps. She's not very keen on anyone really. Including most of the readers."

The park was full of people making the most of a bright February day. I sidestepped an elderly gentleman guiding a little girl along on a tricycle, and looked over at a young woman in a thin coat who was wheeling an enormous pram. She was trying to get it across the grass, while keeping her two boisterous little boys within reach. She wasn't much older than Bunty and me, but she looked exhausted. One of the boys pushed his brother into the snow and within seconds they were fighting and wailing.

"There was a letter this week from someone who's having a baby by the wrong man," I said, which did rather come out of thin air. "But don't tell anyone, will you?" I added, sounding like Kathleen.

"Mum's the word," said Bunty, no stranger to an unfortunate turn of phrase. "Um, as it were."

I grinned but ploughed on. "Mrs. Bird wouldn't help her. She's quite narrow-minded."

"Mmm," said Bunty, who seemed to be looking for something in the distance.

"Which is quite unfair," I persevered. "Some people are having a rotten time."

"There is a war on," said Bunty, not unreasonably.

"So they need help," I said eagerly. "Don't you think? It's part of doing your bit, isn't it?"

"Well, yes," said Bunts, still staring into the distance and fidgeting with her hair. "But there's not much you can do if Mrs. Bird doesn't want to, is there?"

"Actually," I said. "There is, sort of."

Bunty turned round. I looked at the children, who were still shrieking at each other.

"Emmy," said Bunty. "What are you planning?"

She had known me a long time.

"Well," I said. "It's all absolutely under control."

Bunty closed her eyes. "That's not what I asked."

From the look on her face I decided downplaying things would be a good move.

"There was this girl," I said. "And she sounded like Kitty. Or like she could be heading towards Kit's situation . . ."

Bunty opened her eyes slowly, as if she was afraid of what she might see.

"So I wrote to her," I blurted out.

Bunty stared.

"As if I were Mrs. Bird," I added.

Bunty's mouth fell open. A lone duck quacked as if to say Oh Dear.

"Em," said Bunty. "You didn't. You . . . good grief."

I decided not to mention putting Confused's letter into the next issue.

"It's all going to be perfectly fine," I said brightly. "I'm just trying to help out."

"Well, you mustn't." Bunty looked at me as if I was a lunatic, her grey eyes huge, like a cartoon. "Emmy, this is your big chance. A step nearer what you really want to do. How is this in any way perfectly fine?" Her voice grew higher. "You'll mess everything up. Oh, Em."

She looked incredulous. I went into my rehearsed argument.

"Mrs. Bird doesn't even read the letters. I can reply to them and she'll never know."

"But what if she finds out?"

"She won't. Oh, Bunts, you should see some of them," I said. I really wanted her to understand. "They're so sad. People are ever so worried about things—you've just said yourself about the war. Everyone's trying their best, but some of them are in a fix. And Mrs. Bird just throws their problems in the bin. It's not fair."

"Emmy," said Bunty. "I know it must be hard. But you have to stop. I'm serious."

She glanced over my shoulder again and I turned round.

"I say," I said. "Is that William?"

I had never been so pleased to see Bunty's boyfriend.

Bunty herself appeared entirely unsurprised, which was strange as she had been staring in that direction for ages.

"Don't change the subject," she said. "Emmy, promise me."

"It is him," I said, delighted at the chance to ignore her. "Isn't it? And who's that with him?"

"No one," said Bunty, looking frustrated. "Nothing."

"Nothing?"

"I don't know," said Bunty.

"What's going on?" I said, smelling a rat and fixing her with a stare.

She had gone pink.

"Nothing," she said. "Well, possibly something. Anyway, Emmy, you *can't* get involved with readers' problems."

Bunty gave me a last hard stare, straightened my scarf as if she were my mother, and gave an impatient Hmmf.

"Now look nice and smile," she ordered.

William was marching towards us at a pace. Beside him, in army uniform, was the most enormous man I had ever seen.

I'd thought Bunty had rather overblown preparation for our trip to the ducks. She'd made me change out of my wool skirt with the patch on it and swap my perfectly adequate pullover for an entirely too thin mohair one you'd only really want to wear in the spring.

"Oh, I say, that must be Harold," she said gaily.

"We don't know a Harold," I said. "Bunty, have you planned this?"

William waved jauntily, as did the big fellow.

"Not really," said Bunty, looking guilty. "Well, yes, really. But William says Harold is lovely."

"Have you met him before?" I said.

"No. But look, he's nice and tall."

She could say that again. If the sun made a proper effort to come out, it would be in danger of an immediate eclipse.

"They're getting near," said Bunty, waving wildly and looking vivacious. "Smile." She was grinning like a loon and speaking through her teeth like a ventriloquist.

I did as I was told.

"Hoot at his jokes," advised Bunty, rather assuming this Harold was going to tell some. "And flutter your eyelashes." When I didn't respond, she looked at me sternly. "Blink a lot."

"Look, Bunts," I said, still smiling like an idiot as instructed, "this is awfully kind of you, but I've already said, I'm not interested in meeting anyone. I'm concentrating on my career."

"That's rich," said Bunty. "I'd say you're trying to wreck it. And anyway," she added, "I bet he's divine."

Bunty had never used the word *divine* in her life. She was using a peculiar voice too, which was very high and really far too loud.

The boys had covered some ground and were now right by us. Before I could say anything more, a huge voice boomed out.

"DIVINE? ARE YOU TALKING ABOUT US? MARVELLOUS!"

Had Harold come with a foghorn?

It was too late to escape. As Mr. Bone the newsagent would say, I'd been stitched up like a kipper.

"Hello, Bunty, hello, Emmy," said William.

I gave in.

"WHAT HO!" shouted Harold.

"Hello," I said in a weak fashion that I hoped would not be mistaken for feminine excitement.

"This is Harold," said William.

"YES," bellowed Harold, unnecessarily.

"And this is Emmeline," said William.

"How do you do?" I said. "This is Bunty."

So far we'd managed to confirm our names and shout a lot. I certainly didn't want to be rude to Harold, but I hadn't the first clue what to say.

Harold was definitely striking. He stood at least six foot three and could easily have played rugger for England. He was wearing possibly the largest uniform the British army made and was grinning widely.

He held out a large ham about the size of a tennis bat, which, it turned out, was one of his hands.

"TERRIFIC," he shouted, even more loudly than before. He shook my hand with vigour and I tried to join in, despite the likelihood of him dislocating my shoulder. I decided Harold was an enthusiastic type.

"Harold and I were at college together," said William. "He's now in the Royal Engineers. Bomb disposal."

He said it with admirable pride. It was never easy for William to be reminded that all his friends had joined up, but he hadn't made the cut. Bunty worried incessantly that he thought himself a failure, and while I always told her she was wrong, we both knew she wasn't.

And now here he was, doing his best to show off his behemoth of a chum, in case I should like him and because if I did, it would make Bunty happy. It was actually terrifically kind and I couldn't be cross with any of them. Harold was far from a dismal article.

"It's lovely to meet you, Harold," I said, making Bunty look faint with joy. "Shall we take a walk over towards Kensington?"

Everyone declared this The Most Tremendous Idea. Harold said he'd heard that the bookshop had been blown up the night before last but no one had been hurt, and we all agreed this was a huge relief. Then William chipped in to say that a man with a ukulele had been entertaining the people sleeping in Kensington Tube station and we all said this must be an absolute tonic. The four of us were making a lovely effort to be gay about things, even though the news reports about the raids had made sobering reading. By the time we got to the High Street, we were a cheerful party indeed.

Harold seemed a good egg, even if his laugh did make your ears ache. He even made a decent fist at being interested in *Woman's Friend*, and he put up with silences when I couldn't think of anything to say. But I didn't go weak at the knees or want to flutter my eyelashes at him.

I reasoned that quite probably he wasn't awfully interested in me either. All I'd done was grin a lot as directed and talk about the people at work. I hoped he wouldn't think I was an entire dud, though, as William had made the effort to introduce us and I didn't want to reflect badly on him.

"How funny that we ran into you," I said, walking next to William as we went past Barker's department store and I remembered I had run out of blue cotton. "Are you coming with us to tea?" I asked, giving in to the fact that everything had already been planned.

"Only if you want," he said, brown eyes earnest. He looked over to where Bunty was telling a funny story to Harold. "Bunty wanted to see if you two might like each other. I've told Harold we'd just go for a stroll. You should give him a chance, Emmy. He's a good chap. Saved tons of his men. Awfully brave."

I sighed. Bravery was the most important thing in the world to him.

"Bill darling, I want to show you this coat," said Bunty, dragging him away from me. Harold and I looked at each other for a moment.

"SHALL WE WALK?" he suggested loudly. "IT'S TOO COLD TO STAND."

"Let's," I said, adrift for something to say.

"We've been set up, haven't we?" said Harold at very nearly normal volume.

We looked at each other again. He pulled a rueful face and I burst out laughing.

"Sorry about this," he said. "I met Bill in the pub the day before yesterday. He talked about Bunty a lot and suggested we meet up with you both. Is this very awful for you?"

"Oh no, not at all," I said. "Is it for you?"

"DREADFUL," he said, back at usual pitch, and then laughed just as loudly. "NO, OF COURSE NOT. DON'T FEEL BAD," he added as I winced. "I'M RUBBISH AT ALL THIS. GIVE ME AN UNEXPLODED BOMB TO SORT OUT ANY DAY. BY THE WAY, AM I SHOUTING?"

"You are a bit," I said.

"SORRY. RINGING NOISE IN THE OLD LUGS. NOT PERMANENT. I'VE GOT TWO WEEKS OFF UNTIL IT GOES AWAY."

"Oh gosh, I'm so sorry," I said, mortified I'd thought he was a shouter.

"It's all right," he said, lowering his voice right down again. "It happens. Work gets a bit loud and all that. Shall I whisper for a bit or does it make me sound like a maniac?"

I laughed again. Harold was nice. I still didn't feel a blossoming romance, but I was pretty certain neither did he so that was all right.

"Sort of," I said.

"Look," he said. "Would it be very rude if I suggested we just become friends?"

I could have kissed him. It was such an enormous relief.

"HAROLD," I shouted, and three pedestrians turned round. "I SHOULD VERY MUCH LIKE TO BE FRIENDS. THANK YOU."

"MARVELLOUS," he shouted back, looking delighted and relieved in equal measure.

We marched back to Bunty and William, and I broke the distressing news of our nonstarter courtship. Bunty took it bravely and Bill asked Harold if he should like to go to the pub. They walked us to the Tea House and I braced myself, knowing that as soon as they left I would be at the mercy of Phase Two of Bunty's interrogation about *Woman's Friend*.

"Come on, Bunts," I said as we waved them goodbye. "I'll buy tea. All the buns you can eat."

"All right," said Bunty, who had assumed an ominous look. "But bribery won't work. I'm crestfallen about Harold."

I nodded, thinking I had been let off the hook.

"And don't forget," said Bunty. "I want the whole story about what you've been doing at work."

Chapter 10

PLEASE CALL ME CHARLES

Craning our necks to try to see what cakes the Tea House might have mustered up, we joined the back of a long queue to be seated. The line moved terribly slowly, which was dispiriting, especially as we were both now ravenous, so Bunty and I grumbled and threw hard looks at the people already sitting down.

"Look at those two," said Bunty. "A table for four and they aren't even eating."

I looked over to where she was jabbing her forefinger and had rather a shock.

"Good grief, it's Mr. Collins," I said, because it was.

He was sitting facing us, dressed in his tweed suit but with slightly neater hair than usual. The two men—the other in uniform with his back to us—were chatting, and Mr. Collins was nodding in a sympathetic way, which threw me completely.

Bunty scrutinised them. "*Your* Mr. Collins?" she said, and I went unnecessarily red.

"He's not *my* Mr. Collins," I said, and before I could say anything else, he glanced away from his friend and saw us. For a moment he seemed not to be able to place me. When he did, after a moment's pause he gave a small but friendly wave. Then he turned back to his friend, said something, and to my astonishment, beckoned us over.

I waved back feeling self-conscious and Bunty rose to the occasion by giggling and saying, "Well, it looks as if you're his Miss Lake," which was uncalled for and I quite rightly ignored.

"Go on," said Bunty. "It might mean we could join them and get out of this queue. I say . . . who's that chap he's with?"

The man in the uniform had turned in his chair to see who Mr. Collins had rashly gestured at. He had the same dark hair and slim build as Mr. Collins but was lots younger, in his late twenties perhaps.

Bunty and I made our way over to their table.

"Miss Lake," said Mr. Collins politely as both men got to their feet. "How nice to see you."

"Hello, Mr. Collins," I said. "This is my friend Miss Marigold Tavistock."

"How do you do?" said Bunty, quite beautifully. "Please call me Bunty, everyone does."

"How nice to meet you, Bunty," said Mr. Collins, shaking her hand and being chivalrous to the point where I wondered if I had the wrong person. "May I introduce my half-brother Captain Charles Mayhew? Charles, this is Miss Lake, who works with me. I may have mentioned she is the young woman presently giving Henrietta a run for her money."

I felt rather self-conscious at the thought of being Mentioned and we all shook hands and Captain Mayhew said Please call me Charles, and Mr. Collins said Everyone Does, and we all laughed. It was odd thinking that Mr. Collins had a brother or any kind of life outside of the office. One always had the feeling he existed purely to sit at his desk writing furiously and in a terrible mess.

With the four of us standing up, none of the waitresses could get past and we were in danger of causing a scene.

"Ladies," said Mr. Collins, going berserk and saving the situation. "This is dreadful etiquette as most of us have only just met, and Miss Lake and I are colleagues, but may I invite you to join us? I am in danger of boring my brother to the stage where he will throw himself out of the window if someone young doesn't speak to him soon. We have ordered cake," he finished, with a flourish.

"That's very kind. Thank you," said Bunty, smartly wiping out any chance of a decline.

I was mortified to be having a spontaneous tea with a senior member of staff and his brother, on a Saturday and everything. Kathleen would go into shock, and Mrs. Bird would probably burst. But I was terrifically hungry.

"Thank you, Mr. Collins," I said, grateful that at least he had not entirely taken leave of his senses and said Please call me Guy, which I knew was his first name, as then I should have died. "That would be lovely."

"Thank heavens for that," said Mr. Collins. "We can stop this hovering."

With the speed of a panther, Bunty whipped her hat off and shot round to sit next to Mr. Collins, leaving me to sit next to Captain Mayhew, who I didn't yet feel I could call Charles.

"I should like to say," said the captain, who had a quiet but friendly voice, "that I am not in the least bored. Although it is lovely to have you join us, of course," he added quickly. "Have you been out walking, ladies?"

Mr. Collins had now lapsed into one of his silences. Anxious to avoid a conversational lull, I felt compelled to try to appear interesting and not let him down.

"We *have* been walking," I confirmed. "We've had a look at the bookshop that isn't there now, and before that we threw bread at the ducks. Bunty managed to hit one," I added, which made it sound as if we had been doing it on purpose.

"Actually it was two. I wasn't even trying," said Bunty, attempting to rescue things but making it worse.

"Right," said Captain Mayhew desperately. "That's, um . . ."

"One of the milder blood sports," said Mr. Collins.

Bunty motored on.

"Really," she said. "It was only the crusts that would have hurt them and we'd eaten most of those on the way."

"We didn't have any lunch," I said.

"Good God," said Mr. Collins, flagging down the nearest member of staff. "Waitress, could you please double up on our order with some urgency, if you would? Thank you. My treat."

He gave Bunty a look that suggested he thought she was about to start rooting around in a dustbin for food.

"Oh, how terribly kind," she said with the most enormous dignity and giving him her loveliest smile. "They were only very small crusts."

I turned to Captain Mayhew, feeling I should apologise. But before I could say anything, I realised he was trying terribly hard not to laugh.

"I'm so sorry," he said, failing and letting out a guffaw. "But this is like having tea with Flanagan and Allen doing one of their skits. Not to look at, of course. Oh dear, that's come out wrong." He stopped abruptly and looked horrified at himself.

"Do forgive me," he said, blushing. "I just meant that you've really cheered me up. My regiment has had a bit of a time of it and poor Guy has been saddled with a misery guts all day."

"Don't worry, Captain Mayhew," I said, thinking how decent he seemed. "You must think we never get out."

"Not for a moment," he said. "Though please call me Charles."

"All right, Charles," I said, feeling reckless. "And please call me Emmy. Shall we all start again?"

"Let's," said Charles and Bunty at the same time.

"Do we have to?" said Mr. Collins. "I'm not sure I can face the story about the duck for a second time. Oh thank God, here's the waitress."

He waved absently at the girl who had arrived with a full tray of food, and then gave us all one of his most theatrical glares.

"Now come on you lot, stop being so jolly polite and tuck in."

He raised a teapot at us.

"Ladies, I salute you. This is the first time I've seen my brother laugh since he came home. Now, who wants first dibs at the mustard and cress?"

With the ice broken and the prospect of food, Bunty and I regained our faculties and stopped acting as if we were blithering oafs. Although it was odd to be chatting to Mr. Collins and I couldn't help but think at any moment he might bellow "BLOTTER, MISS LAKE," I told myself we could all get blown up by tomorrow so we might just as well enjoy ourselves. Captain Mayhew was quieter than his half-brother and seemed a little shy, but he joined in the conversation, which, as ever with people you don't know, was terrifically genial. We all downplayed anything to do with the Blitz ("My aunt's friend Gwyneth was bombed out and lost everything, but then they found the cat—what a boon!") and stayed on safe ground.

"Are you going to be in London very long, Charles?" asked Bunty.

"A few more days," he said. "If my brother can put up with me for that long."

"Won't you be fearfully bored?" Mr. Collins asked, looking genuinely concerned.

"Guy," said Charles fondly. "You're forty-six. That's hardly the Elgin Marbles. Ladies, please ignore him." He took a sip of tea and raised an eyebrow at me over the brim of his cup. I smiled.

"Do you like the cinema?" Bunty blurted, out of the blue.

I looked at her in alarm.

"It's just that we're planning to see *The Mark of Zorro* after tea and I wondered if you might like to come? You'd both be welcome of course," she added, looking at Mr. Collins and not meaning it.

Charles laughed. "Thank you, Bunty, that's terrifically kind. I shouldn't want to gate-crash the party, though, or desert my brother?" Bunty said Of Course Not very gaily, and Mr. Collins said Not At All and looked pleased.

"That's sorted, then," said Mr. Collins. He frowned. "You know it could be a heavy night, don't you?"

"That's all right," I said, gathering my things. "We know all the shelters on the way home."

"I must say I admire your pluck," said Charles. "I find it more alarming back here than when I'm away."

"My brother says that too," I said. "But I reckon you may as well be a moving duck as a sitting one."

"Miss Lake," said Mr. Collins, "even if you do enjoy being a moving duck, it will make me feel better if Charles is with you. I should be most annoyed if you were blown up. I'll settle things here. Be careful," he said to us all, and as we thanked him profusely for tea, with a continental wave of his hand he sent us on our way.

The blackout had started and it was pitch dark outside, but we all had torches and Bunty and I had our white scarves on to avoid getting flattened by a bus. Nonetheless, Charles insisted on walking on the outside of the pavement.

"Chivalry's all very well," I said through my scarf as we walked carefully along. "But if you get run over, it won't be any good for the war effort."

"I'm not going to get run over," said Charles in a kind voice. "And anyway, you are both important to your jobs and it would be just as bad if it were you."

"I just type things," I said as Charles said I'm Sure There's More To It Than That, and Bunty shot me a stern look as if to say I Haven't Forgotten Our Earlier Conversation, You Know.

We walked on in amicable silence for a while, and not for the first time today did I wish I had my sensible pullover on. It was wretchedly cold. The weather had been poor for the last couple of weeks, but tonight the sky was clear as anything. Mr. Collins was right: the Germans would be busy later.

As older people and those with children had gone home before dusk, the bus was full of young people like us, chatting and looking forward to their Saturday night. Shop girls who had put on their lipstick and heels before leaving work talked about boys and dancing, and boys in uniforms discussed girls and the war. As the bus crept its way cautiously around Hyde Park, Bunty quizzed Charles about the army, while I looked out of the window into the darkness.

Once we had arrived at the Odeon and found our seats Bunty announced loudly she had to visit the lavatory and was gone ages, so Charles and I watched the newsreels, which were relentlessly upbeat about everything. There was a short film about the girl drivers in the ATS, showing them opening up lorry bonnets and confidently poking around engines. When it came on, a group of people in the front stalls cheered and someone shouted, "That's you, Mavis," and a female voice said, "No it's not, Vincent, I'm thinner than that," and everyone in the cinema laughed.

But I felt self-conscious, especially sitting next to Charles in his uniform. During tea I'd told him about the fire station and now I whispered to him that I had been wondering about becoming an AFS motorcycle courier one day if I could get on the course.

"Good for you," Charles whispered back. "Very exciting."

"Isn't it?" I said. "I just need to learn how to ride and then I'll be in, though I think it's a bit of a wait."

Then Charles spoke again, in a light fashion.

"I could teach you if you like. If you don't mind learning on quite an old bike."

"I say," I said, overcome. "That's awfully nice of you."

At that moment Bunty finally returned to her seat.

"Are you all right?" I asked surreptitiously.

"Yes of course," said Bunty as if being in the lavatory for twenty minutes was perfectly acceptable.

"Charles is going to teach me to ride a motorcycle."

"Gosh," said Bunty with a level of awe which suggested he was organizing a day out to the moon.

I turned to look at her. She was staring fixedly at the screen, where

Max Miller was cheering up a canteen full of nuns. He must have been on first-rate comedy form because Bunty was grinning about as broadly as was possible for a face.

"Honestly," she said under her breath. "Who would have thought?"

Halfway through the film, the cinema manager came onto the stage and announced there was an air raid. A year ago everyone would have grabbed their gas masks and rushed off to the nearest shelter. Instead, as always happened these days, nobody moved, and several people in the balcony shouted Get On With It and Bring Back Tyrone Power. The cinema manager got two wolf whistles and a small round of applause. Bunty and I were happy to stay as it was in the middle of a particularly gripping bit of the plot. By the end of the film the all clear hadn't gone.

Bunty announced she was off to the lavatory again.

"Goodbye, Charles," she said, shaking his hand. "I do hope we shall see you again. Emmy, say goodbye to Charles, and when he has gone, wait for me here," she ended rather bossily, which wasn't like her. Then she disappeared behind a large woman in a fur coat.

Although they always played the films at louder-than-usual volume, even *The Mark of Zorro* had not entirely blotted out the crump crump sound from the bombers above. Now that we were out of the auditorium and right at the front of the building, it was far louder. Charles and I shouted at each other over the din.

"You're not really thinking of catching a bus home, are you?" yelled Charles.

"Oh, we always do, it's fine," I shouted back, just as there was a horrible whistling noise. Everyone in the foyer stood still for a second until a huge crash shook the building. "That was a thumper," I added unnecessarily.

"Now then," said Charles over the din. "I don't want to appear a stickler for safety, and I don't care if you two usually get out deck-chairs and watch the city go up in smoke, but tonight, if I can find one, we will be getting a taxi."

He was still smiling, and still unerringly polite. I opened my mouth to argue but thought better of it and shut it again like a goldfish. Kind eyes and quiet charm aside, Charles struck me as a man who knew what he was about.

There was another whistle, lower-pitched so further away this time, but still followed by a shuddering crunch as a nearby building took a hit. Although the glass frontage of the cinema was fully boarded up and we were quite safe, Charles had moved to stand between me and a possible blast.

"Now," he said, ignoring the noise. "Do you think you should check if Bunty is all right?"

She had been gone ages again.

"Good idea," I said as Charles took my arm and we weaved our way through the people queuing at the ticket booth. "She'd rather die than be blown up in a lavatory."

Charles looked at me sideways. We both burst out laughing.

"Oh dear," I said. "I'm not usually this stupid."

"You're the least stupid person I've met," answered Charles. "Look, there she is."

Bunty was loitering behind the refreshment stand, acting as if hiding when it was time to go home were perfectly sane.

"We're getting a taxi," I said as we about-turned and headed back. "Or Charles says he will have some sort of fit."

"I will," said Charles. "Now you two wait here and I'll go and find one."

Taking a small military torch out of an enormous coat pocket, Charles marched confidently across the marble floor and out through the blackout curtains by the exit.

"Goodness," said Bunty. "He's nice, isn't he?"

There was another ominous rumble from outside.

"Bunty," I said, now we were alone. "Is it a dicky tummy?"

Bunty looked bewildered.

"You keep going to the lavatory," I whispered. "For ages."

"Oh that," she said, grinning. "It's good, isn't it?"

I looked at her blankly.

"I'm leaving you two alone, you idiot," she groaned. "He likes you."

"Oh shut up," I said. "That's absolute rot."

"No it isn't. And anyway, you like him, I can tell. I was trying to get him to ask you out before he left."

"Bunty . . ."

"Now then." She gave me a conspiratorial look. "When we get to Granny's I'm going to run like anything for the front door feeling terribly ill. You'll have to rush after me, but before you do, say how awfully sorry you are to leave it like this."

I rolled my eyes at her.

"He'll say he absolutely must see you again and you can look lovely and say you must go as I could be seriously ill—that will make you look caring—but that if he liked, you could give him your telephone number."

"Oh, Bunts," I said. "No one says I Must See You Again in real life. You've been spending too much time watching films."

"Haven't I?" agreed Bunty. "It's given me heaps of ideas. This is so exciting. I've very nearly forgotten Poor Harold, haven't you?"

"I've very nearly forgotten we're friends," I said severely.

"Charles!" shouted Bunty, as if stranded on a rock in rough seas.

She hooked her arm into mine and dragged me towards the main doors, where Charles had appeared, looking cold around the ears. Bunty shamelessly grabbed his arm.

"Thank you *so* much, you *have* saved the day," she said gratefully. "You see, I'm not feeling terribly well."

Chapter 11

A BAD NIGHT AT THE STATION

The next evening, I strode down Rowland Street, warm in my AFS greatcoat and swinging the string bag that held tonight's sandwiches. It was the second clear night in a row and the moon was being quite traitorous and showing off all the best bits of London to bomb. With other things on my mind, I marched to the fire station in a thoughtful fashion.

I was in the middle of a bout of what artistic people called Mixed Emotions. Saturday had been the loveliest day. I had gone along with Bunty catapulting herself out of the taxi, and for his part, Charles just said Goodness and what a lovely evening it had been and might we do it again, apart from Bunty being ill? I said Bunty loved the cinema, but then Charles said that although he liked Bunty very much and he hoped she would soon be quite well, if it was all right with us both, might he and I go out on our own?

So I gave Charles my telephone number and then we said goodbye and shook hands for longer than strictly required and it all went ever so well.

Bunty was thrilled about it of course, but it had been a temporary reprieve as the next day she had given me a stiff talking to about the letter writing at work. She thought I was utterly mad to be doing it, and even if I was just trying to help, the possibility of losing my job should make me think again.

It was no surprise then that as well as feeling a little giddy about Charles, I was also nervy. Tomorrow the new issue of *Woman's Friend* would be delivered to the office, complete with the letter I had sneaked into Henrietta Helps.

Even though I had been writing to as many readers as I thought I could help, I was painfully aware that putting a letter into the magazine had been a different move altogether. I told myself not to think about it. I'd have lots more to worry about tonight if there was a raid.

Carlton Street fire station was only three streets from Bunty's granny's and I could get there with my eyes closed, which was just as well. Now and then things got a bit close and with the streets lit by the huge orange glow of London's fires from the German incendiaries, I would run flat out to get home. I wasn't being panicky, but I reasoned even Mr. Churchill would think getting a move on was a sensible idea. When the ack-ack guns were on top form, though, I would stay at the station until the all clear went. There was no point going out if it was raining shrapnel, and it was absolutely deafening as well.

Walking around a big crater in the pavement, I crossed the street and called a hello to Mr. Bone, who was locking the door of his boarded-up newsagent's. He had his warden's overalls on and as he turned towards me, he blew on his fingers to keep warm.

"Evening, Mr. Bone," I said. "No gloves? You'll get frostbite."

"Evening, Emmy. That daft paper boy's got them. How's that young brother of yours? Still bashing the enemy?"

"Trying to, Mr. Bone," I said, playing things down.

"Good lad," said Mr. Bone kindly and I asked after his wife. Their only son, Herbert, had been a rear gunner in the RAF. He had been shot down over the Channel and never been found. I tried not to think of the day they heard. Mr. Bone stacking newspapers so you couldn't see his face, and Mrs. Bone standing by the till in the shop as she always did, only with tears pouring silently down her cheeks and a look in her eyes that told you absolutely everything was lost. Bert was their only child.

"Don't come home until the all clear, will you?" said Mr. Bone, looking concerned.

I promised him I wouldn't and he told me he knew I had my fingers crossed behind my back, which was true.

I waved goodbye, turned the corner, and walked on to Bellamy Street, just past a big hole where the bicycle shop had been. You could now see through to the street behind it, but I always said a Hello in my head to a handwritten sign propped up on some rubble that said "GONE ON HOLIDAY—BACK IN A BIT!" Its owner, Mr. Dennis, used to live above the shop with his family, but luckily when it was bombed they'd been visiting his sister in Southsea. Mr. Dennis came back to see if anything could be salvaged, which it couldn't, but he put on a very brave face.

"I always said I should get away more," he said, and everyone who'd turned out to see him cheered. Then he'd shaken everyone's hand, and as a couple of his friends took him off to the pub before he caught a train back to Southsea, Mr. Dennis said, "We'll be back in a bit. If Hitler asks, tell him I've gone on holiday."

The next day a local wag had put up the sign. It raised a smile, but most of all it made everyone think of the Dennis family. We knew they'd be back.

William would be on duty tonight, as he very nearly always was. He had just been promoted to Sub-Officer on B Watch, which was very much deserved and we were all thrilled to bits for him. He worked harder than anyone and was enormously brave too, although sometimes I had to admit that scared me. I was all for bravery; it was part of his job. But I was also all for Bunty still having the chap she adored at the end of it all.

I hurried on. Thelma and Joan would already be at the station—they were the B Watch full-timers—and then there were young Mary and me, the volunteers. We'd all sit in a row at our desks and chat and pretend everything was completely normal until the siren went and the phones would start ringing with people calling to tell us that their house had been bombed or an incendiary had gone off and set fire to half the street. Then it would get busy. Mary and I volunteered for three nights a week although often it turned into four or five.

But it was nothing compared to William and the boys. If it was quiet in West London, you could bet your last penny that the docks would be crying out for relief crews. I'd see him at the start of my shift, but it was rare he was back by the time I left at six the next morning, and if he was, he'd often be soaked through, exhausted, and his mind still in another world. When I got home, I would always make a bit of a racket on purpose so Bunty would know I was back, then she'd pop out of her room and offer to put the kettle on. It meant I could tell her everything was all right without either of us making a fuss about it. Whatever had happened, I always told her William looked entirely well.

Now, in good time for my shift, I opened the station side door and walked in past two of B Watch who were mending a trailer pump that a wall had collapsed on last week.

"Morning, boys," I called, even though it was the afternoon.

"Evening, angel," one of them yelled from under the pump. "Thanks for popping in. We're dying of thirst here."

"Kettle on first thing, Fred," I told his feet as I unravelled my scarf. "You too, Roy?"

"That'll do it. Good girl." Roy sounded puffed out. "CLOCKWISE, Fred. I'll get flattened if you turn it that way."

I squeezed past the wonky piece of machinery and climbed the steep stairs to the call room, where the girls were already in and chatting. Thelma was pulling at the waistband of her uniform skirt and showing the gap.

"See—that's no cheese for you. If they start rationing sweets, I might give all this up and become a model." She cracked a big smile.

"Hello, girls. You look smashing, Thel," I said. I knew Thelma didn't eat a thing so she could give more of her rations to her children. "Anything exciting happening?" I took off my coat and cap.

"Adolf's been waiting for you," said Joan. "Any minute now, I reckon."

"Well then, we'd better have some tea and a gossip while we can," said Thelma. "How was your walk yesterday, Emmy? Did you meet anyone while you were out?"

Ever since Edmund had finished with me, the girls had been relentless in their campaign to find a replacement. I didn't mind—it gave us something frivolous to talk about. On nights when there wasn't a raid, we were allowed to sleep in the volunteer room, so we'd sit on our bunk beds and drink cocoa and talk nonsense. And on the nights when the raids were bad, if we had any breaks, we'd talk nonsense even more to take our minds off it. Finding me a husband was perfect on that front.

"Actually, yes," I said. "A very tall man called Harold."

All three of them looked innocent and said "I say" and "Smashing" at the same time. I was quite sure they'd all been in on the plan.

"But he's not the chap for me," I said, dashing their hopes. I had decided not to mention Charles. We had only just met and I didn't want half of B Watch getting overexcited.

"Was he horrible?" said Joan, who thought that men were for the most part a waste of time. Mainly her own husband when it came down to it. She patted me on the shoulder. "Never mind."

"And you're still quite young," said Mary, who was nineteen and thought I was ancient.

"Someone will want you," assured Thelma.

"Oi, where's our tea?" yelled a voice from downstairs.

Joan dropped her voice to a sensitive tone.

"Don't lose hope, Emmy," she said, looking grave.

I was a spinster, not an invalid, but as ever, this had passed everyone by.

Joan and Mary hurried off to sort out the teas and Thelma and I began the usual routine of getting ready for the shift. William put his head around the door to say hello, wearing a look of determination that said he'd rather be with his crew. Then he disappeared.

Thelma was a keen magazine reader and had taken to buying *Woman's Friend.* She thought I was just being modest when I said my job wasn't remotely glamorous.

"Last week's What's In The Hot Pot?" Thelma mused. "The lamb's brain stew. I can't get the smell out." We both laughed. "Still," she added, "it filled up the kiddies. How are you getting on with the problems? Anything good?"

She grinned, used to me saying I couldn't tell her, but my stomach gave a lurch and it wasn't about the stew. I hadn't told Thelma about writing the letters, of course, even though she would be a handy person for advice. Thelma was nearly thirty and had three children. She was bags more qualified to help people than I was.

"I'm not supposed to say," I said. "But . . ."

Thelma's eyes widened. She pulled out the chair and sat down next to me.

"Oh, it's nothing dreadful." I kept my voice lighthearted, but actually I was thinking about a reader whose letter I hadn't had the heart to throw out.

Dear Mrs. Bird,

I am eighteen and my parents are awfully strict. We live very near a military camp and the men are always very friendly.

I have become friends with one who is the same age as me. We are just friends but my parents say I mustn't have anything to do with soldiers and they will forbid me to leave the house on my own. I have been going to the pictures with this boy but they don't know it. All my friends go out with boys, and I don't want to lose him. Please tell me what I should do?

Fed Up, Hull

I knew Mrs. Bird would give Fed Up very short shrift, but I felt sorry for her. I wasn't sure what to advise, though. Eighteen was definitely old enough to be seeing someone in my view, but I certainly wouldn't encourage going against her parents' wishes. I was stuck as to what to suggest.

I could hear Joan and Mary chatting and laughing in the volunteer room as they made the tea. The boys were still downstairs and Captain Davies was locked in his office. I leant forward and lowered my voice.

"Thel, what would you say if someone was eighteen and wanted to go out with a soldier? What if it was your Margaret?"

Thelma's daughter was only nine, but anyway, I gave her the low-down without referring to Fed Up.

Thelma narrowed her eyes.

"I'd want to shut her in her room until there's Peace," she said, smiling. "Bless her. I first met Arthur when he was in his navy uniform. Turned my head in a second. If her parents lock her up, she'll only be out the window." She mulled it over, enjoying the challenge. "She should get her mum to invite one or two of the boys around for tea—all supervised and that. It's doing your bit." Thelma paused. "And then I'd put the fear of God in him too."

We both laughed, but I was taking a mental note. Thelma's advice sounded practical but not overly severe.

"So," said Thelma. "Would I do for Henrietta Helps?"

If only she knew. She would be tons better than Mrs. Bird. I wouldn't even have to think about sneaking letters into *Woman's Friend* if Thelma was in charge.

The anxious feeling started churning in my stomach again.

"Right then," said Thelma. "Where are the others with that tea? Hold on . . ."

We both listened. The sirens had begun to wail.

Joan and Mary hurriedly returned, Mary carrying the tea tray, as almost immediately we heard the sound of planes and the ack-acks, and then the first bombs of the night.

As Mary handed out the tea, Thelma lit a cigarette and pushed her tin hat down over her hair. I put mine on too and pulled the chinstrap tight.

"Sounds close," said Joan, pursing her lips and echoing Mr. Bone by adding, "It's going to be busy tonight."

She was right.

Within no time my telephone was the first of the four to ring. I answered it quickly. "Fire Brigade, where are you calling from, please?" I said, just as there was an enormous crash outside, which made our little building shake. My new cup of tea let itself down badly by jumping in its saucer and spilling its contents.

"I'm sorry, could you say that again?" I asked, the other phones in the control room now ringing as the lady at the other end shouted information. The house two doors away from her had taken a direct hit.

"Do you know how many people live there?" I asked, scribbling down the details of a street I recognised as about half a mile away. "And children?"

I hated this bit.

"Six," she told me. "We can't see anything for the smoke."

"Don't worry," I said. My voice was steady but I was glad the caller couldn't see me wince. "Stay where you are. They'll be with you as soon as they can."

I thanked her and said goodbye, as if I had just taken a restaurant booking rather than the details of half a street that had been razed to the ground. When I had first volunteered it had seemed harsh but it was our job to remain absolutely calm no matter how awful the calls were. You couldn't let yourself think about things when you were in the middle of a busy night. As Captain Davies said, that wouldn't help anyone. Afterwards we all did, of course, especially if you found out things had gone the wrong way.

I ripped the paper off my pad and jammed it onto the spike where all the calls went. Thelma and Mary jammed theirs on too and Captain Davies came in from his office.

"Two pumps and a heavy unit, Mary," he said, looking up at the chalkboard and beginning to arrange discs to show which crews would be going where. Mary was already on her feet and heading to the door to start ringing the hand bell outside. One of the crew ran in to take orders. He had the expression on his face that I had been watching for months. It was a funny mixture of looking grave and not being able to wait to get on with it. If the war lasted for twenty years, I wasn't sure I would ever get used to that.

"Tin hats on, girls," said Captain Davies, glaring at Mary.

My phone rang again and so did Thelma's. Joan was trying to get sense out of someone on hers that she couldn't hear. What with bombs going off at their end and the guns going at it nonstop right over our heads, it was a wonder anyone could hear anything at all.

"Fire Brigade, where are you calling from, please?"

We all kept repeating the same things. Thelma's cigarette burned away and died quietly in the ashtray; Mary kept ringing the bell until there weren't any more men to send out, and Captain Davies told Thelma to get on to Lambeth for backup. Everyone had been right. It was one of the busiest nights since New Year and as the evening continued, the noise of the bombers got nearer and louder. We were right in the thick of it. The moaning of the planes overhead didn't stop, and was only interrupted by the noise of the guns and more bombs.

"They're out to get us tonight," admitted Thelma in a matter-of-fact way during one of the few pauses on the phones. "I hope Mum's got the kids in the coal cellar."

"I hope Bunty's all right," I said. I knew she'd be in the shelter next door. If one of us was on our own, we would bolt down the garden and through the gate into Mrs. Harewood's. Mrs. Harewood was a widow who lived on her own, but as her husband had been in the diplomatic corps, she had opened up rooms to visiting dignitaries. Bunty said you never knew quite who you'd end up sitting next to. It could be Mrs. Harewood's housekeeper Maureen or someone hush hush with a pipe.

On a night like tonight, though, it didn't matter if you were sitting next to the Queen of Sheba. There was a very real likelihood that someone was going to get hit. The worst was if a call came in about a bomb near one of our families or friends. You couldn't do much, just say a quick prayer and get on with it until the end of the shift. We didn't want to let the boys down—after all, they were the ones outside, putting out fires as shrapnel fell about them and the bombs didn't stop.

By midnight we were all in need of a pick-me-up, and in between calls I tried to eat my sandwich as it was beginning to curl up at the edges. You weren't supposed to eat at your desk but Captain Davies was now out on a six-pump for an all hands on deck, so I thought I would be in the clear.

Thelma was standing at the call board, looking at where Captain Davies had chalked in "Church Street, 8:15 p.m." She glanced at the big clock outside his office but said nothing. We all knew what she was thinking.

Worrying about the crews was the worst bit of the job so I began to tell her about *The Mark of Zorro* just to take our minds off how long the boys had been out. The noise of the planes thundered on. Joan and Mary had stuck their fingers in their free ears and were leaning into the phones, still trying to take calls. It was a fruitless task. The bombers were right overhead and they were deafening.

I'd given up on *Zorro* just as there was the most tremendous bang—so loud that it was like being right in the middle of a thunder cloud. We all threw ourselves under the table as the whole building shook to its boots. The big clock crashed down off the wall, bringing a chunk of plaster with it, and tea cups, saucers, and plates clattered, mine falling off the desk and smashing beside me. Mary let out a squeak and then looked embarrassed, but none of us could blame her. The noise was coming from everywhere at once, as if we were being eaten by the very sound itself. There was another enormous explosion and the building quaked again.

If our number wasn't on this one, someone's very near was. Even Joan looked concerned.

"Blimey," shouted Thelma, who was on the floor next to me. She squeezed my arm. "That was a close one. You all right?"

I nodded. "Absolutely." I forced out a grin and looked at the other girls. "Fingers and toes still on?"

The others waggled their hands and Thelma and I waggled ours back.

"Sodding Hitler," bellowed Joan over the guns.

"I think I sat on my pencil," shouted Mary, trying to sound hearty, and shifting to look at her bottom.

"Bad luck," I yelled. I gave her the thumbs up and mouthed, "Okay?"

She thumbs upped back and nodded violently. There was another enormous bang and everything shook again. It wasn't quite as close this time and they obviously hadn't managed to bring down the phone lines, as above us we heard ringing again.

"It's probably mine," shouted Joan. She began to crawl out to answer the phone as the rest of us watched. "Oof, my knees." She heaved herself up as the fighting continued. Joan wasn't frightened of anything.

"Bugger you, Hitler," she shouted as she left our temporary bunker.

The phones were going mad. I didn't know what Joan thought she would be able to do as we could barely hear each other at the top of our voices, but she was the toughest of us all and our leader. Mary, Thelma, and I looked at each other. We could either stay under the table all night, or we could start pulling our weight.

"Ready?" I yelled, and the others nodded.

"BUGGER YOU, HITLER," we roared and clambered up to answer our phones.

Chapter 12

HALF OF IT'S JUST BLOODY GONE

Hitler was unimpressed by our language and continued to bomb the daylights out of West London well into the night.

For hours we took calls nonstop. One man gave me his address as Latham Road, but said it didn't really matter what it was called as we'd be lucky if we could find anything anyway.

"Half of it's just bloody gone, love, it's just bloody gone," he said down the phone.

Fires were reported all around us. The young messengers not already on rounds were sent to track down the crews and tell them not to come back in but go straight to the fires most out of control. By a quarter past three, having done what sounded like their worst, the enemy had headed for home. Soon after, the all clear sounded and someone rang the Women's Voluntary Service and told them to make sure they had sent out the mobile canteens to keep the boys going.

At six in the morning the day-time shift began to arrive and I could finally leave my seat, rolling my shoulders back as they had become stiff with crouching over the phone. I was keen to get home and make sure Bunty and Mrs. Harewood and Maureen were safe. It had been a long night.

"What time do you have to be at work?" Thelma asked as she saw me rubbing my eyes.

"Nine," I said. "I'll get a couple of hours' sleep first." I turned to Joan. "Is there any update on the boys? I'd like to report in for Bunty."

Joan had been in charge of the call board and I had lost track hours ago.

"They're still out in Church Street," she said, looking at her watch. "They've been there awhile." She saw my face and lightened her voice. "They'll be all right."

"Not if Bill carries on like I hear he did last week they won't."

Horrible Vera, one of the permanents on A Watch, had just walked into the room.

"Tommy Lewis said Bill was that gung-ho on a call he was about three inches off losing a leg," Vera finished with a flourish.

She took off her cap and shook her hair in a careless fashion. Vera and I did not always get on. Everyone knew she had a soft spot for William and said nasty things behind Bunty's back.

"Shut up, Vera," said Thelma.

Vera feigned innocence, which must have been a bit of a stretch.

"Well, I'm sure Emmeline would want to tell that Bunty. I know I would if it was my best friend."

I rather thought I would be the one to decide what I would tell That Bunty, but Vera crashed on.

"Oh, did you not know? William had an ever-so-near escape at the warehouses on Shepherd's Bush Road. Tommy said a great big girder came down that close he was lucky they didn't all get killed. Back in a minute." She gave a sickly smile and left the room.

I kept quiet and started packing up my report books.

"She's just stirring it, Emmy," said Thelma. "You know what she's like. It wasn't as bad as all that."

I bit my lip wondering why everyone else seemed to be in the know except me. No wonder Bill had kept a low profile last night and not hung around for a chat.

"Ignore her," ordered Joan, stretching to put the clock back on its hook on the wall. "You know she's a rotten egg."

"Humpty Dumpty in a curly wig," said Thelma, which raised a bit of a grin. "Now you get going, before she comes back. Go on, we'll see you tomorrow. Get some rest tonight."

She shooed me out of the control room.

I tutted to myself as I grabbed my coat and cap from their hook in the corridor and clomped downstairs and out of the station. I was tired, and now cross that I'd let Vera rile me. Everyone knew she made mountains out of molehills. I bet everything was fine.

All the same, Church Street was only a short detour on the way home and I decided to head back that way. It was still before dawn but it wasn't long before my eyes adjusted to the darkness and I started to see the results of last night's activity.

No wonder the station had shaken like a leaf. I had never seen anything like this.

Hatch Road wasn't really there anymore. Buildings were just charred shells, with piles of rubble still smouldering and the smell of burning everywhere. Some of the houses were partially collapsed, and by the dim start of first light you could see some of the rooms were still partly intact. A bedroom clung on to the side of a house, a chest of drawers oddly untouched but the rest of the room missing, as if it had been hacked away with a blunt knife. Two firemen stood on top of a heap of smoking debris, dampening it down with a hose. They were wet through, not speaking, just concentrating on finishing the job. I didn't recognise them so they must have been from another station called in to help.

I walked on, unnoticed by the rescue workers. An ambulance driver was helping an old man into the van and telling him not to worry and that it was all going to be all right. The man said he might be old but he wasn't stupid and what did he think was under those blankets? The ambulance man ignored him and promised him tea.

I looked away and caught the eye of a middle-aged woman wrapped in an eiderdown and sitting on a kitchen chair in the middle of what had once been the pavement. She was all on her own. I went over to her.

"Hello, I'm with the Fire Brigade," I said, stating the obvious in my uniform. "Can I help?" She was covered from head to foot in soot and ash and had a big cut on her chin.

She shook her head and gave me a weary smile. "Don't worry, dear, I'm just getting my breath," she said. "This is the third time I've been bombed out. I'll be all right."

"Are you sure?" I said, feeling useless.

"Oh yes. You go on. You looked like you were going somewhere in a hurry."

She was right. I had to admit I wanted to get home, make sure my friends were safe, and then put on my work suit, go to an office that wasn't in the middle of an air raid, and be a civilian who talked about patterns and romance stories and what best to do with half a pound of tripe.

I felt ashamed. Some War Correspondent I'd make.

I'd seen tons of burnt-out buildings, bomb craters, and people's homes still on fire or being pulled down. But I hadn't walked straight into the scene of such devastation before. Not when there were people on stretchers and wardens crouching beside them and writing out tags.

I took a deep breath and told myself to brace up. Then I asked the woman on the chair if she was sure there wasn't anything I could help with and when she insisted she was all right I headed on towards Church Street to find William and the boys.

"Come on, Lake," I whispered to myself. "Pretend you're at work."

I straightened up and stuck my chin out a bit.

"You don't want to go down there, miss," said an ARP warden as I got to the corner of the street. "I should go the other way if I were you."

"Thank you, but I've been sent from the station," I lied, patting the badge on my coat. "We've run out of dispatch riders."

He looked hesitant but said Good Girl and told me to Go On Then, so I did.

If Hatch Road had been grim, it was nothing compared with the scene when I turned the corner. Church Street was unrecognizable. It wasn't a very big street to start with, and the whole middle section had entirely disappeared. Where a terrace of proudly kept little Georgian homes had once stood, now there were just piles of bricks and glass, smoke coming out of them as fires were still burning underneath. There was water everywhere, some from the brigade's hoses of course, but also, by the look of the water spurting out of the middle of the road, one of the mains had burst.

I walked on, noting four pumps and two heavy units still there, and the crews busy working. There was still no sign of William and the boys. A WVS canteen was parked up and volunteers were handing out sandwiches to a couple of policemen, but our boys hadn't stopped. One of the teams had their pump on full go at a fire in a collapsed building. The flames lit up the whole street and as I got nearer the heat was enormous. I tried to look brisk and efficient in case someone questioned what I was doing there, but no one had time to take any notice.

Someone slammed the door of an ambulance and banged on the back as it drove away, squeezing between a crater and the remains of a house. When it had gone, a van carrying a team of Heavy Recovery men arrived in its place and they jumped out into the street, big chaps with shovels, their sleeves rolled up and determined looks on their faces.

I stopped to watch as a fire captain greeted the team and shook hands with a man in charge.

"Be really careful, lads," said the captain. "It's unsteady as hell. We think there are people still down there and one of the boys is trying to get to them."

"Bleeding 'ell," muttered one of the big men, "they're on a bloody death wish."

"Look at that wall," said his mate. "Captain, that thing's coming down in about three minutes. Your boys need to get out bloody quick."

They were staring at the remains of someone's home: half a three-storey house which looked as if it was about to fall over, and with what had been an adjoining wall now listing horribly to the right, propped up by a small mountain of smoking rubble and splintered wood. Two firemen were lying on top of the mound with ropes tied round their waists, peering into a hole. Two more were standing over them, holding the ends of the ropes. My stomach tightened as I saw that one of them was Roy from the station, who was a picture of thunderous concentration. He couldn't have looked less like the Roy I was used to, asking for more tea and telling funny stories about his ferrets.

I hesitated but then crept nearer, hiding behind the team of rescue workers and aware that as female station staff I shouldn't be there, let alone when I was off duty. If he saw me, Roy would be furious and order me to go home.

"Hold it," shouted the other man standing at the top, who I realised was Fred. He signalled with his hand for the rescue crew to stop and then pointed down into the hole. "I can't hear him. Can they turn off the pumps for a minute?"

Within a few moments, the hissing of the water jets stopped as the lads on the hoses stood down.

"Everyone belt up," yelled Fred as the recovery gang were still murmuring to each other. His voice had an urgency that made everyone shut up and stand stock-still. You could still hear the crackling of the fire that wasn't out, and a clank when the lady in the canteen van put down a stainless-steel teapot.

The recovery team looked grim-faced as the older one walked carefully around the rubble and considered the listing wall. Etiquette meant the recovery boys wouldn't issue an order to a fire team. But I knew everyone listened to their advice and the captain was waiting for his view.

The recovery man didn't take long.

"It's going to go," he yelled. "Get them out. Now."

The captain gave a brief nod.

"Fred," he shouted up to him. "He's had long enough. Bring him up. Fast as you can."

Fred did a thumbs up and then cautiously bent down into the hole. I didn't want to watch, but more than that, I didn't want to listen.

I knew what I would hear.

"Bill," yelled Fred. "Bill, mate, are you there?"

No one moved an inch as Fred paused, listening. Then he turned and called back down to everyone else.

"There's two kids down there. Alive. He's going to send them up. Chuck us more rope."

For a moment this sounded good news, but my optimism was short-lived.

"Bleedin' hell," said the recovery man in charge. "It's never going to hold. Not for three of them." He looked up at the listing wall. "If anything holding that moves, the whole bloody lot's coming down."

I stood on my own, wanting to help but all too aware I was a spare part.

"Everyone not Service or Recovery move back," ordered the captain, and they made me and the wardens and the police and the volunteers get out of the way. All the brigade boys stayed; even ones who weren't from our station refused to budge. Together with the recovery lads, they tried to make a structure out of wood that might shore up the rubble.

Roy fed the first rope into the hole. "All right, kids," he yelled. "Nice and still, for the fireman. Steady, Fred."

I crossed my fingers as they began to pull up the rope.

"All right, littl'n, easy there," Roy was calling, almost singing, to the child. "No, love, don't go kicking. That's a cherub. There we are."

And then we saw her. A terrified little girl in a nightie, clutching onto the rope and covered from head to foot in grey dust, which made her look like a tiny ghost.

"Stay still, princess," said Roy.

The child clung on as she was told, blinking in the dull morning light and then opening her eyes wide as she saw the group of men at the top of the rubble. Her face began to crumple.

Fred lifted her from Roy. "It's all right, Uncle Fred's got you."

The child grabbed at his uniform jacket with her small fists.

"Mabel," she began to wail. "Mabel."

"It's all right, we'll get her," promised Fred as he managed to pass the child down to the others on the ladders.

I leapt forward, but an ambulance lady put her hand on my arm.

"I've got her," she said, moving in front of me as one of the men handed her the little girl, who was still calling out for Mabel.

Roy and Fred had already sent the rope down again to Bill. Interminable seconds passed. Then we saw them pull out a boy, bigger than the girl, but with the same preternatural appearance from all the dust. His right arm was hanging by his side and he couldn't hold on to the men as they lifted him out. His right leg looked awful too.

The men carefully got the boy down and a craggy-looking fireman carried him away as I watched, sick with fear, my heart pounding, for the boy and for William, who was still nowhere to be seen.

Bricks were beginning to topple from the adjoining house and the big wall began to sway.

"Bill," shouted Roy down the hole. "We're bringing you up. It's bad out here. Get hold of the bloody rope."

I held my breath. It was one thing to pull out children who only weighed a few stone, but a grown man would be another matter.

"What's the problem?" shouted the captain. "Is he all right?"

"He won't be when I get hold of him," said Fred to his superior.

The big wall listed. Everyone watching gasped.

Roy was leaning down into the hole.

"Here he comes," he called. "Easy does it, Fred, easy now."

They both pulled on the rope, scattering bricks as they did so. The mound of rubble began to move from underneath them.

"CLEAR OUT, LADS," shouted the chief recovery man. "EVERYONE CLEAR OUT."

The men who had been trying to prop up the wall with wood and girders began to back away. You couldn't credit them with anything other than huge bravery for what they'd been doing so far, but their boss was calling them off and as bricks fell they had no choice but to scramble to safety.

At the top of the rubble, we could at last see Roy and Fred dragging Bill out. He was barely recognizable.

"I'm out, boys. GO."

He was shouting as loudly as I had ever heard anyone in my life.

All three of them half scrambled, half fell down the heap, scattering bricks, glass, and bits of broken woodwork as they went. Like a volcano gone wrong, rubble seemed to get sucked inwards as they went, and the whole thing began to collapse, the big wall coming down after it, making the most almighty noise.

Roy and Fred were on their feet first and running as fast as they could. I must have moved towards them, as an ARP warden grabbed me by the coat and dragged me back with him.

William was a second behind. As the last part of the building came crashing to the ground and a huge cloud of dust and smoke went up he emerged coughing badly, blood all down his uniform and clutching a small bundle.

I shook off the warden and ran through the others to him.

"He's all right, love," said Roy as I pushed through. "He'll be all right."

"What the hell do you think you're doing?" I screamed. "You could have been bloody killed."

William held up the bundle. It was a doll wrapped in a blanket.

That's when I really saw red.

"I'm supposed to tell Bunty you nearly died rescuing A DOLL?" I shouted.

"Where's the littl'n, Roy?" said William, ignoring me and catching his breath. "She'll be wanting her Mabel."

I glared at him. Saving children was one thing, and a wonderful thing at that. But nearly getting half of his team flattened in order to pull a toy out of the rubble was quite another. Fred was kneeling down on what remained of the pavement. He was holding on to his arm and swearing under his breath.

I tried to remember I was wearing my uniform and mustn't make a show.

"You'd saved their lives; you didn't need to go back for the toy box." I wiped my eyes. Dust from the collapsed building was everywhere. "You could have died."

"Calm down, Emmy," said William. "They've lost everything. You wouldn't understand."

"No," I said, trying to sound calm. "I probably wouldn't. But don't go pretending it was a one-off because I know that it wasn't. Do you want to tell me about Saturday night? The ever-so-near escape at the warehouse?"

As I repeated Vera's words, I knew I was in the wrong. William was a hero and I was spoiling it. But I had been frightened, unable to help, and hopelessly out of my depth.

"Emmy," he said, "you won't mention this to Bunty, will you?"

I wanted to hit him. Not only had he taken an entirely unnecessary risk but now he wanted me to act as if it hadn't actually happened.

"Do you ever think of anyone other than yourself?" I said, looking daggers at him. "Because it doesn't seem like it to me."

William shot me a furious look.

"Oh, don't worry," I said. "I won't say anything. But only because I don't want my best friend to know that you just risked your life *for a doll.* You should have a long, hard look at yourself, though, Bill. You're not thinking of her and it isn't fair."

And then I turned my back on him and, wiping the dust from my eyes, headed towards home.

Chapter 13

AN ABSOLUTE COMFORT TO KNOW

By the time I got home, Bunty had left for work, which made it easier to stay true to my word and not tell her about the rescue or what had happened with William. I didn't have to explain why I was covered from head to foot in dust and dirt either. I peeled my clothes off and allowed myself the luxury of a morning bath. The inch of water was nearly cold but it was better than nothing and it would help keep me awake and focus my mind.

I knew I had acted badly. I shouldn't have shouted at Bill in the street. I still thought he had been wildly reckless, but I planned to apologise as soon as there was a quiet moment at the station when I could try to patch things up. I also knew that part of my being so cross with him was because I had felt so useless. The lady handing out tea had done more than me.

As I washed the dirt out of my hair, I gave myself a stern talking to. I'd hated being a spectator in an emergency and was embarrassed about my overemotional response. I had avidly read the autobiographies of fearless female journalists in Spain during the Civil War. Now I marvelled at how they managed to stay detached, do their jobs, and file their reports without wanting to wade in and get involved.

Could I do that? I wasn't sure. I kept seeing the children's faces as Roy and Fred pulled them out of the rubble. How did one stay uninvolved about that? William had taken it too far last night, but even ignoring the stupid doll, he and Roy and Fred, and *all* the men, had put themselves in enormous danger in order to rescue the children. And they would be out doing the same thing tonight. I was proud of working at the station, answering the calls with the other girls, but I wanted to do even more.

It was time to pull myself together. As I arrived at the office, I made an extra-big effort to appear chipper.

I didn't want to tell Kathleen about the previous night so I watered down the raid to a few crash bang wallops at the fire station and, to change the subject, mentioned the briefest of How Do You Do's with Mr. Collins and Charles. This, as it turned out, may have been a mistake.

"I say," gasped Kathleen, goggle-eyed at the idea of Mr. Collins having a relation or even just existing outside of work. "I'd have died a death. Was he shouty like You Know Who can be?" she added in a whisper.

"Mr. Collins' brother was very polite," I said, hoping this was enough information. It wasn't.

"And what did he look like? Older or younger?" Kathleen perched on the side of her desk, a reckless move should Mrs. Bird suddenly come in.

"Oh, gosh, I don't know," I said, being vague to a point of amnesia. "Quite tall. Quite young. Like anyone really."

"Imagine!" said Kathleen. "And what did he say?"

"Oh," I said. "You know. 'Hello.' "

Kath shook her head at the revelation. "Fancy! Mr. Collins with a brother."

"Half-brother," I said rather primly. "It's perfectly normal."

Kathleen narrowed her eyes and smiled. I'd got myself in a fluster.

"You look like Clarence," she said.

I made a scoffing noise to show how ridiculous this was and started on my pile of work.

As ever, acceptable letters had been thin on the ground. There had only been a few to give to Mrs. Bird, and even then she had rejected several as Entirely Unacceptable. The only problems she had agreed to answer were a query from an awkward fourteen-year-old ("You're being rather silly, I suggest you join the Girl Guides") and a helpful hint for a woman whose bicycle seat had made her warden's overalls go shiny ("We are at war. It hardly matters if they are shiny or not. However, if you must insist, use an old beret to cover it up").

One other letter had been worth taking a chance on, and to my surprise it had been given the go-ahead. It was from a girl whose boyfriend had a roving eye.

Dear Mrs. Bird,

Please tell me what I should do. My young man always looks at other girls we pass in the street. He says he doesn't but he does because I've seen him. Should I make a fuss or ignore it? What if he sees someone he likes more than me?

Yours,

Feeling Left Out

I had risked Mrs. Bird blowing her top over lewd behavior, but it turned out that Men Looking At Other Girls was one of her pet subjects. Her reply of "The young man in question is a thoroughly unpalatable sort. If he continues to do this, I suggest you either forget him or call the police" was on the threatening side of robust.

I had just finished typing it up when at half past nine we heard the corridor door bang open and Mr. Collins arrive. He was humming something by Mozart which I couldn't quite place, but it was a sign he was in a good mood. When he didn't whistle, it meant he would go straight to his office, bash about for a bit, and then do one of his Shouts. Today, though, he put his head around the door to our cubbyhole and appeared very nearly smiley.

"Good morning, ladies. How are you? Glad to see you survived last night's festivities."

He always referred to raids in this way.

"Yes, thank you, Mr. Collins," said Kathleen politely as I suffered an attack of fearful self-consciousness. After all, on Saturday we had shared cake.

"I hope you were all right, Mr. Collins?" she enquired.

Kathleen was usually quiet as a mouse around Mr. Collins as she thought him quite mad. I knew she was dying to ask about Charles.

"Snug as a bug, Kathleen. Thank you."

She beamed at him. "And did you have a lovely weekend, sir?"

Honestly, she was beginning to sound like a waitress angling for a big tip.

"Capital, thank you, Kathleen," said Mr. Collins, who in the few weeks I had known him had never admitted to having a capital anything. "How about you?"

Kathleen picked up some speed. "Oh, very good, thank you. We didn't mind the bombs at all, me and Mum. My little brother was there, you see, and we always feel very safe around him, even though he is *quite a bit younger than me*."

I considered throwing myself out of the nearest window.

"Is he indeed?" said Mr. Collins. "Fancy that." He glanced over at me, but I was looking at the pot plant with my mouth open.

"Good weekend, Emmeline?" he asked.

"Um, yes, thank you," I managed. What if he mentioned Charles? Or, even worse, the trip to the cinema? Kathleen would probably pass out.

"HOW IS YOUR BROTHER?" I shrieked, making everyone jump. "WHO WE MET IN THE STREET."

It sounded as if we had been in the East End, dogfighting or betting on horses and eating chips wrapped in the *Daily Express*.

Mr. Collins seemed bewildered, which was a fair response when you looked at it, but then gathered his wits. Reaching into his pocket for his cigarettes, he turned to Kathleen.

"Ah yes. Did Emmeline mention that she bumped into me and my younger brother on Saturday afternoon?" he asked.

"IN THE STREET," I shouted, just in case it wasn't clear.

"Yes. As Emmy has so geographically pointed out, *in the street*." Mr. Collins smiled.

"THAT'S RIGHT," I bellowed, wondering if people could actually die of self-consciousness.

"In the street," echoed Kathleen in a whisper, clearly in the hope this would bring an end to the whole torturous conversation before someone's ears started to bleed.

Mr. Collins grinned, lit his cigarette, and having decided we had all been put through enough, created a welcome diversion by asking what I was working on.

"It's next week's problem page, Mr., um, Collins," I said, trying to sound In Control. The last thing I needed was for Mr. Collins to start taking an interest in the letters. I told myself to remain calm.

"Ah," he said, picking up the notes. "Good grief," he added as he saw Mrs. Bird's answer to Feeling Left Out. "We can't print that. Half the young men in Britain will end up under arrest. Emmy, take it out. Henrietta won't notice, and if she does get up any steam, tell her I told you to do it."

I must have looked uncertain. Mr. Collins exhaled a stream of smoke and made an impatient face.

"The typesetters will know how to make everything fit. I'll be in my office."

Then he snorted and strode out of the room.

"Right ho," I said. "I do hope he's right," I added to Kathleen, who was trying to get some pencil shavings out of her sharpener.

"I think he is," she mused. "Mrs. Bird hasn't mentioned the Odo-Ro-No advert that got left out. And once I forgot whether I'd given her an issue, and when I asked, she said she didn't have time to flimflam about reading, and anyway, the only parts she hadn't already seen were the romances and Mr. Collins' Trifles That Could Look After Themselves."

Kathleen stopped and looked traumatised by the memory.

"Dark days," I said sympathetically. "Still, isn't it nice to know that if something accidentally goes wrong, it is almost entirely unlikely that Mrs. Bird will find out?"

"Yes." Kathleen turned to me and beamed. "That's a real comfort to know."

"Isn't it?" I said, beaming right back.

Feeling Left Out had left the perfect space in the Henrietta Helps page. As my friend returned to typing up "How To Make A Charming Tray Cloth," I took the folder of Unpleasant letters from my drawer and found the one from eighteen-year-old Fed Up that Thelma had helped me with last night. Trying carefully to remember what she had said, I began to type a reply.

Dear Fed Up,

Isn't it a disappointment when one's parents feel rather strict? I am sure they want what is best, so perhaps there's some middle ground you could find . . .

Anyone might think that having got away with putting one letter into *Woman's Friend*, doing it again would be easier, but it wasn't like that at all. Even if I felt confident that Mrs. Bird would not see, it was rotten of me to ignore Bunty's advice. I hadn't exactly *promised* not to write to more readers, but I had nodded my head a lot and said, You're Right, Bunty, Of Course, which was essentially the same thing. And that was just about sending letters to them. She didn't know about my putting replies into the actual magazine.

What was worse, I wondered, keeping something from your best friend or ignoring people who were desperate for help? I felt sure that if Bunty could only see the letters every day as I did, she would agree that I was trying to do the right thing.

In need of a break, I muttered something to Kathleen and hurried out to the stairwell, where I could have a few minutes to think. My head in the clouds, I slammed straight into Mr. Collins at the top of the stairs.

"Ah. I'm glad I found you, Emmeline," he said as I apologised. "Ahem." He paused, stared at the wall, and ran his hand through his hair, making it stick up. "So. Yes. This is highly unprofessional, not to mention hideously awkward, but there we are and all that. Charles would be furious if he knew. Hmm."

He stopped and looked sheepish.

"Ahem," he said again. "So. Yes."

"What is it, Mr. Collins?" I asked as he trailed off again. Then I realised. "Oh. Gosh. Is it about Captain Mayhew?" I said in a rush before being struck dumb by the social horror of it all.

"Ah," said Mr. Collins. "Ha. Yes."

We both looked at the floor in abject misery. Finally, Mr. Collins did the gentlemanly thing and pulled himself together. He glanced behind him in case anyone was coming, which they weren't.

"So," he managed, with some effort. "Didn't mention earlier. Rather realised I should. Just to say, Emmy, er, Emmeline, or indeed, Miss Lake, that my young brother Charles was as happy as I have seen him for some time following your jaunt to the cinema." He cleared his throat. "And. So. Right then. I just wanted to say that if, for any reason, you think that working for, that is, *alongside*, I should say, in many ways, er, me, here . . ."

He pursed his lips and looked me in the eye. Then he gave a big sigh and hurled himself in.

"Emmeline, Charles very much enjoyed meeting you. I know he would be delighted if he were to do so again and I don't want you to think you mustn't, just because we work in the same office. I don't think it is something people here need to know about, and I certainly won't mention it again. So if you did want to . . ." He paused. "Or perhaps not . . ."

This was unbearable.

"It's all right, Mr. Collins," I said. "I thought I might rather like to," I managed.

Then I returned to looking mortified again. This was worse than when Father caught Bunty and me laughing at the drawings in one of his medical books when we were twelve.

"Oh right. Good. Yes. Good oh," said Mr. Collins, looking enormously relieved. "That's sorted, then. I'm so sorry to put you through this. Dreadful. No idea how parents manage. Not really my thing. Hmm." But he smiled at me and looked proud. "He's a good chap, young Charles," he said. "Good chap. Goes without saying, of course."

And then Mr. Collins marched briskly down the stairs in exactly the same direction from which he had first appeared.

It was a relief to go back to my desk and begin typing up a new romance series. I'd just got to a part where a young Wren had been posted to a naval base and immediately fallen in love with two officers at the same time when Clarence arrived, sporting a new hairdo, which featured an enthusiastic amount of Brylcreem, and clearly electric with the hope that it might make an impression on Kathleen.

"Good morning," he called, starting well in a gruff voice before squeaking out "ladies" in an unexpectedly high finale. "House copies," he added gravely. "And post."

I was up in a flash, pushing my chair back so that it scraped loudly across the wooden floor.

"New issue. Thank you, Clarence," I bellowed, grabbing the bundle from him. "Post. Smashing."

This was the issue with Confused's letter in it. So much for me blithely writing a reply for Fed Up and thinking it was easy to just keep sneaking things into Henrietta Helps. With proof of my insurgency now in print, I was jumpy as a frog.

"Gosh, Emmy, you're keen," said Kath. "Hello, Clarence, you look nice."

Clarence looked stricken to the core.

"Thank you, Clarence," said Kath gently, feeling sorry for him. "Are you all right, Emmy?"

"Fine, thanks," I said. "Loads to do."

I could feel perspiration on my back as I put the bundle of magazines on the floor by my desk and started to go through the post. What if Mrs. Bird decided to read this week's *Woman's Friend* as a one-off? I told myself to show some backbone. Everyone was convinced Mrs. Bird didn't look at finished copies. Confused's letter would be fine and so would Fed Up's.

But my heart still raced and I reasoned that it might not be a bad idea to take a short breather from putting any other letters into the magazine. And perhaps even from writing to the readers as well. After all, I had been pushing my luck recently. The idea of lying low for a bit did rather appeal.

I looked at the door nervously. Mrs. Bird was in her office and might launch herself at us at any moment. It would be best to act as if everything was perfectly normal. I would open her post and then take Acceptable Letters and a copy of the new issue into her office.

I told myself everything would be fine and opened the first letter.

Dear Mrs. Bird,

I have just spent an endless ninety minutes holding a skein of wool as my wife untangled it. A thoroughly wretched business indeed. Why on earth is this not sold in balls?

Yours,

T. Leonard, Esq.

A wool enquiry was right up Mrs. Bird's street. I relaxed slightly and opened the next one.

Dear Mrs. Bird,

I am in love with a young Polish airman who is stationed nearby. We have been going together for nearly a year, and he has asked me to be his wife. My mother wants me to wait until after the war because she thinks we won't last, but I love him and I know he loves me. He has a good education and is a gunner so has a serious job. The thing is, if he was English I don't think Mother would mind in the least.

Please tell me what I should do.

In Love

Poor In Love. It was desperately sad, not to mention unfair. It wasn't the first letter I had seen on the subject either. I had read several like this—girls who had met and fallen in love with Allied soldiers from overseas. Mrs. Bird ignored them all.

Last week I had tried to get her to answer one, from a lovely girl very much in love with a man who had come from Czechoslovakia to fight. "He is one of the very best men you could ever meet," the girl had written.

I'd chanced it with Mrs. Bird, asking as a General Query if we took letters about Foreign Beaus.

"I have no doubt he is a very brave young man indeed," she replied. "We are all most grateful to the Allied servicemen." Then her tone changed. "But when the war is over, no one will want them here and almost certainly no one will want her over there either. Don't pull a face, Miss Lake, it is how the world works. Such suggestions are best left alone."

There was no point showing her In Love's letter, but I hated having to ignore another girl who had every right to be with whoever she chose. Especially now, when no one knew how long they might have, least of all the airmen. Why shouldn't they be happy? It was hard enough holding on to love in the middle of war as it was, without people who didn't understand making it even more difficult.

I thought of Edmund. We'd known each other's families for years and he'd ended up being absolutely rotten to me. Or Charles? I didn't know anything about his background—other than being Mr. Collins' half-brother, and that didn't shed very much light. But I was jolly well sure that if I might grow to like him, no one in my family would give a hoot where he was from, as long as he was a good man and decent to me. I was beginning to realise how lucky I was.

A magnificent rustling noise from the corridor heralded the looming of Mrs. Bird from her office.

"Balaclavas for the troops," she announced, to no one and everyone at the same time. "I shall be an hour and a half."

"Yes, Mrs. Bird," called Kathleen, who was proofreading a recipe for a curried vegetable medley.

"Miss Knighton, I do not like shouting," shouted Mrs. Bird.

"Sorry, Mrs. Bird," said Kathleen.

"What?" shouted Mrs. Bird, before giving up. "Young people."

And with a loud Hmmph she was gone.

As Kathleen shook her head and returned to the recipe, her face a picture of concentration, I looked down at the parcel of new magazines on the floor. Thinking of Edmund had made me remember my reply to Confused, whose fiancé had gone off the boil. The more I put off looking at it, the worse it felt. In my mind it now took up half of Henrietta Helps. A great big letter that Mrs. Bird had not even seen, followed by advice she would never have given.

With the same feeling of trepidation as waiting for exam results to be read out at school, I picked up the scissors from my desk, cut through the string, and unwrapped the package. There it was. The new issue of *Woman's Friend.*

I turned immediately to the second to last page, almost surprised when I had to look for Confused's letter rather than seeing it leaping out of the page in letters at least ten inches high.

I am very much in love with my fiancé, but he has suddenly become very cold . . . Should I marry him and hope that he comes round?

It looked exactly like any other problem. A few lines long, with my answer neatly below.

"What an unfortunate disappointment," I had written—briskly like Mrs. Bird might.

And a sadness all round. I suggest have a jolly good chat with your fiancé and if you aren't convinced his heart is in it, then I am afraid it may be time to move on. It could feel quite rotten for a while, but I promise things will *get better. Marriage is for a very long time and you deserve to be with someone who very much wants to be with you. I do hope your chap will step up, but if not, I am sure you will find the one that is really for you.*

So, there it was in print.

It was the strangest feeling. Partly I felt like a fraud. After all, what did I know about marriage? But when I read it again, I could see that I had offered some hope. Confused could give her fiancé a chance, but if he didn't make more effort, she wouldn't have to get stuck. All in all, I thought it wasn't too bad a reply. I hoped Confused would agree and either sort him out or push on and one day find her true love.

I had to stifle a smile in case Kathleen saw. It felt good to have done something. I couldn't fix it for Confused, but I'd tried to be something of a friend. And other readers might take comfort from it as well.

Galvanised, I thought of In Love again. She deserved to be happy. She deserved to be allowed to make up her own mind.

My plan to lie low had lasted less than three minutes.

I had become too involved in the readers' lives to just throw In Love's letter away—or any of the others I might help, for that matter. Putting their letters into the magazine was horribly risky, but I had been writing back to them for over a month and no one had suspected a thing. That part of things was watertight, I was absolutely convinced.

I wasn't working at the fire station tonight and I knew Bunty was going to the cinema with William so I would be alone in the flat. I hid In Love's letter under some papers until Kathleen went out and I could slip it into my bag. Then I quietly got on with my day.

Chapter 14

TO US, EMMY LAKE

On Monday afternoon, when I had returned home from work, Captain Mayhew—or rather, Charles—called me on the phone. He had a lovely telephone voice and it all went very well. Charles said how pleased he was that I had been all right during last night's raid and I said it wasn't that bad really and didn't mention seeing two children and a Fire Brigade nearly get squashed to death in the street.

There was a bit of difficulty getting to the issue of seeing each other again, but after a tricky period where we both said different things over each other at the same time, and then a looming threat of neither of us saying anything at all, Charles took the bull by the horns.

"I say, Emmy, do you enjoy dancing?"

"Oh yes. Enormously," I said. "As a matter of fact Bunty and Bill are planning to go out the night after next." I stopped and cringed. It sounded as if I was fishing for an invitation to go along too.

"Not that I'm fishing for an invitation to go along too," I said.

Charles laughed. "I wouldn't mind if you were. In fact, do you think you would mind if I asked you to go with me, just to be clear?"

I laughed as well. "I would love to," I said.

"If Bunty and her chap won't mind?"

"Bunty will be thrilled," I said, absolutely sure. "They both will."

Then we sorted out what time Charles should come over to the house and chatted a bit more before saying goodbye. After I put the phone down, I stood in the hall grinning like a loon. I had to admit it, Charles Mayhew certainly had a way of perking me up.

I was right about Bunty too. When I told her about the dance, she thought it quite the best idea in the world, even if adding "And I bet he won't go off at the drop of a hat with some nurse or another like That Edmund" wasn't entirely in the spirit of Forgive and Forget. I wasn't sure I would be able to forgive Edmund, but I was doing my very best to forget.

Still, if it helped Bunty move on from being in a fury with That Edmund (as she now always referred to him), then it was all the better. I didn't say anything but I thought it would be a good opportunity to make it up with Bill too. The more I thought about it, the worse I felt about giving him such a telling off when actually he had been incredibly brave.

On Wednesday evening Bunty and I were ready early. She had put on a pale green day dress she'd worn for her twenty-first birthday and updated with a layer of chiffon that looked awfully nice and floated about when she danced. I had decided on a midnight-blue silk frock which, though several years old, was my most favourite article in my wardrobe and when Bunts and I had a quick waltz around the flat as a practice, I was hopeful that I would pass muster.

With time on our hands, the two of us did have a rather wet outbreak of worry over where we should greet Charles and William, as dragging them all the way upstairs to the flat when we were about to go straight out again seemed daft. We thought about using one of the reception rooms downstairs, but they had been covered with dust sheets since Bunty's granny had left last year. The windows were all taped up and the blackout curtains permanently drawn. The rooms were fusty too and, more than that, seemed grand and showy compared to our flat upstairs.

We decided we would invite the boys up as, after all, that was where we lived, and as William was in and out of the house all the time seeing Bunty, he would think we had gone mad to do anything else. Bunty suggested we offer sherry as a reward and I suggested we have one ourselves to get into the swing of things. Bunty put on a Joe Loss record and turned the volume up while I bolted my sherry and unnecessarily rearranged a china duck on the mantelpiece.

"Don't be nervous," Bunty said kindly as the doorbell rang and I nearly dropped the duck. "We're all going to have the loveliest time. Now go and answer the door."

It was twenty-nine minutes past seven, and having flown down the three flights of stairs to the door, I paused for a second to pull myself together and arrange my face into a welcoming smile.

"Oof," I said out loud in the large and freezing cold hall. My mouth was dry and my lips had stuck themselves to my gums. "Good evening," I whispered to myself just as I had rehearsed. "Good evening, Charles," I added more flamboyantly to a large Chinese urn.

It was a simple enough greeting. I switched the hall light off so I wouldn't get shouted at by a passing ARP warden, pulled back the heavy curtains, and opened the front door.

Charles was standing on the doorstep in the dark, smiling a little shyly from under his army cap.

"Hello, Emmy," he said. "You look lovely." It was ever so kind as he couldn't really see me with the light off.

"Good evening, Charles," I managed, which came out very formally and rather as if I was about to start broadcasting the news. I wondered whether to say he looked lovely as well, but wasn't sure it was the Done Thing, so I clung on to the curtains until I was struck with inspiration and asked him if he should like to come in. With the door safely closed, I switched on the light and led him up to the flat.

Bunty, who I knew had been practising looking casual, was in the living room, standing with one hand on the mantelpiece while staring into mid-distance. She looked as if she were modelling an evening-wear pattern for *Vogue*.

Before I could announce him, Bunty burst into action and exclaimed, "Charles!" and Charles exclaimed, "Bunty!" rather as if they had discovered gold, and then they shook hands in relief that they had established first-name terms again and avoided the difficult You Must Call Me Charles, Do Call Me Bunty business. Then the doorbell rang again.

"Are you well?" said Charles as Bunty ran off downstairs.

"Oh no," I said without thinking. "I was going to say that. What an idiot. Me. Not you, of course." I grimaced. "It *is* nice to see you," I said in the end, because really, it was.

Charles laughed. "It's nice to see you too," he said. And then he took hold of my hands, which was tons better than the handshake he and Bunty had done, but meant that then we were standing in the living room holding hands when Bunty and William came in.

"Well now," said Bunty, which was unhelpful.

I snatched my hands away from Charles and immediately wished that I hadn't. I couldn't see how I might shove them back at him, though, so I said hello to William instead. It was the first time I had seen him since the row, so I was self-conscious and wondered if he felt the same. It may have been my imagination but he did seem a little uptight.

Remembering my manners just in time, I introduced the two men, somehow managing to do it without appearing an absolute nitwit.

Charles and William both looked splendid in their uniforms and immediately expressed admiration for the other's work in The Current Situation.

"I don't know how you chaps do it," said Charles seriously as they shook hands. "Fire terrifies me. I very much admire you."

I couldn't help thinking that Edmund had never said anything complimentary about the Fire Service to William and how nice it was that Charles had. It was lovely to see Bunty beam with pride too.

I offered everyone a sherry, pleased that Bunts had had the presence of mind to hide the two glasses we'd already used so there was no suggestion of an unfortunate dependency. As it was my second drink in ten minutes it was also a nerve-settler if ever I'd had one.

With everyone relaxing, the conversation became gay. We chatted about how there wasn't enough jazz on the BBC but it was super when they did do some and wasn't Tommy Handley a real card on *It's That Man Again*. I made a big effort to be lovely to William, and he made an equal effort to be chivalrous back, while Charles showed great interest in Bunty and she was adorable to him in return, until anyone would have been forgiven for thinking we were all about to go dancing with completely the wrong person.

It was a damp evening, but as we headed off to the West End we were all in high spirits. William seemed especially keen to get going and the four of us arrived at the dance just as the queues were beginning to build for the evening session. It was a mixed crowd, lots of service men and women, and a real jumble of accents. We waited in the drizzle by some friendly New Zealanders, who made funny comments about the posters advising "Be Like Dad, Keep Mum" and even more colourful ones about the adverts for land girls. Charles raised his eyebrows at me and I laughed. So much for my plan to be a career woman with no time for men.

By the time we got inside, the dance floor was packed with couples. At the far end of the hall, the band were playing their socks off and if it hadn't been for the absolute sea of different uniforms and the fact that the civilian girls were in day dresses rather than evening frocks, for a second you could have forgotten that there was anything awful happening in the world at all.

Straightaway a determined William swept Bunty onto the dance floor, and for a few moments Charles and I watched. Bunty looked so happy as they started fox trotting, with the chiffon on her dress flying out like a ladybird about to take off. I laughed out loud and gave them a wave.

"I think they've left us to it," shouted Charles over the noise of the band and the chatter around the bar. "Would you like a dance, or shall we have a drink to celebrate the evening first?"

"A drink sounds lovely," I yelled. "Although what are we celebrating exactly? Quick, there's a free table." A couple were moving onto the dance floor so I grabbed Charles by the arm, pulling him with me. We rudely pushed past a short man chatting to a tall girl and hurled ourselves into the tiny velvet booth that had just become free, falling into it without any semblance of decorum.

As the other couple looked defeated, Charles and I turned to each other.

"Hurrah!" we both said at the same time and burst into laughter.

"Well done," said Charles, flagging down a waiter. "I bet you're a demon when you dance. Would you like champagne?" He paused and pulled a face. "I'm sorry, am I being an awful Flash Harry?"

"Not at all," I said as if I drank champagne and went dancing every Wednesday and this was all par for the course.

"Good," said Charles and ordered a bottle. He turned to me and smiled. "You do realise I'm trying to look as if I do this all the time, don't you? Please tell me it might be working just a bit?"

Actually, I had a feeling it might be working rather a lot.

"Oh yes," I said in a supportive way. "I think you're doing very well."

"Thank goodness. Quite honestly I'm not sure what's come over me. I'm showing off terribly. I shall hate myself tomorrow at this rate."

"Ah, but we're celebrating," I said, coming to his rescue. "Aren't we?"

He laughed. "I'll say."

"Only, I don't really know what," I added, thinking that I didn't actually care.

Charles paused and leant forward to speak. Even sitting in the booth, we were surrounded by noise. "Well," he said as the waiter reappeared in double quick time with a bottle and two glasses, "I think we should celebrate you making my leave quite the jolliest ever."

I could feel my cheeks turning red.

"I haven't done much really," I said. "Just the cinema and talking on the phone. Oh, and this."

The waiter showed Charles the bottle and, after he had nodded, poured the champagne.

Charles handed me a glass. "It's been a bit of a year," he said, frowning, his brown eyes very serious for a moment. "Not always huge fun." He didn't appear at all Flash Harry now. He cleared his throat. "Emmy, I hope you don't mind my saying that you've cheered me up no end. I just wanted to say that. I hope you don't mind," he said again.

He fiddled with his glass and looked embarrassed, but in a rather dashing way. I clutched at the stem of my champagne glass and forced myself to look him in the eye.

"I'm having the loveliest time," I said, which came out so quietly I felt sure he wouldn't hear. It wasn't the sort of thing I wanted to bellow. "Thank you ever so much."

Charles had the nicest eyes I had ever looked into. It must have been a funny sherry at Bunty's as I could hardly breathe.

He raised his glass.

"To us, Emmy Lake," he said as we clinked glasses and stared at each other.

"To us," I said, and then, just to make sure of it, said again under my breath. "Goodness. To us."

Then neither of us said anything and it was the most natural thing in the world when Charles put down his glass and reached across the table to hold my hand.

This was how Bunty and William found us a few minutes later, which elicited a loud Oh from me as I sat bolt upright and snatched my hand away from Charles again. If he minded that I seemed to keep doing this, or thought I was rude, he certainly didn't let on, just raised a surreptitious eyebrow at me with a smile.

As it turned out, Bunty only had eyes for William. Although all of us tried, the conversation didn't really take off with the music and hubbub, and anyway, William kept fidgeting and clearing his throat. He looked even more jumpy than earlier, but both he and Bunty were more than happy to stay in the booth when Charles suggested he and I go off to dance.

The band were well into their stride, and even though it was packed, no one got in the way and it was as if the entire dance floor was ours. Charles was a good dancer, confident and practised, and you didn't feel as if you were a sack of coal being heaved onto a float, which sometimes happened with a partner you didn't much know. Dancing with Charles was exciting and I wished we could carry on through the night. I'd never felt like that with Edmund, who didn't like dances anyway.

We waltzed and fox trotted and it felt as if we cut quite a dash, and for once there was no thought of work or the station or air raids or worries. Just dancing and laughing with a man who was rather lovely, and, I thought, very handsome as well.

When the band leader announced a short break we headed back to our table to catch our breath. William had stopped looking nervy and was grinning like a Cheshire cat and Bunty was sniffing and looking happier than I had ever seen her.

About fit to burst, she held up her left hand.

"Look, Emmy, look," she cried.

My best friend in the world was engaged and the expression on her face was enough for me to know that her dearest dream had come true.

Within a second there was absolute pandemonium with Bunts and me shrieking and hugging and trying not to cry in public, and Charles pumping William's hand up and down and saying Well Done, Old Man, as if he had known him forever. Then Bunty and I pulled ourselves together and she properly showed me the most beautiful emerald ring, which had belonged to William's mother, and it was quite hard not to start crying all over again.

It was the loveliest surprise.

"Bill says now he's been promoted, he doesn't have to wait any longer," said Bunty, beaming. "He is silly. I'd have married him whatever he's doing."

"Someone's got to keep you in champagne," grinned her fiancé. "We might all get used to this sort of high life."

We all cheered in agreement and then Bunty turned to me.

"Emmy, there is one thing I need to sort out," she said, putting on a serious face for a moment. "You will be my chief bridesmaid, won't you?"

Of course I said yes, and then we both went slightly to pieces and Charles ended up giving me his hankie. William had ordered a second bottle of champagne and we all started making toasts to the happy couple and the future and Peace and even a mention for The King and Queen.

William had his arm around Bunty and was holding on to her as if he would never let her go. Bunty kept gazing at him, and even though they were sharing the marvellous news with Charles and me, you could tell it was really as if there was nobody else in the whole hall. Finally, Bunts whispered to me that would I mind if they left as she wanted to telephone her granny straightaway? Of course I said she must, so we hugged again, and they galloped off into the night, leaving Charles and me to stay dancing on our own.

Their happiness was catching. We danced for ages, and although we both said our feet hurt like anything, at the end of the evening, we happily walked home, arm in arm in the dark. Although there were raids over the north of the city, it didn't bother either of us very much and it was past midnight when we got back to the house and stood whispering on the doorstep. Charles had to be on a train back to his regiment at five the next morning and there would be no chance to see each other again for some time. It was a horrid thought and hard not to feel low, but we chatted as perkily as we could and agreed we should both very much like to write to each other while he was away.

"I'm not going to be gloomy," he said. "Because I will look forward to your letters, and anyway you never know when they might dole out some more leave."

This was an admirable lie so I went along with it and said I would write him hideously dull letters if he liked so that he'd be far happier being away. Then I shut up and we looked at each other in a brave fashion, because actually it was horrible having to say goodbye seeing as we'd only just met, and I for one thought that I might like him very much.

"You're funny and lovely and couldn't be dull if you tried," he said. "Write to me every day and I bet you still can't do it. I'll write too of course."

And before I could think of anything funny or lovely or not dull to say back, that was when Captain Charles Mayhew leant forward, and very gently, we kissed.

Chapter 15

I KNOW WHAT I'M DOING

Charles was as good as his word about promising to write. The day after next, a letter arrived which I read while Bunty paced up and down, pretending she wasn't dying to know what it said.

Dear Emmy,

It isn't very long since we said goodbye, and as I put off packing for just a little longer, I wonder will you think me too horribly keen if I write to you tonight?

Well, I chewed it over all the way back to the flat and have decided it is a risk I shall have to take!

I so very much enjoyed going out with you tonight. I wish I could stay in London longer, but what a send-off it was—laughing and talking and dancing our feet off! I can't remember when I had such a grand time.

Emmy, I am terrifically pleased we have met. I should like very much to get to know you. I shall post this tomorrow, so that you have proof I intend to write as often as possible—and to hold you to your promise to write too!

Well, I said this would just be a note and I'm afraid I had better get my kit ready for the off. I will try to write again before I leave England—it may get a little patchier after that, but they do try to get post to us as it gives such a boost.

Please pass on my sincere congratulations to Bunty and William again, won't you? I wish them the very greatest of happiness.

Cheerio for now.

Yours,

Charles x

I thought it was lovely. I put Bunty out of her misery by reading it out to her and she was pleased as anything too. Then I let her read it herself and when she saw he had signed it with a kiss, she very nearly went into orbit.

I kept my side of the bargain and began writing to Charles, trying to send chatty letters that might make him laugh or at least brighten his day. He would be away for goodness knew how long before his next leave, and while hugely upbeat about everything, neither of us was under any illusion about the job in hand. My first letter took all evening to write and rewrite several times in order to look entirely spontaneous. I started off tremendously well with "Dear Charles," but then ran aground as I panicked and couldn't think of anything remotely interesting to say and was pretty sure I never would again. Somehow I pushed on through and ended up with four sides of chatter even though it had only been a day since we had said goodbye.

Finding a suitable end to the letter was a trial, as I didn't want to just copy him and say Cheerio For Now back again before signing off, and Bunty didn't help by going berserk and suggesting Ever Yours as if it was something out of one of Mr. Collins' romance stories. In the end I took a grip of myself and settled on Yours, Emmy with a kiss, so it did match after all.

While we had only seen each other a couple of times, I liked Charles very much. I cursed the stupid war for making him go, even though if it hadn't been for the stupid war I probably wouldn't have met him in the first place.

And anyway, I wasn't going to moon around pining like a hopeless schoolgirl. It was one of the few things I absolutely agreed with Mrs.

Bird on. We might be back home and not actually fighting, but we women needed to pull our weight. I had tons to be getting on with, what with *Woman's Friend* and the shifts at the fire station and helping plan Bunty's wedding.

At work I continued to answer as many of the readers as I could. I would read their letters on the bus home, terrified I might drop one without noticing, and then type out answers like fury in the living room on afternoons when Bunty was still on her shift at the War Office. *Woman's Friend* was still far from overwhelmed with letters to Mrs. Bird, but there had been a few more in the last couple of weeks. Some said they had heard about the magazine from their friends. I had to admit I had edited one or two of Mrs. Bird's real replies in Henrietta Helps to make them sound slightly less brusque. The advice was the same and that was what mattered.

Occasionally, if it was a quiet night at the station, I would casually ask Thelma for her views, especially about the problems from older readers. One lady had sent in a stamped addressed envelope for a reply but I didn't have a clue what to advise.

Dear Mrs. Bird,

Me and my two friends are all in our late thirties and beginning to worry about The Change. We have seen advertisements in your magazine that say a woman's forties are the most difficult time in her life. Is this an old wives' tale? Our friend Irene gets Menopax from the chemists for hot flushes but she doesn't look any different and is still a right old misery guts half the time if you ask me. What should we do?

Yours,

Winnie Plum (Mrs.)

I'd asked Mrs. Bird, who had snorted and said Winnie Plum was A Very Silly Woman Indeed, but Thelma was far more sympathetic and said that according to her older sister, middle age wasn't exactly a day at the seaside but it wasn't the end of the world either, especially if you took the odd gin and lemon and a double Jimmy Stewart feature at the Odeon. And if that wasn't enough, Her Majesty The Queen was forty and she looked smashing.

I couldn't quite put this in a letter but translated it into a supportive reply to Mrs. Plum, finishing it with an upbeat *Don't you let any stage of life stop you from doing all the things you want to do anyway. Good luck!*

I hoped it might help and that it was better than nothing. I just wished I knew more about Life. Mrs. Bird received quite a number of letters about The Change, and although it was one of the few subjects not to feature on the List of Unacceptable Topics, invariably readers were told to stop making a fuss and crack on.

No wonder people preferred the more modern magazines. They sent you a pamphlet about very nearly anything if you wrote in to them and included a stamp. Kathleen knew someone who worked at one of the biggest ones and she said they had teams of people sending out information all the time.

Often it felt as if I was wasting my time. There I was, secretly trying to come up with answers on the bus home while the other magazines were doing it on an industrial scale. I told myself to stop being a gloom bag and keep going.

And anyway, there was now tons to be cheerful about. Even though spring had been dragging its heels about getting started and not pulling its weight in the least, the promise of Bunty and William's wedding was the best-ever tonic. Since the war began, no one had long engagements anymore (which might have given me rather a clue about Edmund now I thought about it) and as Bunty and William had known each other forever, there was no reason to wait. They had set the date for Wednesday 19th March. It meant less than a month to get everything done.

Bunty's excitement was infectious. The wedding was going to be a quiet affair, at Bunty's granny's village church, followed by an informal luncheon up at Mrs. Tavistock's house. Roy from the station was beside himself to be William's best man, and Mother and Daddy would be there of course, although Jack would be unlikely to get leave. After the lunch, the new Mr. and Mrs. Barnes would leave for a two-night honeymoon near Andover before William had to be back at work on the Friday afternoon. There was talk of pork loin for lunch.

As a jovial sort of engagement present, I bought Bunty *The Guide Book for the Modern Bride*, which had been written three years earlier and was full of practical advice and ideas that were now quite hopeless in the middle of war.

"'No house is a home without a piano,'" Bunty read out loud, adding gravely, "That's Bill and me up a gum tree then." She roared with laughter.

"I don't think you're taking this seriously enough," I said, reading the book over her shoulder as she flipped through the index. "Look up how to become the perfect hostess by using Exciting Sandwich Fillings For An Informal Supper."

Bunty snorted.

"Crikey," she said, reading the page. "I had no idea you could do that many things with a tin of sardines. I'd better get up to speed. I don't want to let myself down."

We laughed even more at that. Everything listed was now impossible to find, but we did study the chapter on "Cocktail Suggestions" so that we could both confidently run up a Stinger as soon as Peace was declared. The combination of brandy, peppermint syrup, and absinthe sounded quite vile but we wouldn't know until we had tried.

It was all huge fun and even though it would have been nice to spend months talking about a fancy white wedding as perhaps we might have in a different place and time, Bunty was so very happy and in love that it didn't matter. She just wanted to get on with it and become Mrs. William Barnes. Whenever he popped in to see her at the flat, which was whenever he had time off between shifts, you could see that Mr. William Barnes felt very much the same too.

With less than two weeks to the big day, I was frantically making

Bunty's dress, in a very elegant green crepe which we had been terrifically lucky to find and she would be able to get good wear out of at other occasions. I wasn't too wretched on the sewing machine, and so far it was going to plan. Bunty had chosen the material in the Army & Navy, and Mother and I had clubbed together to get it. Bunty was thrilled. Mrs. Tavistock surprised us all by sending the most glamorous pair of brown suede court shoes ordered from Lilley & Skinner, and a friend of Bunty's at work was lending her a tiny velvet-ribboned brown hat that went wonderfully with the shoes. Whatever the weather, Bunty would look lovely.

One evening, William called in to the flat on his way to the station with some news. I still hadn't had a chance to speak with him about our silly row. At home he was stuck like glue to Bunty, and at the fire station there were always lots of people around, or he was horribly busy. So busy, in fact, that I was beginning to wonder if he was avoiding me.

Bunty let him in downstairs, and the two of them came racing up to the kitchen, William with a spring in his step and Bunty skipping up the stairs behind him, laughing and telling him he'd gone quite mad.

I looked up from where I was cutting a slice of herring pie to eat on my overnight shift.

"Evening, Bill," I said pleasantly. "It's nice to see you. Would you like a jam square? Bunty's been baking."

I reached into the bread bin and handed over a pastry with a friendly smile.

"Don't go getting jam on your uniform now," said Bunty behind him. "I'm not having a husband who lets himself go. And it's a waste."

William turned and put his arm around her. "Yes, darling," he said, looking proud and as if they'd already been married a hundred years. "Just think. In less than two weeks you can boss me around as much as you like."

"Never," said Bunty, and we all laughed.

"Anyway," said Bill, managing to stop grinning at his fiancée for a moment. "I have an important Social Announcement."

"Oooh," said Bunty and I together.

"Yes," he said, used to us speaking at the same time. He fished inside his uniform pocket for a moment, before pulling out some tickets and clearing his throat. "Ahem. This Saturday evening. Nine o'clock sharp. The Café de Paris. Ladies, you are cordially invited to a pre-wedding celebration on behalf of the beautiful Miss Marigold Tavistock and her greatest admirer, Mr. William Barnes."

"No!" shrieked Bunty.

"Goodness," I gasped, hugely impressed. "I say!"

Bunty and I looked at each other with our mouths open. The Café de Paris wasn't the kind of place any of us normally went to. It was the sort of evening out that rich London types had all the time, but it was very swank for us. I knew Bunty had always wanted to go there as the band was supposed to be top drawer, and although she said a girl at work reckoned it wasn't quite as fancy as it used to be what with the war on, it was a smashing effort for William to have arranged it.

"Is that all right, then?" asked William as Bunty came to her senses and started hugging the breath out of him.

"YES PLEASE," said Bunty into his coat. Then she pulled herself away, her face suddenly sad. "Oh, but I do wish Charles was here for Emmy."

"Don't be daft," I said, shoving my supper into my bag and playing things down. "I've only seen him twice, and once was with you."

"What about all the times you've written to him already?" challenged Bunty, kissing William on the cheek and looking for some bread and butter for him to take to work. "I've never seen anyone write so many letters as you."

"Rot," I said, doing an unnecessary inspection inside my bag.

"You'll be next," she laughed, which was a bit keen.

"Actually, I've lined up a sub," said William, stepping into the breach. "For this special event, I felt it appropriate to invite my best man. I do hope Captain Mayhew won't mind Fireman Roy Hodges joining us and accompanying Miss Lake for the evening if she will allow."

"Of course," I said, slightly giddy and thinking of the hysteria this was going to cause with the girls. "It will be my honour." Then I remembered. "Oh no," I said. "I'm on a shift Saturday night."

William grinned. "I've sorted it," he said. "Vera said she'd cover for you if you don't mind doing a double for her in return."

I was taken aback at that. I had to admit it was a kind thing to do.

"Hurrah!" said Bunty.

William couldn't stop smiling. "And you'll be surprised at Roy. He may be knocking forty but I'm told he cuts a bit of a dash on the dancing front. He's been to the Café de Paris, so he can show us the ropes."

It was an unlikely turn up. Roy had an allotment and liked murder mysteries. He was an absolute good sort.

"Watch out, Captain Mayhew," said Bunty. "Here comes Fireman Hodges on the inside."

I pulled a face at her and then looked at the kitchen clock.

"I say," I said, throwing William a smile. "Would you mind if I come with you to the station?"

"Oh," said William rather sharply. "I was going in early."

My heart sank a little. William had seemed so cheery that I had hoped he had forgiven me for falling out with him. I ploughed on, trying to keep my voice light. "It is a bit, but what with Roy turning into Fred Astaire, the girls are going to need at least twenty minutes to get over this before they can start the shift."

"Go on, darling," said Bunty. "But don't ask Emmy any questions about my dress. I want it to be a surprise."

William smiled gamely, unable to say no. I picked up my bag and raced off to fetch my coat and cap.

William and I were wrapped up well against the early evening damp as we set off together on the short walk to the station.

"Thanks awfully for inviting me next week," I said as we picked our way along in the dark. "I'm looking forward to it such a lot."

"Bunty wouldn't have it any other way. And, obviously, er, neither would I of course." He added that quickly, but I was sure meant no harm by the afterthought. "Watch out, there's a bit of a dip there."

I manoeuvred my way around a large hole in the pavement where part of a house had landed when it was hit in a raid a week or so ago. Mr. Bone had told me three families had been bombed out and one of his regular *Daily Mirrors* had had a leg taken off at the knee.

"Nasty one," I said, looking into the hole. "Mr. Bone said."

"I've no idea," answered William. "George's boys on A Watch took it. They're a really good team."

"Absolutely," I said keenly. "You all are, of course."

I heard a Hmm in the darkness but nothing more.

I chewed the inside of my cheek as we walked along. Once they were married, William was going to move in with Bunty and set up a little home in three rooms on the first floor of the house. Bunty had insisted that I should continue to live in the flat upstairs, which was lovely, but this tricky atmosphere just couldn't go on. I might have been one of their oldest friends, but I was also going to be their lodger. More than that, though, I wanted William to know that I was terrifically glad things had worked out for Bunty and him and I had only been cross because I wanted him to be safe. We just needed to clear the air and get on.

Now was as good a time as any. I'd get it out of the way and then we could talk about going to the dance and the day of the wedding and be normal with each other again.

"Nice and cloudy, looks like it'll—" said William, just as I launched in.

"The thing is," I said, interrupting him. He stopped speaking abruptly.

"I'm sorry. I, um, well, I just wanted to say."

William had speeded up a bit and I had to trot to keep up, which wasn't easy in the dark.

"Thing is, Bill," I said in a half gasp. I reached out and touched his arm. If he could just slow down for a moment, I could apologise properly.

"We're going to be late," he replied, which was a very big hint to shut up, but he did at least stop striding on.

"I just wanted to say I'm sorry we rowed," I said in a rush and in case he decided to push on again at a pace. "And I'm really so terribly happy for you and Bunts."

He nodded. "Thanks," he said, and then paused for a second before continuing. "You do know how much I love her, don't you? And I'm not an idiot."

"Absolutely," I said.

"And, Emmy, I'm not going to do anything to spoil things for her. So to be honest, you don't need to tell me how to do my job."

"I know," I said. "I'm sorry about that."

"You don't need to go nagging me about things."

"Yes, all right," I said. He'd made his point.

"Good," said William somewhat shortly, and started to walk off again. I kept up beside him, trying to remember where the road got really wonky. My torch was so dim that it didn't show anything very well and I stubbed my shoe on a stone and had to do a little jump so as not to trip. William was still talking.

"I know what I'm doing, Em. You don't. While you've been sitting there at the station, we've been out doing this every night for months. You don't know what you're talking about. It's not as dangerous as it looks."

I thought this was rather rich. I knew what I'd seen at the bomb-site. Fred had broken his arm in the scramble and it had been poking out at an angle that would make most people feel sick. And the bombed-out house had been on the brink of caving in on all of them. You didn't need to be an expert to know the danger they had been in.

We were at the corner of Bellamy Street and only a minute or two from work. I'd hoped we would be chatting about the Café de Paris by this point.

"Anyway," I said, trying to move on in a positive way even though William was speaking to me as if I were soft in the head. "I'm looking forward to the Café de Paris enormously."

". . . and actually in Church Street it was completely under control."

He still hadn't accepted my apology and now it was turning into a lecture.

"For goodness' sake, Bill, that's rubbish," I said, overtaken with frustration, my good intentions flung out of the window. "You and the boys were nearly buried alive."

He stopped walking.

"Really, Emmeline," he snapped. "Can't you just leave it alone?"

He hadn't called me Emmeline for years. And I *had* left it alone—at least until trying to say I was sorry. I hadn't even mentioned Church Street since the morning of the bombing and I hadn't breathed a word to Bunty. You'd think I'd written it on a big sign and pasted it up at the station.

"No, Bill," I said. "I can't. Not when you're acting as if it's perfectly reasonable to mess about saving a dolly, which very nearly got you and half the crew killed."

As soon as the words came out, I regretted them. No one would ever say William didn't admire and even love his crew as if they were his family. I shouldn't have put it like that. I shouldn't have mentioned the others. I opened my mouth to apologise, but he got in before me.

"That's low, Emmy," he said. "That really is low."

He turned his back and marched off towards the station.

"Bill," I called, but he didn't slow down. "Bill, please."

I stood on my own in the middle of a pothole, staring into the darkness as he disappeared from view.

"Hello, is that you, Emmy?" Footsteps crunched unevenly along the road behind me. "Wait for me, won't you? My batteries have gone and I can't see a thing."

It was Thelma, with rotten timing. I said hello back, trying to make my voice appear chirpy.

"You all right, love?" asked Thelma, who had a very good nose for a brave front. "Has our William gone off on his own?"

"Oh, it's fine," I lied. "We're both running a bit late so I told him to go on ahead."

"Bless him," said Thelma, making me feel worse. "He's so excited about next week. Has he told you his big surprise?"

Thelma took my arm and we followed the light from my dim little torch up the road.

"The Café de Paris," she marvelled, oblivious to the fact I hadn't answered her. "He asked me last week if I thought Bunty and you would be pleased and I said you'd be cock-a-hoop. Are you excited?"

"Yes," I said in a small voice. "Neither of us can wait."

"I'll bet," said Thelma, squeezing my arm. "And old Roy is over the moon. Honestly, your Bunty is the luckiest girl. Isn't it smashing she's marrying such a lovely chap?"

I nodded and felt like a heel. Of course Thelma was right. William loved his job and was mad keen to prove he was doing his bit. But I knew full well he loved Bunty more than anything else in the world. I could have kicked myself for snapping at him again—we'd been chums for years and he was about to marry my best friend. Thelma continued to chat as I chewed my lip and walked in silence. In ten years William and I had not had a cross word, and now this. I felt a surge of anger, but not at William—or even at myself. It was this stupid war. Stupid, stupid, bloody war.

"You sure you're all right, Emmy?" asked Thelma in the dark.

"Yes, of course. Just a bit cold," I said. I put my arm in hers and hurried us both along to the station. If I was quick, I could get hold of William before the start of the shift and try to make things right once and for all.

Chapter 16

IMPERSONATING AN EDITRESS

I couldn't get hold of William. Ignoring the Café de Paris–induced excitement of the girls on B Watch, I went to look for him, but he was deep in discussion with Captain Davies about equipment, so I was forced to go back to my phone. Thelma and the girls were following Bunty's plans for the wedding as if it were one of the serials in *Woman's Friend*, and you could tell everyone was pleased to have something cheerful to focus on, especially details about outfits and the possibility of the sort of food we rarely caught sight of anymore. There was something about planning a wedding that felt like one in the eye for Hitler. He could send over as many Luftwaffe planes as he liked, but he couldn't stop people being in love and everyone getting excited.

At the end of the shift Captain Davies wanted to discuss rotas with us so I ended up having to rush to get home and missed the chance to speak with William. As usual it would be a quick change before going to the office and I would sleep later. Mother always worried about how we kept going. I had no idea. We just did.

Even though I desperately needed to sort things out with William, I was looking forward to telling Kathleen all about the Café de Paris and I arrived at the office early, squeezing into our tiny shared room and noticing that the pot plant needed watering. As I only worked in the mornings, Kathleen had left yesterday's last post on my desk and I was pleased to see a slightly bigger stack of letters than usual for Mrs. Bird. Hanging my overcoat on the hook on the back of the door, I settled at my desk and began to open the little pile of post, hopeful that there would be enough to pass on. I was lucky and struck gold straightaway.

Dear Mrs. Bird,

Your magazine has run several articles about shorter hair being safest for war work, but my husband won't have it. He says if long hair is good enough for Dorothy Lamour, then it should be good enough for me. He says I shouldn't have to pin it back at work.

What should I do?

Married To A Fan Of Miss Lamour

I grinned. It was the sort of letter that sent Mrs. Bird up the wall but I thought she secretly liked. I was quite sure she wouldn't know who the Hollywood actress was and would probably think she was a bad influence who lived next door, but I was equally sure she would tell Married To A Fan Of Miss Lamour to belt up and fetch a hairnet.

I put it in the Mrs. Bird folder straightaway.

And then the oddest thing happened. I opened a letter from a reader who didn't ask for any advice, although she'd got up some steam telling her story.

Dear Mrs. Bird,

I am writing to thank you for printing the girl called Fed Up's letter in this week's issue. I wouldn't have had the nerve to write in but I was ever so glad when I read your answer to her.

You see, I was like her—my parents are very strict too, even though I am going to be twenty this summer. They didn't want me to have a boyfriend, especially not if he is in the army or anything—not even ones that everyone says are nice boys you'd want for a son-in-law any day. I was really worried because I met ever such a lovely boy at a church dance that I'd gone to without my parents knowing. You see he is in the navy and I knew they would be cross.

I'd been worrying myself sick thinking what if they caught me seeing Leonard (that's his name), but then I read where you told Fed Up to be brave and talk to her parents and so that's what I did. And it turns out that my mum's friend Edith is second cousin to Leonard's mum and she told my mum that you couldn't wish for a better boy for anyone and that he is nearly as good as marrying a vicar and everything.

So anyway, now my mum is happy and Leonard came to tea like you said he should and they got on so well my dad called him Son at the end and now we're going out properly and I'm so glad.

Anyway, I wanted to thank you very much for giving me the courage to pipe up.

Yours sincerely,
Lilian Banks (Miss)

PS: I have told my friend Jennie to write to you as her mother is being properly horrible.

It was a lovely letter, but it knocked me for six. This was the first time a real, live person had actually said she found my advice useful. And she wasn't even the one I'd answered. Until now the *Woman's Friend* readers had been a faceless mass, soothed and entertained by Mr. Collins, and treated as one great slow-witted child by Mrs. Bird. I had known that I liked them and wanted to help, but this was different.

I wouldn't have had the nerve to write in but I was ever so glad when I read your answer to her.

I hadn't thought of the letters in the magazine like this before. I'd been concerned I might come a cropper and give the wrong advice to the person who had written in. I hadn't thought that hundreds, even thousands of people would read my advice and other readers who were having a rotten time of it might be encouraged as well. I was pleased as punch.

All the sneaking around, walking on hot coals, even lying about it to Bunty. Lilian Banks' letter made it all feel worthwhile. I wondered how many other readers might have been reassured too?

As I heard the door to the corridor open, I quickly put Lilian's letter back in its envelope. I would read it again when I got home.

"Morning, Emmy," called Kathleen as she came into our office, removing her hat and letting her hair bounce out of control from its clips. She took off her coat to reveal a bright yellow cardigan with leather buttons that looked like little footballs.

"Morning, Kath," I replied. "That's a smashing woolly. Thanks for putting the post on my desk. You'll never guess what. I'm going to the Café de Paris."

I started to chat, keen to tell her about it, but Kathleen looked preoccupied. Before she'd even sat down, she looked at the letters on my desk and interrupted me. Her voice had a nervy edge in it.

"That's almost a pile," she said. "Are there any good ones?"

"Oh, nothing exciting," I replied airily. "One about hair. Bound to be lots of Unpleasantness to go in the bin."

Kathleen nodded.

"It's funny, isn't it," she said. "Don't you think that Mrs. Bird is becoming, well, almost nice? She was very patient with one reader whose fiancé was being difficult. I thought Mrs. Bird would have called her an idiot but she was actually quite kind."

Kath smiled briefly. Her voice was higher than usual. I shifted slightly in my chair.

"I don't know," I said. "I can't remember exactly."

"There was one this week," she continued. "About a girl who was seeing a soldier behind her parents' back. I was surprised she didn't give the girl a real telling off."

I went hot and began to take off my jacket.

"Oh, that one? I say, spring is on the move, don't you think?" I said, getting one arm stuck behind my back as I tried to get out of a sleeve. "It's so much warmer now than it was last week."

There was a stiff breeze outside, and the day before, Mr. Brand in Art had been off with his chilblains. Kathleen carried on.

"It just seems strange. You know, she's very clear on things like that. Quite a turnaround. Don't you think, Emmy?"

My stomach lurched. I had always thought that if anyone was likely to find me out, it would be Kathleen. She read *Woman's Friend* from cover to cover and was sharp as a tack. I must have been mad to think I could fool her. My brain raced around, weighing up whether I could confide in her. It would be awful not to tell the truth, and actually, I desperately wanted to confess, get her on my side and be in it together.

But it wouldn't be fair. Kathleen was the most honest person I knew and terrifically strong on Moral Fibre. I had been impersonating the Editress. I couldn't expect her to keep this from Mrs. Bird.

"Emmy?" said Kathleen again, as I felt hotter than ever and couldn't look her in the eye. "I'm not being horrid, honestly. But there's nothing you're keeping from me, is there?"

The thought of dragging her into this with me was dreadful. It just wouldn't do.

"Actually," I said. "There is something. Kath, can you keep a secret?"

Kathleen looked as if her nerve would fail, but nodded bravely.

I took a deep breath.

"It's just that, I've, um . . . I'm seeing Mr. Collins' brother, Charles."

It came out in a big rush. Taking Kathleen into my confidence about something exciting but not terrible was the most diversionary tactic I could have found. Even if using Charles as a front made me feel an absolute pig.

For a moment Kathleen hesitated, and then as her eyes grew wider than ever, she managed to whisper, "NO!"

I nodded back with the most two-faced smile in history. Through habit we both glanced at the door in case Mrs. Bird might appear. When she didn't, and with an expression of absolute delight and even greater relief, Kathleen clasped her hands to her cardigan and said Gosh, Mr. Collins' Brother and Fancy That, several times in a row.

Kathleen and I talked nineteen to the dozen for the next ten minutes as I gave her the full story about Charles and hinted that having a secret might have made me seem a bit shifty recently. I even went close to the mark and innocently asked her what had been concerning her about the letters, but she waved the topic away and said she was being silly and it was nothing. Kathleen was so good-hearted and thoroughly thrilled for me that she had completely fallen for the Charles excuse. In the space of a quarter of an hour I had gone from being on a high about a thank-you letter from a stranger to feeling quite sick with myself.

As I tried to enjoy what should have been a lovely chat about romance, I made a proper promise to myself. Absolutely no more letters in the magazine.

I had meant well, but I'd nearly put dear Kathleen in the most difficult position. The thought brought me up short. It was bad enough not telling Bunty I was writing back to the readers, but if Mrs. Bird ever thought Kathleen had suspected me of tampering with advice in the magazine and not reported it to her, it would be very serious indeed. I just couldn't risk getting Kathleen into trouble.

I would carefully continue to write back to readers, but in terms of printing things, that really would have to be that, even if it did seem to help people like Lilian Banks.

A door banged loudly as it was flung open in the corridor, and as if to prove my point, Mrs. Bird appeared in our office, looking determined in tweed.

"I cannot stay," she announced. "There has been a farming accident."

"I'm so sorry," I said as Kathleen and I both stood up.

"The man's own fault," replied Mrs. Bird rather brightly.

There wasn't much to be said to that so Kathleen and I nodded and looked stern. Mrs. Bird glanced around the office.

"I shall return from the country on Monday. I trust you both have enough to be getting on with? Do you have Acceptable Letters for me, Miss Lake?" She looked at my desk, where Lilian's thank-you letter sat in its envelope. My heart started to beat faster. "Dreadful handwriting," she muttered. "No Unpleasantness, I trust?"

"Absolutely not," I said with huge conviction. "In fact there's a very interesting one from a lady who has been worried by a palm reader," I said. "She is most keen to be helped."

Mrs. Bird frowned. "I shouldn't wonder," she said. "I shall consider it on Monday. Are you sure you are both busy? I thought I heard Chatting."

Kathleen and I looked injured at the suggestion and issued a wild denial.

"Very well," said Mrs. Bird. "Then I must go. Miss Knighton, there is correspondence in my out-tray. Please ensure it is dealt with. Good day."

And with that, she swept out of the office.

If the near miss with Kathleen had already given me the jitters, Mrs. Bird appearing out of nowhere like a substantial ghost had tipped me over the edge. Pleading the need for more room to go through the post, I squeezed around my desk, gave Kathleen one last mad smile, and escaped into the corridor.

Then I stopped and leant against the wall, shutting my eyes and hugging the letters to my chest.

"Just got away with something?" said Mr. Collins, who was standing by the door to his office. For anyone else I would have described it as lurking, but somehow Mr. Collins could pull off standing around in what should be a suspicious manner. He had a journalist's ability to make himself unnoticeable.

"Me? Oh, gosh no," I said, following up with an unlikely laugh. "It's just been a bit hectic, that's all. TONS to do," I added, hoping to look industrious.

"Well, that's good," said Mr. Collins. "We may all have work for another week or two if for some incomprehensible reason we're busy." He gave a little laugh, almost to himself. "Don't tell me people are actually buying the magazine?"

"Well, I think so," I said, hoping to head off another possible inquisition. "It's probably down to the gypsies," I added wildly.

"The gypsies?" He raised an eyebrow at me and sighed heavily. "I sense a crushing inevitability that I will regret asking this, but really, Miss Lake, what gypsies?"

It always seemed to amuse Mr. Collins to call me Miss Lake.

"The ones in your stories. Gypsies. And foraging. In woods. Readers are mad for it, sir."

My diversionary chatter wasn't going half so well as it had done with Kath, and now I'd called him sir, which I never did.

Mr. Collins came a little nearer. "Is everything all right, Emmy?" he asked.

"Absolutely," I said. "I'm about to sort the post. I was just taking it to the old reporters' room if that's all right. Ours is so small, it seems silly not to use it sometimes. I wasn't sure if Mrs. Bird might mind."

"I don't see why not," he said. "In fact, if you want a bit more space, why don't you set up a desk in there? Tell Henrietta I made you, if you want." He flashed a smile at the thought, as I thanked him and said I would go and see if Kathleen would mind.

Kathleen thought it a jolly good plan and wished she could use the bigger office too, only Mrs. Bird liked to be able to hurl herself across the corridor at her and wouldn't want the walk. She came with me to do a little housekeeping, and with Mrs. Bird away, I finally managed to tell her about the night out at the Café de Paris.

Mrs. Bussell the tea lady popped in bang on time as usual and managed to produce a rare Garibaldi biscuit, for which she apologised, What With It Being Bloody Italian.

"At least it's not called a Mussolini," I said, trying to help and hearing her say something unprintable as she wheeled the trolley back off to the lift.

"What are you going to wear?" asked Kathleen, who was picking the currants (there were two) out of her biscuit and eating them very slowly. "Will it be evening dress?"

I nodded. "I've got a silk gown from when I was twenty-one." I smiled. It felt like a very long time ago. "I think it will do."

I shifted around as I sat on an abandoned desk. "It seems a bit showy what with everything else going on," I added, feeling self-conscious.

"Oh no," said Kath. "It's lovely. And you should enjoy every minute. Anyway, it's our duty to celebrate things like this, isn't it? The Nazis would hate it."

I laughed, pleased that we were chatting like we usually did and I didn't have to be cagey about the letters.

"I'm not sure Hitler will be terribly worried about me going to a nightclub," I said. "But I know what you mean. I promise on Saturday I'll flounce about the West End like mad."

I struck a pose with my hand behind my head and tried to look like a mannequin out of a society fashion magazine.

There was a polite cough from the doorway.

"I take it Henrietta is still out?" said Mr. Collins, as Kathleen and I jumped to our feet looking guilty. "Oh, come now, you don't need to start standing to attention, I'm only joking. What's all this about gadding around the West End?" He threw me a mock Hard Stare.

"Oh, not really gadding," I said. "Bunty's William is taking us out on Saturday as a sort of pre-wedding treat. They didn't have an engagement party."

"To the Café de Paris," added Kathleen, who had recently become braver about talking to Mr. Collins and was buoyed by the excitement of the event.

Mr. Collins let out a long whistle. "Miss Lake," he said. "I say. Good band. Overpriced champagne."

That stopped Kathleen and me in our tracks. Mr. Collins knew about dance bands?

Mr. Collins rolled his eyes. "I'm not entirely ancient, you know."

"Of course not," I gasped as Kathleen nodded emphatically.

"In fact, really quite *young*," I carried on, which was clearly taking it too far. Kathleen gave me a look.

"All right, Emmy, don't go mad," said Mr. Collins. "Youth's not all it's cracked up to be anyway. Well, I'm sure you will have a very fine time. If there's a raid, you should be as safe down there as anywhere," he added.

"Have you been to the Café de Paris, Mr. Collins?" asked Kathleen.

I could see she was carried away with the promise of stories about dancing and music and frocks. I wished Kathleen was coming with us as I knew she would love it and I promised myself that in future I wouldn't wait for momentous reasons to do dashing things. A common or garden birthday would be enough.

I was sure Mr. Collins would draw the conversation to a close, but to my surprise, he just smiled and, crossing his arms, leant back against the door frame.

"Once or twice, Kathleen," he said. "Not recently, I should add. What with me being so terribly old." He raised an eyebrow just slightly. "But yes, back in the days when it first opened. I was rather snazzier then."

Kathleen and I stared, agog.

Mr. Collins, snazzy?

I didn't even think he would have known the word, let alone use it. This was a turn up! We hoped for more, but after the briefest of moments, when he was clearly thinking of a very different time, Mr. Collins stopped leaning, jerked the bottom of his waistcoat down, and made a Hmm noise.

"Long time ago," he said briskly. "Now then. You'd better get on with some work or we'll all be for the high jump." He snapped back into work mode. "Emmeline, I have a stack of typing for you if you can spare the time. A story set by the sea. Rather dull but it has a happy ending. I'm going to be out for the next couple of hours so I'll see you on Monday. Have a good time on Saturday. I'll see you later, Kathleen."

He turned to leave and then had second thoughts and came back into the office.

"Be careful on Saturday. It may be busy up there." He raised his eyes to the ceiling. Then he gave a brief nod and left.

Kathleen turned to me. "Gosh," she said. "I think he's trying to look after you while his brother is away." She giggled and then looked nervously into the corridor.

"Oh, shush," I said. "He was just trying to be nice. And look at you, asking if he'd ever been to the Café de Paris."

"I don't know what came over me," she said, putting her hand to her forehead. "I really don't." Then she beamed. "But, oh, isn't it going to be lovely?"

I nodded. It was. Now I had managed to smooth things over at work, my mind went back to the wedding plans and Bunty. I just needed to sort things out once and for all with William, and then everything would all be all right.

Chapter 17

THE SAFEST AND GAYEST RESTAURANT IN TOWN

As much as we didn't get on, I was immensely grateful to Vera for covering for me on Saturday night. In return I was doing her shift with A Watch earlier in the day. I was hopeful I might even get a chance to have a quick nap and be fresh for the Café de Paris. The firemen had their bunk rooms of course, but there was also a tiny back room for us girls if we needed it, which had two camp beds and some mice who had eaten three ounces of cocoa that Joan had brought in and rashly left in the little wooden locker overnight.

The plan was that I would race back home after the shift, try to make myself presentable, and be ready for William and Roy to arrive for drinks at the house before setting off to the club to be there by nine. It was tight but doable.

I marched off to the station on Saturday morning, early so that I could find William, who I knew had changed his shift round as well. As usual, Roy was already at work when I arrived, head inside the engine of one of the pump vans and whistling away to himself.

"Morning, Roy," I called. "Are you thinking through your steps for our waltz?"

Roy straightened up from the van and greeted me with enthusiasm.

"That, Ginger Rogers," he said, "was a quickstep." He pulled a daft face.

I laughed. "Don't panic, Mr. Astaire, I knew." He looked relieved. "Are you all ready for the big night?"

Roy looked down at his arms, which were covered in grease from elbow to fingernails. "In a few hours you won't recognise me," he said, picking up his wristwatch from where he had balanced it on the windscreen. "Blimey, I'd better get motoring." He looked back into the engine. "That'll have to do."

"Is Bill about yet?" I asked, trying to keep my voice light.

Roy shook his head as he shut the bonnet. "No, he's over the river. They're three men down and need a Watch Leader." He noticed my face fall. "Don't worry, love, Arthur Purbridge is standing in for him tonight. Arthur's probably glad to get away from his Violet. Gawd, she can talk."

I managed a laugh and headed upstairs. There was nothing for it but to wait until tonight to see William. I told myself the champagne and excitement would help. I would tell him what an idiot I had been and make him promise that we were still lifelong friends. Despite everything, I was confident. On such a special occasion, how could we not patch everything up?

It was a quiet day on the phones and Captain Davies let us take it in turns to get some rest during the afternoon, but I was anxious to leave on time and relieved when Mary arrived for the evening shift, followed by the B Watch boys, who were full of jokes and colourful warnings to me about Not Wearing Roy Out.

Six months ago they would have made me blush, but I was used to them now and let them go on for a bit before asking if they wanted me to forget about putting the kettle on or not. Everyone was on good form and I didn't notice until gone six o'clock that there was no sign of Joan or, more concerning, Vera and her friend Mo, who had swapped with Thelma so she and Vera could be on the same shift. Captain Davies emerged from his office, did a quick scan of the room, and frowned.

"Mrs. North is ill," he said, referring to Joan. "I've only just heard. Where are the others?"

It was poor to miss a shift, but unforgivable if you didn't give the station a chance to find a replacement, so Joan must have been in a grim way.

"Would you like me to make some calls to find someone to cover for Joan, sir?" I asked.

"I certainly would, Miss Lake," answered the captain, sounding no happier. "Straightaway, please."

"Yes, sir," I said, and went over to the noticeboard and unpinned the list of numbers for people who had telephones at home or nearby. I started with Jocelyn Derrick, who was a good sort and might be able to come.

Just as I was dialling the number, Vera's friend Mo breezed into the room, stopping abruptly when she saw Captain Davies standing by her empty chair with his arms folded.

"I'm so sorry, Captain, the buses kept playing me up," she cooed.

The buses tended to play Mo up on a very nearly permanent basis, at least as far as getting to the station was concerned.

"I see," said Captain Davies with a distinct lack of emotion. "And are we to assume Miss Woods is experiencing a similar challenge?"

"Oh no, sir," said Mo, who did amateur dramatics. "I'm afraid Vera might be a little bit late. She's Not Been Well," she added, dropping her voice to show the gravity of the illness.

"Good of you to let me know," said Captain Davies drily.

"I could call her mother," said Mo in a small voice.

"I should," said the captain, and with one last glare at us all, he walked into his office.

There was no answer from Jocelyn. I rang the next number on the list while eavesdropping on Mo.

"For goodness' sake, Vere, he's in a right mood," she said in a whisper. Her face clouded over. "Oh, suit yourself," she added, and put the receiver down with a loud tut.

"She's going to do her very best to get here as soon as she can,"

Mo announced and, with the greatest of dignity, huffed away to give Captain Davies the news.

I couldn't leave with just two girls on the phones. There was nothing to do but keep trying to find a replacement for the absent Joan. I called Bunty and told her the news.

"Oh dear, no. But never mind," she said, being a trouper and almost managing to disguise the disappointment in her voice. "I'll put your things in a bag, then if it gets hairy timewise, Roy can bring them over and you can both come on from there."

"I'll be there, Bunty," I promised. "You know I wouldn't miss this for the world."

"Don't worry, Em," said Bunty. "Now, I'd better go. I'm still in curlers and look a sight. I'll see you later, and if a raid starts, don't do anything madcap, will you?"

"I won't," I said, planning to ignore her if required. I looked at the clock and picked up the phone to try Jocelyn again.

This time I was lucky. Although she had just got in, the good-natured girl said she would come as soon as she could. It was super news. I just needed Vera to get a wiggle on and then I would be free.

But Vera didn't get a wiggle on. In fact, I was fairly sure Vera wasn't worried about hurrying in the least.

At a quarter to eight, she still hadn't turned up. Jocelyn arrived in a rush, and moments later, following a mighty cheer from the boys downstairs, in came my date for the evening.

"Ladies," said Roy. "I have a fashion delivery for Miss Lake." He waved the holdall that Bunty had packed with my things.

"I say," said Mary as we all stared.

Roy gave a short bow to acknowledge the attention. He looked smashing. His uniform had been carefully steamed and pressed, its buttons under orders to make an even bigger effort than usual to shine, and it looked as if he had scrubbed his face half to death with a Brillo pad to ensure he was top-notch. Brylcreemed to within an inch of his life, he had a real sparkle about him.

Jocelyn let out a loud wolf whistle, suggesting she wasn't a stranger to its use. "Doesn't he scrub up?" She grinned.

"He certainly does," I said as he handed me the bag. "Thanks ever so much, Roy. You look very handsome."

I was touched he had made such an effort, even though I was sure it was more for William and the brigade than for me. A lot of the men there tonight would be in military uniform and I knew he wasn't going to let the Fire Service down.

"Hurry up, Cinders," said Roy, who made an unlikely Fairy Godmother. "Glad rags on and we can get off."

I smiled my thanks and rushed to the Ladies'. As fast as I could, I wriggled out of my uniform. My hair was rather dreadful, but Bunty had sent along some grips and a diamanté hair slide so I was able to pin it back and make not too bad a fist of the thing.

A brief check in the little mirror above the sink said I would hardly turn heads, but hopefully I wasn't too bad. After a quick teeth brush, I swapped my thick work stockings for a precious Going Out pair, anxious not to put my fingers through them in the rush, and then I threw my best dress on over my head. Evening shoes buckled with fingers trembling under pressure, a dab of lipstick I could improve when we got there, and I was ready. I had taken all of three minutes.

"Blimey, girls, who's this?" said Roy as I walked back into the control room, which was ever so kind, and Mary and Jocelyn joined in with some oohs.

I was quite out of place standing by my seat in a full-length evening gown and dancing shoes, especially with all the girls in their uniforms, but I felt a buzz of excitement all the same. In a disloyal fashion I wished it was Charles standing there as I bet he'd look the bee's knees in black tie or dress uniform, but I was honoured to be accompanied by Roy. Now I just wanted to get into town, clear the air with William, and have a jolly time of it all celebrating with my best friend and the boys.

And then the sirens began. My heart did a nosedive.

"Don't you worry," said Jocelyn, indefatigable to the last. "We'll be

OK. Vera should be here in ten minutes. We can manage until then, can't we, girls?"

I didn't trust Vera as far as I could throw her. With a raid on I wasn't leaving until she arrived.

"I don't mind," I said. "We'll wait until Vera gets here. Roy, is that all right with you?"

Roy agreed and said he'd go and check if there was anything he could do to help the lads in the meantime.

Within minutes we could hear the drone of enemy planes. I put my tin hat on over my hair and the fancy slide, and it was business as usual as a call came in about a High Explosive, which had made quite a mess. The gunfire had started right over us too.

Vera Woods finally wandered into work at twenty-five past nine, and despite declaring that she probably had pleurisy, a healthier type you couldn't have seen. She was three and a half hours late.

I jumped up from my chair and grabbed my overcoat as Captain Davies appeared with a face like thunder.

"Miss Lake, find Fireman Hodges and leave. Miss Woods: I would like to see you in my office. NOW."

It took some effort not to throw Vera a look, but there was no time for silliness. Roy was ready to go, and with a hurried goodbye to the girls, we raced from the station and out into the darkness of the street. With the planes and gunfire rumbling overhead, we were heading out into what had turned into a very nasty raid.

To the east, the sky was already turning pink. Later it would go orange and red as the fires took hold, but for now the moon was lighting up London for the Luftwaffe and they were taking full advantage of it. Outside the station, the drone of their planes was far heavier and even more oppressive, like a monster calling to its friends. Which was pretty much exactly what it was.

I clutched my torch in one hand and Roy's arm with my other. It wouldn't be easy to find a cab, but as they always kept going unless things got horribly sticky in the immediate area I held out hope.

Then we saw one. Creeping along the street with a tiny shaft of light pathetically acting as its headlights.

"TAXI!" Roy and I shouted at the same time, both of us breaking into a run towards it and then cheering as we saw it slow down.

"Any chance of Coventry Street, old son?" said Roy through the wound-down window. The driver grimaced. It was slap bang in the middle of the West End.

"Sorry, governor," he said. "It's a right stinker tonight. I wouldn't go into town if I were you. You'd be best off making a night of it at home." He winked at Roy and put the cab into gear to drive off. Roy ignored him and leant in further.

"It would be such a favour. We're AFS," he added in case the cabbie hadn't noticed the uniform and badge. The driver rolled his eyes, but he put the handbrake on rather than run over Roy's foot. Roy carried on talking and I couldn't help thinking he could make a fortune selling encyclopedias after the war.

"You see, one of our brigade is getting married next week. This one's chief bridesmaid and I'm his best man. I wouldn't normally ask, but . . ."

Just as I was about to say that we could all get hit by a bomb in the time he was taking to make up his mind, the driver said he'd give it a go, nodding at us to get in. He launched into a story about his cousin who was a fireman in Limehouse, where you wouldn't believe the show when the docks took a direct hit.

As Roy joined in with some gusto, I sat back in my seat. We'd struck lucky and if that luck held, we would be with Bunty and William just after ten.

Before the war, if one was feeling swank and wanted to take a taxi, Pimlico to Piccadilly Circus was not a huge fare. But roadblocks, bombed-out streets, and the blackout meant any journey might take three times as long as it should and even that could change if someone dropped a bomb on the route you'd planned. Once you were on your way, there was nothing much you could do other than become wildly philosophical and hope to get there at some point. London's cabbies were awfully resolute and if there was a fare to be had, invariably they'd give it a go even when the raids were on. Chat with any of them and you'd learn that the last few months had meant that if they didn't, there was an awful lot of sitting around drinking tea and going home with empty pockets.

Tonight we did well, despite the horrible noise surrounding us. Bombs were going off thick and fast, great flashes lighting up the street for a second before another enormous bang took our concentration elsewhere. The jovial chat became forced and then nonexistent as we crawled, queued, and jolted our way through cratered streets, taking back routes that were unrecognizable from this time last year. Every now and then we'd have to do a U-turn due to a new roadblock where a shop or an office had been blown into the street.

I hadn't been out in anything this bad for weeks. It was on a different scale altogether from the night at the cinema with Bunty and Charles. It was far from the best idea to be heading into the West End on a night like this, but I wasn't going to miss it for the world. I sat quietly and concentrated on not flinching at the noise.

We made progress to Hyde Park Corner, where we'd hoped to then head along Piccadilly and on to Coventry Street and the Café de Paris. But even though we were all acting as if everything was just fine, it was impossible for any of us to pretend we hadn't heard the aching whine of bombs falling. Seconds later the whole road shook and the cab jumped almost out of its skin.

We ground to a halt just before Green Park.

"I'm sorry, it's getting too lively for me," the cabbie said to Roy. "I should give it a miss. Anywhere towards home you fancy instead?"

I shook my head violently, even though he hadn't directed the question at me.

"We'll be all right," Roy said, fishing in his pocket for his wallet. "Thanks for getting us this far."

I added my thank-you and, clambering out into the street, wished the driver a safe journey back.

As soon as I opened the door I could smell burning. A rumbling noise a couple of streets away backed it up. Someone had taken a hit. The noise of the guns was deafening now. They were fighting right over our heads.

"You've got a plucky one there," I heard the driver shout at Roy, trying to make himself heard. "Take care of her."

Roy laughed and, thanking him, shouted back that he would. Then he gave a wave and took my arm.

"Come on, Emmy," he yelled, knowing he didn't have to ask if I was all right. "Once we're there, we'll be safe as houses."

"I know," I bellowed back. "*The safest and gayest restaurant in town.*" I was quoting the Café de Paris advertisements that ran in the London magazines.

"*Even in the air raids. Twenty feet below the ground!*" finished Roy. But then he looked up at the sky where a vast marker flare had lit up the city. "Damn it," he said, more to himself than to me. "The buggers can really see what they're doing now."

Neither of us needed more encouragement to move on. You got used to being out during raids, but this was unnerving. Evening shoes were not the ideal footwear and I'd have given anything to be back in my brogues, but lifting the bottom of my dress up with one hand and holding fast on to Roy's arm with the other, I broke into a jog as he lengthened his stride.

The Germans were having a fine time of it, and although we could hear the British machine gunners going at them full blast, the horrible whine of their bombs didn't stop. We both knew it was getting worse. At first Roy made jokes as we went past the shops. "Hamper for Ascot?" he shouted as we passed Fortnum's. "Two!" I yelled back as if we were on an absolute lark, but it was hard to keep it up, and by the time we were at Piccadilly Circus, the comedy routine had almost petered out. Despite my high heels, we were running at a pretty good lick.

"Fancy a new cricket bat?" I shouted at Roy, relieved to be nearly there as we made it to Lillywhites, its windows blacked out but advertising signs still up and announcing garments for all services and ranks.

Roy stopped. The ear-splitting whistle of a bomb falling was right over our heads. There was no point trying to cover it up with jokes. This one was terribly close.

Roy pulled me against Lillywhites' locked doors and we held on to each other as we braced ourselves against the oncoming blast. I pushed my head into Roy's uniform, my face pressed against one of the silver buttons he had polished and polished until it shone. We were so very near to making it to Coventry Street and the safety of the Café de Paris.

I was not ashamed to say I closed my eyes in the last seconds, but even with them tight, tight shut, I couldn't block out the vast flash of light.

Roy flattened me into the door, using himself as a barrier without a thought for the risk, and I pulled him in even more, trying to will him out of the way of the oncoming blast.

We clung to each other. If they were going to get one of us, they would have to get us both.

And then the bombs landed, threatening to burst our eardrums with the noise and making my insides feel as if they were being turned upside down as everything around us shook to the foundations.

But they didn't get us. We hadn't taken the direct hit.

I looked up. While still holding on to me for dear life, Roy had half turned and was looking over his shoulder across Piccadilly. He now had the same expression I had seen at the station when the crews were called out for something awful, like when a hospital or a school had been bombed. Only this time, for us at least, it was worse.

I knew where he was looking. They had hit Coventry Street.

And that's when we started to run.

Chapter 18

SOMEONE SHONE A TORCH

Even in the blackout, the sky was so bright we could see our way easily. Holding hands, we ran towards the bombs at full pelt. Roy was nearly dragging me, but I kept up, always a good runner since school and not even conscious of my high heels or silly, impractical dress. As we got nearer to the Café de Paris, we had to slow down. Crowds of people had already started gathering. Desperate to get into the club, we began to push our way through.

I kept telling myself perhaps we had been wrong. From the outside of the building you couldn't be sure. The street was full of glass as windows in all the buildings around had been blown out, but perhaps we had overreacted and guessed it wrong. It would still be awful for other people of course, but we would know Bunty and Bill were safe.

It was wishful thinking.

I could just see the main entrance of the Café. The double doors weren't there anymore. Someone was trying to pull down what remained of the thick blackout curtains to get them out of the way. Shocked, injured, dishevelled people were stumbling out into the street, helping each other or being helped by the people outside.

"Fire Service," shouted Roy. "Coming through." He pushed his way past a large man who was trying to get a better view and, in doing so, lost hold of my hand. Roy immediately looked back for me.

"Keep going," I yelled at him. "I'm coming." He nodded and disappeared into the club.

I tried to follow, shouting into the back of the fat man's coat to let me get through, but the gap had closed and I couldn't force myself past. People trying to get in were blocking the way of people trying to get out. Someone called out to Give Them Some Room. Above us the planes still roared and the guns kept booming.

I stopped pushing for a second and stood on my toes. A slightly built man in grey was half carrying, half dragging a lady out of the Café. She was also entirely grey. But it wasn't their clothes; it was the dust covering them and their hair and their faces, as if they'd been dipped in ash.

Someone shone a torch at them and the woman cried out, putting her hand over her face and then recoiling from her own touch. Blood was coming out of a huge wound on her forehead, the red looking all wrong against the monochrome of everything else.

My friends were in there. What if Bunty was hurt like this woman?

"LET ME PAST!" I screamed in a voice that came from the bottom of my gut, and I punched my fists into the thick overcoats blocking my way. Roy had got through and now I couldn't. Just because he was bigger and stronger than me, and wearing a uniform that showed he was trained and knew what he was doing and could properly help. That wasn't the point. In the horror of everything, the injustice sent me into a fury. Roy was William's friend. Bunty was mine. It was my job to find her, my job to make sure she was safe. I would *not* be a bystander.

I kept pushing and then shouted again, this time with more authority. It still didn't work. I pushed harder.

Somebody gripped my arm, and without looking round I tried to snatch it away. But a man's voice I vaguely recognised kept saying my name.

"Emmy. Emmeline. Emmeline . . . MISS LAKE."

I turned, disorientated, my mind already inside the building, looking for Bunty.

"Emmy," came the voice again. "It's me."

Mr. Collins took hold of my shoulders tightly, pulling me back from where I needed to go.

"My dear girl, thank God," he said. "I thought you were in there. I was on fire watch at my friend's restaurant." He stopped. "Where are your friends? Miss Tavistock?"

"I have to get in," I said, half to Mr. Collins and half to myself, as I pulled away from him and started trying to push through the crowd again, managing to move a couple of paces closer to the door as would-be helpers made their way into the club, either disappearing into its depths or getting as far as the door and helping more of the grey people trying to get out.

"All right, miss," said an air-raid warden who was blocking my path. "No need to go in there now."

"Let me through," I said, staring him down.

The warden looked at me in my civilian overcoat, my silk frock poking out underneath and the stupid diamanté clip in my hair. He probably thought I was drunk or one of the women who hung around the streets in the area looking for an easy opportunity to loot.

"Run along, love," he said. I started to argue but he stood firm.

"For Christ's sake, man, let my wife through."

Mr. Collins was by my side, barking the order in his most imperious voice.

"She's a nurse, you idiot. Let us both through."

He waved an identity card very quickly at the warden.

"Dr. Richard Green," he said, violently shoving the card back into his coat. "Now stand aside, so we can help these people before they drop any more on us."

The warden hesitated and I took my chance. Ignoring him and with a face that made Mr. Collins' assertiveness appear benign, I bunched up my fists and shoved my way in.

As the shocked and injured continued to escape into the street, I slipped past. Only later I would think of how selfish I had been, how

I chose who I wanted to help. But at that moment I just wanted to find Bunty.

Inside the Café it was pitch-black and I fumbled in my coat pocket for my torch. Now I was inside, my rage disappeared. Nothing existed other than to find Bunty and Bill. My heart was still racing like anything, but now I became armoured with a single-mindedness and even a sort of calm.

The air was almost entirely smoke and dust and immediately I started to cough. Hand over my mouth, I somehow remembered my training at the station, where even the admin staff were taught what to do if we were hit.

More people die from asphyxia than burning.

Keep calm.

Breathe through your nose and don't gulp.

I felt my way down some stairs, stepping around debris and shining my torch ahead. Its little beam caught a line of four people coming up towards us, holding on to each other, making a human train to the exit. They weren't grey like the others but black from the blast. A man was crying. I thought perhaps his dinner jacket had been blown off, but then I saw he had put it around the shoulders of a woman with him. Her dress was in tatters. No one was running or shouting.

I knew Mr. Collins was close behind me, holding his torch over my shoulder and swooping it around to see where we were.

"Emmy," he said. "Would they have been dancing, do you think? Would they have been downstairs?"

I didn't know. Bunty and I had talked about whether we should have a table on the dance floor or up on the balcony and which would have the best view of the band. The most frivolous of chats had become the most important thing in the world.

I thought she had said downstairs. I was almost entirely sure it was downstairs.

I shone my torch along the balcony to my left.

The balustrade leading along from the stairs had been twisted and mangled, like a roll of black liquorice. And then nothing. The balcony wasn't there anymore.

I nodded, more to myself than in answer to Mr. Collins, and holding on to the banister, clambered down the stairs, my shoes crunching on broken glass as I went.

"Bunty," I called. "Bunty, it's me. We're here, darling. It's all right, we're here."

It was the voice my mother had used when I was little and had nightmares. I would call out for her and as soon as I heard her voice, even though the monsters were still in my room, I knew I could be brave enough to hold on. I would hear her voice as she came along the corridor, calm and soothing and telling me it was all right. Not stopping until she was in my room and the light was on and the monsters had gone.

"Bunty, we're coming," I called again. "Tell us where you are, sweetheart, we're coming to help."

I kept calling and then I stopped and listened for her. There was no response. I could hear cries and moaning, someone shouting for help, people calling for each other, someone saying the ambulances were on their way.

Mr. Collins and I paused for a moment when we reached what had been the dance floor. His hand was still on my shoulder. He asked me what Bunty was wearing and I remembered her blue dress and told him. It had ruffles on the hem. I said that William would be in his AFS uniform. Mr. Collins said to just think about Bunty and, whatever I saw, just to keep thinking of her and to keep calling and listening and not to think of anything else and that he was right behind me.

I shone my torch and kept searching. There was rubble and glass and what may have been the balcony or the ceiling but was now all over the floor.

And there were bodies. I heard myself say Oh and then Oh again. Mr. Collins' hand did not move from my shoulder.

"Keep calling her," he said when I stopped for a moment, shining my torch at something. I knew it was a person but I couldn't really tell.

"It's not her," Mr. Collins said, terribly gently, and I nodded, then kept nodding because, unimaginably awful though it was, to be told that this poor soul wasn't Bunty was the best possible news. I started calling for her again.

We kept going, climbing around tables, past the low stage on our right where people, I supposed the band, must still be. Someone cried out, saying It Hurts, It Hurts.

I ignored them and that was disgusting of me. I ignored people who were dying. At the time, it didn't feel like a decision. If Bunty was alive, she would need help, so I kept going.

There were people and debris and dust and so much glass. We had to bend down to look at each person to see if they were Bunty or Bill. When they weren't, it was as if there was one more person to stack the odds in our favour. Not everyone could be dead. It was a warped logic. For months afterwards, I would lie awake in my bed and wonder how, in a matter of moments, I had become someone who could think like that.

Madly, wildly, while some people had been blown to pieces, others were still in their seats at their table. Black from the blast, dead, but unmarked. A man was slumped over a table as if he were drunk. I didn't see his face, but I saw that his hands were gone.

I turned away from the man and kept calling. I didn't need to look round for Mr. Collins. I knew he would not leave. Even as everything around us just got worse and worse, he never suggested we should turn back. I knew that for the rest of my life, even though he was my boss, I would love him for that.

More people had arrived to help. A man shouted for a stretcher. A group of real nurses were helping a lady covered in blood and talking to each other in medical terms. I heard Roy's voice, somewhere further back from the stage. He was shouting for Bill and Bunty over and over again.

As we pushed on, I saw two dancers kneeling over someone. One was ripping a tablecloth into pieces and the other was pressing the material into the body. They were all dressed up in their sequins and not covered in dust or blackened at all.

"Jesus, Amy, another five minutes and we'd have been out here," said one of them. "This poor girl."

Stifling a gasp, I flashed my torch onto the person they were trying to help. She was in her underclothes; her dress had been blown off by the blast. It was hard to see who she might be. But she had blonde hair. It wasn't Bunty.

The dancers must have been backstage or on a break when it happened. I shone my torch behind them. Huge chunks of plaster had fallen just by the stage.

Then I saw. Half buried under one of them, someone in a long frock. You couldn't tell what colour the dress was but you could see that it was long with ruffles along the bottom.

"Bunty," I screamed.

I scrambled over to her like a maniac and threw myself down by her side, not noticing as I knelt in the glass and rubble surrounding her. One of her legs was trapped and she was covered in debris, but I knew it was her.

She opened her lips and said something. A tiny sound and I couldn't understand what she was trying to say, but it was enough to know. She was alive.

"Bunty sweetheart, it's all right," I said, touching her face. "You're going to be all right."

I started to move chunks of plaster from around her. Mr. Collins was on his knees too, doing the same.

"You're not going to die," I kept saying. "We're going to get help. You're going to be all right."

Bunty blinked. Twice. Her eyes were full of dust and she was struggling not to cough. But she looked up at me and, in a wretched, hoarse little voice, managed to speak.

"Bill."

Chapter 19

IT WAS OUR TURN

After the ambulances came and Bunty was taken away, Mr. Collins bribed a taxi to ignore the state we were in and follow the long grey convoy to Charing Cross Hospital. The rest of the night was a bad dream of trying to find out where Bunty was and if William had been located. I borrowed coins from Mr. Collins at the hospital and phoned my parents, but all I could say over and over again was, "Bunty's been hurt, Daddy, Bill's missing and Bunty's been hurt."

My mother and father drove through the night to get to the house, as did Bunty's granny, only her driver took her straight to the hospital. Charing Cross had sent me and Mr. Collins home. They'd been insistent about patching up my cut knees and equally as firm that they couldn't tell me anything about my friends.

Sunday should have been the day that Bunty and I sat around the flat reliving thc glamorous excitement of the previous night and waiting for William to come round for lunch, when we would relive it all over again with him. Instead, while Mother made endless cups of tea and Father insisted on re-bandaging the nurse's perfectly good work, I tried not to relive anything at all.

At ten to eleven that morning, the phone rang. It was Bunty's granny. My father answered it, saying several times in his doctor's voice, "I see," and, "Mrs. Tavistock, these are very good signs." Then he said, "And any news of William?" and after a short pause a quite upbeat, "Well, I'm sure they will tell you as soon as they know."

Then Father said Goodbye and came to sit beside me, taking hold of both my hands.

"She's pretty roughed up, my darling," he said gently. "And it's going to take rather a time to recover. But I promise you, from what I've just heard, Bunty is going to get well, she really is. And while we don't know where William is yet, Mrs. Tavistock says she is sure we will soon. People were taken to several hospitals, so it is taking a little while to find out."

After that, for just over an hour, everything seemed a bit better.

Then, at nearly twelve, the doorbell rang downstairs. Buoyed by the news about Bunty and my faith in my father's words, I headed downstairs to answer the front door. Not cheerful, far from it, but hopeful.

But as soon as I opened the door and saw Roy, I knew.

Still in his uniform from last night, but without his AFS cap and greatcoat, I barely noticed the dirt and grime that covered him. All I saw was the look on his face.

"Emmy, love," he said quietly as he stood on the big wide doorstep. "Can I come in?"

I didn't move.

"Did you find him?" I asked in a whisper.

Roy nodded and gave me the smallest, saddest smile that his eyes didn't join in with. He glanced into the hall. "We should sit down."

I felt my breath catch in the back of my throat.

"Roy?"

"He's gone, love," he said softly. "Bill's dead."

When people hear that sort of thing in films, they gasp or faint or put the back of their hand to their mouth in a dramatic way. But I didn't do any of that. I wanted to say no, that it couldn't be true. I wanted to tell Roy he was wrong. I wanted it to be ten seconds ago, when I still didn't know.

But instead I just stood there feeling as if someone had sucked all the air out of me. And then my bottom lip started to tremble, like it does when you're little and you can't make it stop.

I tried to take a deep breath and be British and brave, but it didn't work, and instead, the tears began. Masses of them. Where did tears like that come from and how did they get there so fast? Were they always there, just waiting for something awful to happen? What a horrible job they had.

Poor Roy. It was awful for him too. He stepped into the house and hugged me into his cold, dusty arms, holding on just like he had when the bombs fell, when he did everything he could to make sure I wouldn't get hurt.

And I clung back, just like before, trying to pull Roy out of harm's way.

But this time we couldn't protect each other. It was too late. Everything was all just too late.

I couldn't stop crying. Roy didn't let go. I heard him say, "There, there, love," and his voice was shaking. I knew he was trying hard not to cry as well. Roy was one of London's very finest. A big old tough fireman. But Bill was his best friend.

I gently pulled away from him as I heard my parents coming down the stairs. Roy's eyes were brimming with tears. I sniffed and tried to stop blubbing as it wasn't fair on him.

Mother and Father didn't have to ask. Mother flung her arms around me and said My Darling but as much as I wanted to cling on to her and howl, I wouldn't leave Roy just standing there.

"This is Roy," I said pathetically. "Bill's friend Roy. My friend."

Roy coughed and cleared his throat, straightened up, and said Sir to my father, offering his hand for him to shake. It must have been dreadful for him to suddenly have to be so polite. Daddy took his hand and gripped Roy's arm with the other.

"Thank you," he said with an urgency, and I knew he meant for looking after me. "Thank you, Roy. Please come inside. Let's get you a drink."

In the living room upstairs, my mother made Roy take his uniform jacket off so that she could put a blanket around his shoulders. He said that he was fine thank you, but she insisted and so he sat with the blanket wrapped around him, like one of the people he normally helped. He held on to a large glass of whisky.

I sat on the sofa next to my mother, who wouldn't let go of my hand. I had whisky too. It tasted as awful as ever. It would be the last time I would ever drink it.

"Are you sure it was . . ." I asked.

Roy started nodding before I finished the sentence.

"The uniform," he said, looking into his glass, and then taking a large swig from it. "It was him." Roy looked even worse than before.

Then I asked the question that I dreaded.

"Who . . . who will tell Bunty? When will she know?"

"I don't know, love," said Roy. "I stayed with Bill until . . ." He stopped. "Until they took him away. Then I went to Charing Cross but they're swamped. Bad night. So I came here. I'll go back to the hospital now."

Roy got to his feet. He looked exhausted.

"Not at all," said Father quickly, also getting up. He glanced over at my mother, who nodded. I knew what they meant. It wasn't fair to send Roy back and it would be better for Mrs. Tavistock to hear it from my father than from a policeman or nurse.

"Let me come," I said. I didn't want to sit around being useless. I wanted to be there for Bunty. "I'm fine. Really," I added. It was a lie but that wasn't the point.

My father shook his head.

"No," he said firmly. "Not this time, Cherub. You and Roy have both done enough. You need to rest. And that's me being a doctor."

He gave us both a serious look as I tried to argue, adding, "Emmy, really, I've more chance of seeing them if I'm there as Bunty's GP."

I knew he was right. I slumped back into the sofa and admitted defeat.

This was happening every day, to people all over London, all over the country, all over Europe. Everywhere people were getting the most dreadful news. We were no different from anyone else. It was our friends' turn. It was our turn. It didn't make things feel any better at all.

Poor, poor Bill. And, oh God, *poor Bunty*. Everything she had dreamed of, everything they had been planning and looking forward to. The living room didn't look any different from this time yesterday. There were unopened cards and presents, and the photographs in their silver frames: pictures of William and Bunty on a summer's day on the common, one of him so proud in his uniform when he'd first joined the Service. Bunty loved that picture. A little blue box on the coffee table which held the Cufflinks she had bought to give him as a wedding present. And now everything was gone.

Then, just as I thought I couldn't feel any more awful, I remembered my silly, pointless, pathetic rows with Bill.

I should have tried harder to tell him I was sorry. I should have found a way to say it sooner. I should have been at the Café de Paris on time.

I vaguely heard my mother saying, "Do go, Alfred, we'll be absolutely fine." And then squeezing my hand and saying, "Won't we, darling? We'll be all right."

I nodded. But nothing would be all right. I couldn't tell her, just as I had no idea how I could tell Bunty.

That I had fallen out with Bill and let Bunty down? That an old, dear friend had died loathing me? I couldn't tell anyone. It was a horrible secret I would just have to keep.

I was desperate to see Bunty, but only family were allowed and we didn't count. Instead, Mother and I put our faith in the fact that Mrs. Tavistock was of a generation and class that would hardly put up with being told what they could or couldn't do. If she felt that us seeing Bunty would help in any way, then it was more than likely that was what we would do.

In the meantime, throughout the whole of Sunday, I sat in the flat, going over and over again in my head what I would say and how I would say it. However badly Bunty was injured, I knew she would battle on. But I wasn't half so sure about how she would take the news about Bill.

How would anyone cope with that, let alone so close to her wedding? I didn't know how I could help her, but whatever she needed from me, I would do it.

On Monday morning, before returning to his practice, as he had patients to see, my father phoned Mr. Collins at the office. Mr. Collins said I should have as much time away as I needed until Father was sure I was quite well. I was to leave Mrs. Bird to him and not even think about *Woman's Friend*. He sent his best wishes, Father said.

After that, Mother and I spent another interminable day waiting for news from the hospital. Finally, in the late afternoon, Mrs. Tavistock rang to say Bunty was conscious and that I could see her for a minute or two if I wished. Mother and I were in our coats and out of the house within seconds.

It wasn't Visiting Hour, so we knew strings had been pulled. At Charing Cross, the Duty Sister looked ferocious, but as Mrs. Tavistock was familiar with at least one of the members of the board of trustees, she was having to turn a very reluctant blind eye.

Mrs. Tavistock met us in the hospital corridor. Slightly built but straight-backed and still with the elegance that had made her a notable beauty fifty years before, despite clear best efforts, she looked worried and drawn.

"Emmeline dear," she said, clasping my hands and giving me a warm smile. "I hope you have slept." She turned to my mother. "Elizabeth, how terribly kind of you to come. Now. Marigold . . . Bunty . . .

is awake. The doctors have done what they can for the present and the very good news is that they are confident they have managed to save her leg."

I tried not to look shocked. Father hadn't said anything about losing legs.

Mrs. Tavistock gave me a sad, kind smile.

"Emmeline, I am afraid Bunty is rather under the weather and if you would prefer not to see her quite yet, I am sure she would very much understand."

I shook my head quickly and Mrs. Tavistock went on.

"You should know that Bunty hasn't spoken since I gave her the news about William."

Mrs. Tavistock lifted her chin up the tiniest amount, as if to back up the enormous effort going on inside. "They believe she is in shock but I hope she might speak with you as you girls are so close. I didn't tell her you were coming, just in case you felt you would rather not."

Her voice was brave, but she still sounded bereft.

"I would very much like to see her please, Mrs. Tavistock," I said. I didn't care what state Bunty was in. "Might I go in now?"

With a nod of acknowledgement from the Duty Sister, who was still gritting her teeth as Bunty's granny broke every rule in the hospital's book, I was shown the way.

I had only been on a hospital ward once before, when my brother, Jack, had his appendix out the year before the war started. The long room we entered now was much the same, only the windows were all blacked out and the beds were closer together so they could get more people in. When I stole a glance at some of the beds, people didn't have appendicitis or jaundice or the odd broken arm. They had multiple wounds, blackened faces, entire bodies swathed in miles of pristine bandages.

They didn't show this in the newspapers.

Sister briskly walked us on.

"Your friend is going to be fine," she said. "Bright smile, talk about chins up, and do not discuss the event. Here we are, on the right. You can sit on that chair. I will be back in five minutes."

She raised her voice as if Bunty were deaf. "Miss Tavistock. You have a visitor. Five minutes," she said again to me and strode off.

Bunty's bed was at the very end of the ward by the wall. I took the hugest of deep breaths and tried to do a bright smile as instructed. It did not feel a time for anything like a bright smile.

"Bunty?" I said softly.

She was lying almost flat, her right leg hoisted up on some sort of pulley, and bandaged from hip to foot. Her left arm was held together with splints and more bandages, and where she wasn't bound up, everything else was livid bruises and cuts. Nearly two days after the bomb, her face was almost unrecognizable. One of her eyes was a huge puffed oyster shell, swollen as far as the yellow and purple bruised skin could stretch, as if she had been knocked out by a prize-fighter. I fought the urge to gape. I may not have been able to plaster on a pretend smile, but I wouldn't let Bunty see I was shocked.

I sat down rather quickly on the iron chair next to her bed. I should have liked to hug her, tell her that all of us would help make things better, but of course I couldn't. You can't hug someone who looks as if every inch of them hurts. I wanted to hold her hand, but it was hidden in the bandages. I reached forward and clutched at the crisp sheet instead, twisting it and spoiling the perfect effect.

Bunty had not responded to my hello and there was no sign that she had even heard me. The eye that hadn't been battered beyond use remained fixed on the ceiling above.

"Bunty," I said again, as gently as I could, as if the slightest noise might cause further injury—jar something and make it worse. "It's me. Emmy."

Her chest rose and fell as she breathed and I saw her blink. I was sure she knew I was there.

"Oh, Bunts," I said, feeling at sea but desperate to say the right thing. "I'm so very sorry."

Nothing.

"We're all here. Everyone's here and we're going to help you get better. We'll help you and your granny, and Father is going to speak with the doctors to make sure we know exactly what we need to do so that you can be up and about terribly soon and . . ."

It was unbearable. If she could hear me, how would she respond? Perhaps she was trying to say something only she couldn't work out how.

"Um, anyway, darling, the doctors are very confident they've mended your leg and I know it must hurt horribly but I promise one day you will feel better." I paused. What did I know about anything?

"Oh, Bunty," I whispered, hoping my voice wouldn't crack. "I'm so sorry about Bill."

Bunty blinked but still didn't say anything. With her face so beaten, it was impossible to make out any expression. I opened my mouth to go on, but before I could get the words out, Bunty spoke.

"He told me."

She spoke with difficulty, but it was a start. I leant in towards her and pulled the metal chair forward to get closer.

"Bunty, love," I said, reaching for the tips of her fingers, desperate for her to know she wasn't on her own, and ready to say anything that might help.

"Don't."

I withdrew my hand to the side of the bed.

"He told me," whispered Bunty again. Her voice was flat, without emotion. She still didn't look at me.

"What is it?" I said, trying to encourage her to speak. "Don't rush, I know it's hard."

"You going on at him. Shouting."

It caught me unawares. In the enormity of William's death, our arguments made even less sense than before. I scrambled to put things right.

"Goodness," I said. "Yes. We did have a silly disagreement." I stopped. I hadn't meant it to sound unimportant. "I just wanted him to take care," I finished lamely.

"It wasn't silly to him," said Bunty. "You'd no right. You think you can sort people out, but you can't. You interfered."

The bitterness in her voice stopped me in my tracks.

"Bunty, I'm sorry," I said. "I was worried about him. I was thinking about you."

As the words came out, I realised how stupid that sounded.

"No you weren't." Despite being so fragile, Bunty sounded angry now. "I'm supposed to be your best friend. You don't think of other people, you just do what you want."

"Oh, Bunts," I pleaded. "I'm sorry. I didn't mean to."

Bunty's voice was weak but she didn't stop.

"You never *mean to*. But you push in and make things worse. You did it with Kitty. You told her to fight for her baby and it didn't work and she felt even sadder. You even thought you could give advice to strangers at the magazine, but you can't. You shouldn't have interfered," she said again.

I was gripping my hands together so hard, my knuckles looked as if they would pop out of my skin. A feeling of panic rose in my throat. Bunty sounded as if she hated me.

"I didn't want you to know Bill had been in danger," I said. "I told him I was sorry, and we talked and I wanted to say sorry again, but I didn't get the chance. I was going to as soon as I got to the Café de Paris."

It was a poor catalogue of excuses. I loathed myself more with each word.

"You weren't there," said Bunty, and finally her voice wavered the tiniest bit. "He was worried."

"I'm ever so sorry," I said, searching for the right thing to say. "They had no staff at the station. I didn't think I should leave."

"He was worried about you," she said. "He said he wanted to find you in case you were still cross."

"But I wasn't cross," I said, appalled, and scared of what she would say next. "I wasn't cross."

Bunty slowly turned her head and finally looked at me. Her poor broken face was utterly wretched.

"Bill didn't want it to spoil things. He said he would find you and sort it all out."

She looked exhausted, but carried on.

"That's when he died. He was looking for you."

I thought the world had collapsed on Saturday night. That things were dark and awful and at their very worst. It turned out I had been wrong.

I sat back in my chair as the tears came.

I didn't know what to say that could make it better, apart from how sorry I was, sorrier than anything, ever. I would say it a thousand times until Bunty knew. But she didn't want to hear it. As I began to speak, she cut across me, her voice flat again but chillingly clear.

"Don't."

The brisk step of Sister sounded behind me.

"I'll come back," I said. "Another time, when you feel better, and we'll talk."

Bunty looked at me with all the sadness in the world.

"You mustn't come again. I don't want to see you."

Then she turned her head away.

Sister started saying something brisk about leaving, and I rose slowly from the chair.

"I'm so sorry," I whispered as a huge tear rolled down the side of Bunty's swollen, unrecognizable face.

The nurse told me to hurry up.

Bunty said nothing else.

Chapter 20

TRUST ME, WRITE

I wanted more than anything to ignore Bunty's instructions and visit her again. I had to explain what had happened with Bill and hope she would understand. The sight of my friend in hospital, in pain and bereft, would not leave me. Worst of all was replaying over and over again what Bunty had said: that Bill had been looking for me when he was killed.

You could dress it up any way you liked, but it was quite clear. It was my fault he was dead.

Mrs. Tavistock and my mother were waiting for me outside the ward and assumed I was white as a sheet at the shock of seeing how poorly Bunty was. I told Mrs. Tavistock that she didn't want to talk, which was true, but of course not the whole story. Then I said if it was all right with them both, I would prefer to get some air and make my own way home. Mother began to disagree and Mrs. Tavistock held my hands and told me I was such a good girl for trying to help and not to worry and that everything would be right as rain soon.

I could hardly stand it.

Leaving them behind, I ran as fast as I could out of the hospital, flying down the stairs and ignoring the tuts and calls of Steady

Up and I Say as I rushed through the reception and out into the blackout.

Mrs. Tavistock was very kind, but she didn't know her granddaughter the way I did. Bunty did not want to see me. I would keep trying, but I knew she meant it. It was only a matter of time before I would hear from her granny, saying that Bunty wasn't up to receiving visitors for the present.

There was a little café next to the hospital which was open for staff working late shifts. Unsteady on my feet, I called in for a strong cup of tea before facing the bus home. The café was warm and smelt of reconstituted meat and carbolic soap, but it was cosy all the same.

"Young lady, are you feeling unwell?" said the friendly man behind the counter. He was in his fifties with a notable moustache and a strong accent. "You look green along the gills. I'm Czechoslovakian," he added, obviously used to the assumption that anyone sounding foreign was most probably an enemy sympathiser.

"I'm fine, thank you," I said, hoping he wouldn't ask any questions, because I was keeping my end up by a thread. If he was any more kind to me, I would cave in. "Might I have a cup of tea, please?"

"Of course," he answered. "Sit down. I find you secret sugar. Shhhh!" He winked and pointed to a small table in the corner. I nodded and tried to say thank you but it came out as a sort of hiccup and he flapped a tea towel at me in a fatherly way. I wondered how many people stumbled out of the hospital and into his café every day, their lives turned upside down.

He hummed to himself as he brewed the strongest cup of tea I had seen since war broke out and then delivered it with a fig roll resting in the saucer and the clear instruction to "Eat, drink on the house. Stay until red cheeks."

I stirred my tea and studied the encouraging posters pasted to the inside of the walls. One recommended growing potatoes, while another suggested investing in savings bonds. Both implied a guaranteed success in becoming a vital part of the war effort. A third pictured lots of women in uniforms of the different services. "Doing A Grand Job!" it announced.

I kept stirring the tea. I was doing anything but a grand job. My kind Czechoslovakian friend was singing in a soft baritone that in another time and world would have its place in a choir. Instead, here he was, looking after a complete stranger for free while having to tell people his nationality in the same breath as hello in case they thought he was a threat.

The world had become ugly and mad.

Struggling to keep my chin up, I sipped my drink, immediately becoming almost dizzy from the unaccustomed sweetness. I couldn't begin to think what to do next.

Bunty and I would always, *always* chat through a row, rare though they were. We were lifelong best friends and had sworn we always would be. Only now it was my fault that Bunty's fiancé was dead. It was all too big, too awful.

On a table in the corner opposite me, someone had left the day's newspapers and a couple of well-thumbed magazines. *Woman's Friend* did not appear to be one of them, but it made me think of the rotten irony of trying to give advice to the readers while making an absolute hash of my own life. Mrs. Bird would make mincemeat of me if I sent her a letter about this.

I bent down and opened my bag, pulling out the notebook I carried everywhere. I was forever scribbling down ideas for how to answer a knotty problem someone had sent in. Now I wanted to sort out what I had to tell Bunty, how I would put things to her when I had another chance. Perhaps I could write it all down properly and send it in a letter. Then she could decide when to read it.

I didn't have much of a plan, but starting to write at least felt as if I were doing something. I certainly wouldn't give up just when Bunty needed friends most.

Dearest Bunty, I wrote.

I don't know where to start or how I can say the right thing, but in case my seeing you will be too upsetting, I am writing in the hope you may read this. I wish more than anything that you will know how much I am thinking of you and hoping against hope that things will be better for you one day.

I know you are terribly injured but far worse, I really do know, is losing Bill. I hardly dare write his name as you must hate me so much. Words can't even begin to describe how very sorry I am.

He was absolutely right. It wasn't silly. We did row and I said some rotten things to him about trying to be too brave at work and taking too many risks. Bunty, I was so stupid. It came out wrong and when I tried to apologise, that came out wrong too. I was trying to protect you and worried about him getting hurt, but I shouldn't have said anything. It was his job and he was wonderful at it. Everyone knew that. Some friend I was to you both.

The words were tumbling out like mad, but none of them looked up to much. It was all just a bundle of excuses. If I were Bunty, I would probably tear it up and never open another from me again.

I leant my elbows on the café table and felt my shoulders slump down. The manager was still humming to himself as he swept the floor.

He paused for a moment and looked over.

"Drink," he said, nodding at my cup of tea. "Before it is cold."

I tried a half smile in response and he looked at me kindly.

"And write," he said. "Whoever you write, if they love you, they understand."

I wished he was right. I must have looked as bad as I felt as he propped his broom against the wall and came over. Then he patted my shoulder.

"Trust me," he said. "I have many customers. Write."

I was touched by his kindness and how he was trying to help with tea and songs and secret sugar.

"Thank you," I said. "I will."

Because he *was* right. My words weren't very good—in fact I didn't know if they might even make things worse—but all I could do was try my very best to explain so that Bunty knew the truth. I couldn't expect her to forgive me, but she needed to know how much I wished I could change what had happened.

I took a large gulp of the still-warm tea and picked up my pen again.

Bunty, I thought I could patch things up at the Café de Paris. I thought there would be time. I was wrong and I will regret it forever.

I can't imagine how wretched this is for you and I realise you can't forgive me. I would give absolutely anything to change things and swap places with Bill, I promise I would. I mean it, please believe that.

Well then, I'll finish now. You will try as hard as you can to get better and back on your feet, won't you? All of us love you enormously and can't imagine life without you being quite well again.

Please know, Bunty, that you will always be my very best friend in the world and I will always be here just in case you ever might need me.

I am so very sorry.

With much love and yours always,

Emmy xx

I sat back in my chair for a moment. I didn't know what else I could say, but I didn't want to stop. It was as if it might be my last chance to speak to her.

I couldn't bear that. I had to add one more thing.

PS: I will continue to write, just in case you might feel you can open my letters. I will put a note on the front of the envelopes so that the nurses know it is me and they can throw them away if you'd prefer. Em.

I would keep writing.

I shut my notebook carefully. I would copy out the letter and send it as soon as I got home.

Bunty may have lost William and, because of it, hate me with a passion, which I quite understood. But I would not give up on her. I would always be her friend, whether she wanted me or not.

Chapter 21

WAR WAS FOUL

I was right about Bunty. Later that evening, Mrs. Tavistock came to the flat and said that while she was already Doing Terrifically Well and would be better in Absolutely No Time, neither of which I believed, it would probably be for the best if I didn't visit for now. I should let the doctors and nurses do everything they could to help her along.

I had no idea how much Mrs. Tavistock knew, but I said Yes Of Course and even managed to add something about How Tremendous all the nurses were and How Terribly Clever the doctors had been, which sounded as if I were reviewing a show in the West End.

I felt it only right to ask Mrs. Tavistock if I might write to Bunty, crossing my fingers as I didn't know what I might do if she said no. For the briefest of moments I thought she hesitated, but then she regained herself and said Of Course. I had never felt so relieved.

She was also adamant I should continue to live in the upstairs flat, for which I was ever so grateful. Even though I would be surrounded by constant reminders of Bunty and William, which meant battling with my guilt every moment I was there, it meant I was still in some way part of my best friend's life. Most of all, I hoped it might mean that Bunty couldn't have told her granny that William's death was my fault.

Staying in the flat came with a condition, however. My parents insisted that for now, I was to leave London and return home for a rest. I was dreadfully unhappy about this. I didn't need a rest—I wasn't the injured one—and being carted off to the country made me feel like a fake. But it was obvious my parents and Mrs. Tavistock had discussed it, and despite a strong-willed exchange with my mother, I had no choice but to give in. It was either that, or Mrs. Tavistock would close up the house.

Bunty's granny had always been lovely to me, but I knew when I was beaten. Roy had said he would speak with Captain Davies at the fire station, and with Mr. Collins insisting I mustn't return to *Woman's Friend* straightaway, I had no reason to stay. There was nothing wrong with me, but if I was honest, I was relieved not to face everyone just yet.

Even though I wanted to thank Mr. Collins for everything he had done the night of the raid, I wouldn't have known where to start. He had been extraordinarily kind at the Café de Paris, staying with me the entire time and trying to find Bunty. I didn't know if I would have found her on my own. I wasn't even sure I would have been able to get in if he hadn't lied to the air-raid warden about my being a nurse. And now he was being kind all over again about work.

Then there was Charles, of course. Less than two weeks ago he and I had been dancing and laughing and promising to write as we kissed each other goodbye. It had been exciting and fun and something to look forward to. What should I write to him now? How could I explain what had happened to someone I hardly knew? I pushed it to the back of my mind.

On Tuesday morning my mother and I boarded the train at Waterloo. As the rain thundered down, and while Mother made polite conversation with an elderly lady about shortages, I rested my head against the second-class carriage window and closed my eyes. Mother assumed I was tired, but really it was because I couldn't bear the fact that with every minute I was further away from Bunty and further away from being able to make things right.

Returning home could not have been more different from my last visit, when Bunty and I had wrestled with Jack in the snow and everyone had been upbeat about my accidental new job and loudly furious about Edmund's shortcomings. Now the house was shrouded in quiet. Little Whitfield was a small village and everyone knew William and Bunty and how close we all were. Concerned friends knocked softly on the front door rather than ring the bell, and even Father's patients seemed to be spirited to and from his surgery room with nothing to be heard of the usual conversations about the children's measles or grandad's lumbago.

I stayed in my old bedroom, staring at the pretty flowered wallpaper and only going downstairs for meals, which I didn't touch, or to wander around the garden, where I wouldn't have to see anyone. In the middle of the night, with my bedroom in darkness, I would look out of the window and up at the sky, almost willing a plane to appear and do something awful. Not to anyone else, of course, but to me.

I kept telling myself to buck up but I couldn't. The only thing I managed to do was write to Bunty as I had promised; short, subdued, but hopeful letters, every day. I had no idea if she would see them.

I made myself write to Charles too. I didn't want to, but he had been so terribly nice and as he had met Bunty and William of course, it would have been unutterably rude of me not to tell him. I couldn't tell him it was all my fault, so I kept it as short as I could.

Dear Charles,

I hope you are very well.

I don't know if your brother may have written about this, but I am afraid I am writing with rather awful news. I can hardly bear to say it, so just will.

You see there was a raid when Bunty and William and I were out celebrating their engagement. They bombed the Café de Paris and Bill was killed.

Bunty was injured and is quite poorly. I am fine as I was late and missed it, and Mr. Collins (I'm sorry, I can't call him Guy) was there and he helped me find Bunty. He was so kind and you would be very proud.

I'm so sorry to write with such horrible news. I had promised to send you cheeriness.

Please don't worry, because Bunty is wonderfully strong and Father says she will be on the mend very soon. I wish I could help her but he says the nurses are top drawer, and she is in very good hands.

I'm at my parents' for a few days but will be back at the flat very soon.

Do take huge care of yourself, won't you?

Yours,

Emmy x

I didn't know what else to say to him. My mother posted the letter for me as I didn't want to go out of the house.

It was easy being at home. I didn't have to do anything except put on a chipper face for my parents and say I felt better each day. Mother tried to get me interested in things—sewing blankets for the war effort or collecting eggs or even just visiting next door to see their new dog. She meant well but it wasn't doing me any good. I wasn't an invalid and I knew I had far too much time to dwell on everything that had gone on.

A week after going home I was sitting on the damp old wooden swing in the garden and looking at the early daffodils that were pushing their way through the grass. It reminded me of the first time I went out with Edmund. We were seventeen and were only going for a walk, but he arrived at the door with a bunch of flowers for me and looking embarrassed. I shook my head at the memory. In my all so easy, fortunate life, his going off with the nurse had felt like a slap in the face. It was such small beer now.

And what had Bunty done then? Fixed me that drink, told me Edmund was an absolute fool and that he would never do better than me. She was irrefutably on my side—not a moment's hesitation. As ever, being the best friend in the world.

"You idiot," I whispered to myself, and then more loudly. "You absolute bloody idiot."

Had anyone given prizes out for self-pity, I'd have been top of the class. If Bunty had been here and still my friend, no matter how rotten everything was, she would never have spiralled into such gloom. She would have fought on.

I needed to go back to London and to work. It was the only way to shake myself out of this despair. I would have to make Mother and Father understand, after all, I was the one who was lucky enough to be well.

I got off the swing, walked back into the house, and went upstairs to pack.

Coming back to the flat on my own was the first test of my resolve to push on. As I opened the door and switched on the wall light in the late afternoon, almost everything about it looked the same but almost everything about being there had changed. The cold living room was quiet and lonely. Mother had moved the unopened wedding cards and presents and hidden them away. It was unbearably tidy, apart from my writing case and typewriter, which sat on the small teak dining table where Bunts and I used to eat our meals and I would write my secret *Woman's Friend* letters when she was at work. There was a stack of new letters hidden in my room, which I had intended to reply to as soon as possible. I didn't know what I might do with them now.

Before, answering the readers' letters had given me a sense of purpose. Even when Kathleen had nearly found me out and I decided not to put any more into the magazine, I'd thought continuing to secretly write back to people could help. Now Bunty's words at the hospital stung.

You push in and make things worse. You even thought you could give advice to strangers at the magazine, but you can't.

She was right. Rather than flouncing around posting letters, I should be doing something decent for the war effort. Sitting at my parents' house during the past week, I had thought I might stop just talking about it and apply to get on the training course to become a full-time Fire Service motorcycle courier. Or try to join any one of the other services. If I was honest, I didn't really care, just as long as it meant doing something useful.

Whatever I did, it would be more than I was doing now. I'd never have to stand hopelessly by the edge of a street as firemen saved people, or need someone like Mr. Collins to get me through to someone in an emergency. I made up my mind to research the different services properly. I couldn't afford to make another mistake and get into the wrong job. In the meantime, I'd put in for more shifts at the fire station and work my socks off at *Woman's Friend*. And I would absolutely stick to the rules. No more writing to readers. No more interfering in people's lives.

It was the start of a plan and I felt brightened by it.

Tomorrow I was going back to the office, but before that there was something far more important to be done. I had to go back to the fire station for the first time since the Café de Paris.

I felt my nerve falter.

The globe-shaped drinks cabinet in the corner very nearly waved at me. But I shook my head. Dutch courage would not help. Instead, I got up from the sofa and systematically went through every room, switched on every single light, and for absolutely no reason but to avoid sitting down and thinking about things, I cleaned every last inch of the already spotless flat.

At half past six the next morning, having not slept a wink, I was washed and dressed in my smartest work clothes. *Woman's Friend* did not scare me, but facing Roy and the girls and all of William's friends very much did. I knew that the longer I put it off, the worse it would be, so as the Luftwaffe's pilots left London and were, I was sure, being chased back to Germany by our boys, I put on my greatcoat, shoved my woollen beret down to my ears, and headed into the darkness towards the fire station.

The Carlton Street teams were still out on calls with their engines and pumps so I arrived at an empty yard. Having run almost all the way as it had started to rain, it was a moment to catch my breath and get myself in order.

I pulled off my hat and stood alone in the yard, breathing hard. B Watch would just be finishing their shift. Thelma, Joan, and Mary, and whoever was covering for me. My throat tightened. I hoped it wasn't Vera.

Even if it wasn't, this was going to be hard. My friends would be lovely, which would make me feel horrible, but far worse would be facing their grief. Until now I had only thought of Bunty and Mrs. Tavistock. And, indulgently, myself. Not William's friends. He had been hugely popular at Carlton Street, loved even.

"Come on, get into harness," I said out loud. Head up, shoulders back. If they ask questions about how Bunty is, tell them She Is Doing Awfully Well.

I opened the side door and walked in, past the damp wall where everyone parked their bicycles, and up the steep, dark stairs. Yet another deep breath as my heart thumped with apprehension.

The all clear had gone over an hour ago, and as the first sign of dawn was nudging into view outside, the night-shift girls in the call room were still alert, taking messages as Pimlico's residents ventured out and discovered what damage had been done overnight. At this time in a shift it would be calls about people who were trapped or buildings that might well collapse or the cruel late fires that came from nowhere when air got through, just as everyone thought things were safe.

The call room looked exactly as it should, phones and paper pads on desks, call chart on the wall showing which team was going where, big clock by the door ticking the shift to an end. Joan was on the phone, furiously making notes, and Thelma and Mary were writing up call notes from the shift. It was just the three of them. Thel and Mary looked up as I entered the room and immediately got to their feet, chairs grating against the floor. Mary glanced over to Thelma for a steer on what to do next, but Thelma was already on her way towards me. Her face twisted itself into a determined imitation of an Everything Will Be Fine smile. I managed an equal imitation of one back.

"Hello," I said, and ground to a halt as Thelma hugged me violently.

"Oh, love," she said, and then again, "Oh, love," in a trembling voice into my hair. She didn't let go. "Bless your heart. Bless your heart."

Too choked to speak, I fought like mad not to let tears start all over again. I didn't want to let them all down, so I just nodded and hugged her back.

"I'm so sorry, Emmy," said Mary, who had followed Thelma over to me. She patted my shoulder a little shyly and I looked up to see tears in her eyes too. Thelma had run out of things to say, or rather, I knew she couldn't speak either. I hugged her back with one arm and reached out to Mary with the other. Joan finished her call and, having hastily put the note onto the call spike, joined the rest of us.

"Oh, Em," she said, and I pulled away from Thelma to hug her too. Joan had always had a soft spot for William, saying she hoped her young lads would grow up to be just like him.

"I know," I said, trying to sound comforting rather than hopeless, which is exactly how I felt.

Joan's eyes brimmed. She held on to my arms, like Thelma, trying to offer a brave smile.

"Our poor lad," she said, shaking her head.

A big fat tear now defied my orders and ran down my cheek. This wasn't about any of us. It was about the loss of a decent and courageous young man who hadn't even started to do all the things he deserved to. My own feelings of guilt weren't the point. The point was that Bill was gone. Standing in the middle of the call room, it was impossible to believe.

Joan, Thelma, and Mary, like thousands of others, spent day and night after day and night carrying on with their jobs in the most frightening of conditions. Every day they helped save strangers they didn't know and would never meet. But today it was their friend. Stiff upper lips and getting on with things were all very well, but sometimes there was nothing to do but admit that things were quite simply awful. War was foul and appalling and unfair.

For once, not one of the telephones rang.

After a few moments, I carefully let go of Joan, wiping my face and then grasping her hand and Mary's as well. They both reached out to Thelma, and for just a moment the four of us stood in the middle of the call room, gripping each other's hands as if we were a special, secret society.

I spoke first, wanting like anything to make them feel the tiniest bit better or help them find it easier to carry on.

"Come on, girls," I said, voice shaky but doing my best. I looked at Mary and added very gently, "Come on. Chins up."

It was only four months since her brother had gone missing in Africa. I knew Mary's tears for William were mixed with ones for him too. I squeezed her hand harder and hoped I looked like a reassuring big sister. She tried a brave smile back.

"Good girl," I said. "That's the ticket."

Thelma took up the baton.

"Look at us," she said, sniffing. "This won't do, will it? In uniform and everything." She ran out of steam.

Joan tried manfully to carry it on. "What would Bill say, eh?" she said, trying to raise a laugh but wobbling badly. "Oh dear," she finished. "Oh dear."

They were trying so hard. It was difficult to bear.

"Well," I said slowly, "I think Bill would be ever so sad to see everyone so upset, but I think he would understand. And he'd probably try to cheer us all up."

It was despicable speaking on his behalf but it seemed to boost everyone. They all nodded and agreed and tried their hardest to smile.

The noise of an engine sounded downstairs. The first of the team had returned from their calls.

Mary looked panicked and felt in her pocket for a hankie. The others did the same. No one wanted the boys to see them in tears.

"It's all right," I said. "They'll be parking up. I'll go down and see them in a minute."

"Thanks, love," said Thelma, who then blew her nose briskly. She seemed to steel herself slightly before asking how Bunty was.

"She's doing tremendously well," I said, giving her my rehearsed answer. "Though it's probably going to take a bit of time to be fully back up to scratch."

"You will give her our love, won't you?" said Thel, and I nodded, feeling sick.

I could hear the growl of more pumps coming in downstairs and a few shouts and calls between the men. Any second now, one of them would come tearing up the stairs asking for tea.

"I must go down and see them," I said, hoping I sounded plucky and upbeat and all the things I wasn't at all.

"They'll want to see you, of course," said Joan.

Will they? I thought. If only they knew the truth.

But with one last smile at the girls, I headed downstairs to face William's friends.

Chapter 22

YOURS EVER, MRS. WARDYNSKI

When I left the station, being an absolute coward, I walked the long way home in order to avoid going past Mr. Bone's newsagent's. I was pretty sure he would know what had happened and I couldn't face another desperately sad conversation, especially as I knew this would have opened the wound of the loss of his son. People were beginning to fill the streets on their way to work and I kept my head down, anxious to avoid anyone I knew. I was already beginning to recognise an odd expression on their faces when they saw me. A flicker of not quite panic, followed by a well-meaning grimace of a smile as they searched for something to say, or far worse, tried to cover up sadness of their own.

I passed the little playground as usual and stopped momentarily to watch two children playing chase with their dog. The children were shrieking and the little terrier was yapping with excitement, oblivious to the cold, the damp, and the thundering great craters that formed the backdrop to their games. The little girl called the dog and he ran over to her, tail wagging furiously. She scooped him up in her arms and hugged him tightly as he licked her face, his back legs hanging down where she was too small to hold him properly and leaving happy smears of mud on her coat.

I wished I could run around the playground, playing and shouting and laughing as if everything were fine. I allowed myself a moment of wishing Charles were here. He might hold my hand and tell me things would be all right. Even though they wouldn't, I would like to hear him say it. He had a way of sounding sure; not an arrogance, but a calm that made you feel somehow safe and as though there was nothing that couldn't be sorted out.

I checked myself. There was no point in getting soft over him now. Goodness knows what he would think about the whole sorry story once he came home. There was only so long I could bluff about Bunty's recovery. What would he think of me then? We hadn't known each other very long, and although I wrote to him a lot and had received his first letters from overseas, it was still such early days.

I shivered and, crossing my arms in front of me against the damp, set off smartly again. I would wash my face and make myself presentable for the office. Then I could start my plan to keep as busy as possible until I got war work and could leave *Woman's Friend*.

At *Woman's Friend*, everyone, without exception, was lovely on my return. Kathleen was even waiting for me by the lift on the third floor, and after she had given me a huge, worried hug, we walked the two flights to the office together, Kath with her arm through mine and telling me over and over again how sorry she was.

We had barely made it through the doors to the *Woman's Friend* corridor when Mrs. Mahoney and Mr. Brand appeared and offered the warmest of words. Mr. Collins must have told them what happened and they were terrifically nice.

Anxious to move the attention away, I thanked them and assured everyone I was absolutely fine to be back at work. Kath took the hint and chivvied me into her little room. I was just taking my coat off when Mrs. Bird appeared in the doorway. She was resplendent in a black feathery outfit and hat, which made her look like a very large crow just off on its way to church.

"Ah, Emmeline," she said in a matter-of-fact way but at an acceptable volume and using my first name, which had never happened before. "I thought I'd come and see you." She pursed her lips and looked grave. "I hear you've had a grim time of it. Difficult days."

It was most unlike the Acting Editress to actually come into Kathleen's office, rather than bark orders from outside, and the gesture was both surprising and kind.

"Thank you, Mrs. Bird," I replied, "and for letting me have the week off."

"Quite all right," she said, brushing it away. "Mr. Collins gave me the gen. Rotten business. They are not people, they are vermin. Well done for turning up. Wobbly?"

I shook my head. I wasn't used to Mrs. Bird in sympathetic mode. I looked at Kathleen, who was rooted to the spot and staring.

"Thank you, Mrs. Bird," I said again. "I really am fine, thank you."

"Good for you," she replied with a mixture of gusto and probable relief at the fact I was not doing anything hideous like having a cry. "Best thing is to keep busy. Throw yourself in."

I wondered whether now was a good time to tell her I intended to leave *Woman's Friend* and apply for a full-time job in the war effort, but Mrs. Bird ploughed on.

"Now, Mr. Collins tells me he could do with some overtime from you. Perfect to get you back in the swing."

She had returned to her usual, much preferred approach of human steamroller.

"An extra afternoon a week and all day Monday has been discussed. But I still need you to remain on top of my letters. Miss Knighton has enough on with the rest."

I nodded gratefully. It was just what I needed for now. If I added more shifts at the station as well, I could keep myself from thinking about things. All I would have to do would be work and sleep.

"However, I must warn you," said Mrs. Bird, manoeuvring her eyebrows into a stare that would turn milk, "that we have had some very Unpalatable Correspondence lately. Very. Unpleasant. Indeed."

The letters. Not now, I thought. Not now.

Mrs. Bird glowered.

"Nastiness, Miss Lake. I can't imagine what's come over our readers but I'm afraid Miss Knighton has had to cut up several highly Unacceptable letters in your absence."

Kathleen nodded and looked awkward. I waited, holding my breath.

"One obviously hopes this is not An Unsavoury Fad, but I would ask you to be more than vigilant and report any Unpleasantness to me. We shall not move in this direction."

"Of course," I said. "I'm sure it's been just one of those things." I bit my tongue. I should know better than to put in a throwaway platitude as it was likely to make Mrs. Bird more than irate.

"Hmm," she said in a threatening manner, and then turned to Kathleen. "I will be in the boardroom discussing Fire Buckets."

And then she was gone.

Kath and I looked at each other as the doors to the stairs crashed shut.

"She was very nice," I said. "I hadn't really expected that."

"Mrs. Bird really isn't nasty," said Kath. "She's just, um . . ."

"Assertive," we said together, which raised the smallest hint of a smile. It wasn't much, but I had to admit it was a relief to be back. No one at *Woman's Friend* knew William or Bunty, and selfishly, not having to worry about people's grief made things easier.

I sat on the edge of the desk and asked Kathleen if Mr. Collins was in yet.

"Any minute now, I should think," she said. "He's awfully worried about you, Emmy," she added. "He's been very quiet and rather unbearable to be honest." She looked at the door. "He'll be ever so pleased to see you, I'm sure."

I didn't really know what to say to that but hoped he wouldn't make a fuss. To change the subject I decided to take a risk and ask about Mrs. Bird's Unsavoury Fads. I hoped like mad that it hadn't aroused Kath's suspicions again.

"So, has there been some colourful correspondence?" I asked, hoping to look as if I was merely interested in focusing on work.

My head ached from the lack of sleep. I was trying hard to push what had happened to the back of my mind and hoped Kath would allow my line of questioning and not put up a moral No Entry sign instead.

To her credit, she joined in, merely picking some lint off her woolly before pulling a face.

"Well, yes. A few have been a bit much, if you know what I mean. Because you weren't here we had a bit of an All Hands On Deck and Mrs. Bird even went through some of the letters herself. You know we've been getting a few more in than usual." Kath stopped and looked behind her, then reached back and picked up a small pile of letters. "These came in yesterday's second post. I haven't opened them yet, but Mrs. Bird opened about this many. It turns out there were two pregnancies and one asking how to get a divorce. She wasn't best pleased."

I made a sympathetic face.

"Mrs. Bird said if this was the sort of person who wanted to read the magazine, we should have to have a long hard look at what we were writing about, and then do something about Raising The Tone."

I shrugged and looked blank, but it didn't sound good. Kath motored on, sorting through the letters in an absentminded way.

"The sad thing was, there was the loveliest letter from a lady who said Mrs. Bird had really helped her. I tried to show it to her yesterday as I thought she might be pleased, but she said she didn't have time. I kept it as I thought it might cheer you up." Kath looked at me apologetically. "I'm sorry, I know it hardly would. But you always take such an interest in the readers, I thought . . . well. Anyway. I can just throw it away."

"Oh, please don't. I'd love to see it," I said.

Kathleen opened the bottom drawer to her desk and handed me a letter. Thanking her, I added it to the rest of yesterday's second post so I could read it on my own rather than invite further discussion. Then I scuttled off down the corridor to open all the post and wait for Mr. Collins to come in.

I had only spent a few hours in the old reporters' office before my week away, but I already felt fond of it. It made me feel I was at least in a proper journalists' room, the smallest suggestion of my Correspondent dream. I had a romantic notion of what it might have been like when *Woman's Friend* was a success and it had been full of writers in a hubbub of activity, sharing ideas and cigarettes and sandwiches. I rather wished it would be that way again one day, after the war. I turned on the light and opened a window as the musty smell was continuing to mount a stubborn defence against change. Then I sat down at the desk I had chosen. It was just by the door, so I could leap to attention when Mr. Collins called, but also as it gave me a nice, if partial, view out of the taped-up window and over the tops of the buildings across the street.

It was time to get on with things. I opened the letter Kath had kept for me.

Dear Mrs. Bird,

I wanted to write to you to thank you for the advice you so kindly sent in response to my letter some weeks ago.

You will know me as In Love, the girl with the Polish airman, who was told not to marry him by her mother.

My stomach churned. So this was what Kath had wanted to show Mrs. Bird. Talk about a close shave.

Well, Mrs. Bird, I must tell you that my name is Dolly Wardynski, or rather, Mrs. Mieczslaw Wardynski. We were married yesterday!

I heard myself say "Oh" as I clamped my hand over my mouth with surprise. In the midst of everything horrible, this was just lovely.

I read your advice a hundred times and thought about things very carefully, just like you said I must. It made me sure that I don't mind whether I move to Europe with Mieczslaw after the war, or even to America or anywhere else. I know it may be difficult, but as long as we are together, I don't mind. But I did think about it tremendously carefully, and my husband (it is such a thrill to write that!) and I discussed it very sensibly and he gave me all the assurances in the world that it would all be just fine.

I had been worried about Mother, but you helped me be brave! Mother and Father aren't terribly pleased about it, but I am sure they will come round in the end.

Mrs. Bird, I can't thank you enough for your kindness. My husband is in a dangerous job and none of us really know what may happen next, but now I am his wife, I am the happiest girl in the world.

Yours ever,
Mrs. Mieczslaw Wardynski (Dolly)
Scotland

In Love had done it. Outside, a weak but plucky sun was trying to push through the March clouds, and my excitement for Dolly was only tempered by the sad fact that I couldn't tell anyone. Certainly no one at *Woman's Friend*, but my goodness, how Bunty would love to hear of such a lovely, happy ending.

I crashed back to earth with a bang.

Of course I couldn't tell Bunty. How could I have even considered it? A letter from a stranger who now had everything that Bunty had lost could not have been worse. And anyway, I hadn't even been truthful with her about continuing to write the secret letters in the first place. It was a heavy reminder that in terms of best friend behaviour, I was a pretty thin show.

With spirits plummeting, I barely heard Mr. Collins come into the room, only looking up as he took a chair from another desk and set it down beside me.

He didn't say anything but, looking thoughtful, leant towards me, his hands folded between his knees. He was my boss day to day, my new boyfriend's brother outside of work, and now a man with whom I had shared the most horrific experience. Eccentric, moody, funny, and now heroic Mr. Collins. He was not one for shows of emotion, but from the look on his face I could tell he was fighting with quite what to say. It would have been entirely inappropriate but infinitely more comforting if I could have put my arms around his neck and been a watery lettuce all over his coat. But that would have been a world gone quite mad.

In the end he reached over and touched my arm, which for an office situation was radical enough.

"Are you all right?" he said quietly. "You don't need to be here, you know."

I nodded and trotted out my now standard response that I was fine. He did one of his eyebrow raises and didn't reply. One of the things I had learnt in the last few weeks was that you couldn't bluff him.

"I'm going to resign," I blurted. "And apply to join one of the Services full-time."

Mr. Collins nodded.

"I see," he said.

"I've been thinking all week. I want to do something more useful."

I struggled to explain. "This isn't enough. And anyway, they'll start calling up women soon. So I'm going to resign."

I braced myself for a You're Being Too Hasty speech.

"Right you are," said Mr. Collins. "I can understand that. Is this your resignation?"

He took Dolly's letter that I was still holding and, before I could stop him, started to read.

"Goodness," he said, surprised. "Henrietta's actually helped. Wonders will never cease."

"She does sometimes," I butted in quickly.

"Good," said Mr. Collins, putting the letter back. He turned in his chair and looked out of the window. "Pleasant day. Spring's having a go."

He didn't look at me but continued to speak as he contemplated the view.

"Nice to know that old *Woman's Friend* isn't an entire waste of time. It's rather a shame you're off. I had a few ideas I'd hoped you could help me with." He turned and smiled at me very kindly. "Not to worry. I know Bunty must need you."

Mr. Collins could either read minds or had a sixth sense. I did want to join up, but if I was properly honest, and slightly to my own astonishment, I didn't really want to leave him and Kathleen just yet.

"I might want to stay until I actually get accepted," I said.

He nodded absently, looking at one of the noticeboards.

"Good point," he said. "They're frightfully slow on admissions sometimes. Ah now, I remember that article," he added, peering more closely at a yellowing snippet pinned to the wall, and appearing for all the world as if he was infinitely more interested in this than getting me to stay on. "Young chap wrote it. Wasn't too bad."

I wondered if the Government knew what an asset Mr. Collins would be in terms of getting what he wanted out of people. They should let him loose on some spies.

I crumbled. "Um, Mrs. Bird said you might need some more help? I'm sorry if I didn't sound keen."

"Under the circumstances, I think you're being a trouper," said Mr. Collins, finally looking me in the eye again. "Now, tell me how Bunty is doing and then I'll explain to you what it is that I need."

Chapter 23

WITH MUCH LOVE, EMMY

Mr. Collins suddenly had an inordinate amount of work that required my help. It seemed unlikely that he might be in cahoots with Mrs. Bird and on a secret mission to keep me busy, but either way, it certainly did. As well as typing up his work, he wanted me to give him ideas for stories people my age might like. One day he really surprised me.

"Can you write me five hundred words on working for the Fire Brigade?" he said. "It might be of interest to our readers, and an inside view could be quite good."

I stared at him goggle-eyed that something written by me might actually be printed in *Woman's Friend*, and then gave it a go. He said it wasn't bad for a first try and would I help him on a funny piece on The Ideal Secretary? After that he started asking me to do bits of research for him or write letters to organisations for information. He asked for article ideas that young women of my age might like and I came up with lists of suggestions. It was interesting and kept my mind busy. It even made me feel a little bit closer to being a journalist. Not that I was holding on to that dream anymore. But I enjoyed doing it and was grateful to him all the same.

I worked more hours at the magazine, staying long after I was supposed to go home, and I took on as many shifts at the station as they would allow. I went back to the flat to sleep and eat and write to Bunty—and Charles too a little—but other than that I kept going. If I sat down, I would think about what had happened.

I did anything I could to fill my time, but the one big thing I didn't do anymore was write to the readers. It didn't matter how much they needed help or how much Mrs. Bird might ignore them, I didn't write back.

Finally, I was doing what Bunty had told me.

It seemed a hundred years since she'd told me to stop, but even though I had felt bad about it, I'd still carried on. I couldn't bear to do that now.

It was horrible having to snub the readers, but I stuck to it. Mrs. Bird's moral code was still as impenetrable as ever and she either ignored the letters or sent replies that would frighten the life out of most people, let alone if you had written in because you felt a bit low.

I very nearly buckled and wrote back to one girl who I knew Mrs. Bird would make very short work of, but when I got to the signature, I stopped and tore it up. There would be no more writing to strangers and no more lying.

Instead, I wrote and wrote to Bunty—every day—hoping some of my letters might be read. It was like living but on paper, and not in the real world. I liked it better. You could rub things out or start all over again if you said the wrong thing. But Bunty didn't reply.

So I just kept writing. Sometimes about big things, like the memorial service they held for William, because even though I sat in church feeling as if I was the last person in the world who should be there, I thought that one day Bunty might want to hear just how beautiful it was.

Often, though, I wrote about nothing very important, just small things that she might like, and always when someone asked after her or sent their very best wishes. That was most of the time actually. Everyone wanted to know how she was. Everyone wanted her well.

Wednesday 19th March 1941

Dearest Bunty,

We have all been thinking of you today.

Mother phoned to tell me that this morning, Reverend Wiffle held a special service for you and Bill.

Mother did the flowers in the church. She picked your favourite daffodils from the garden. She said both they and the service were lovely. They will still be there on Friday for Bill.

With much love,

Emmy x

Saturday 22nd March 1941

Dearest Bunty,

I know if you read this, it will be dreadfully hard and I am so sorry if it is too much. I thought that perhaps one day you will want to know about the memorial service, so here it is in case.

Oh, Bunts, you would have been the proudest girl in the world yesterday. There were nearly three hundred people at the church. Bill's father came from Cardiff, of course, and the first thing he did was to ask after you.

Absolutely everyone from the village was there. Lots of Bill's old teachers—Mr. Lewis read the lesson and managed it very well.

As many of the boys as could came down from Carlton Street and lots from the local brigades too. Captain Davies did the most beautiful eulogy. He said Bill was one of the very best of men, the absolute *best. Afterwards he gave me the cards he had written it down on. I have enclosed them here for you.*

Roy and Fred brought a book with them. It is full of messages for you and things people wanted to say about Bill. I'm putting it in this parcel as well and your granny is going to bring it all to you to make sure nothing is lost in the post.

We sang "I Vow to Thee, My Country" and then the Brigade Choir sang "O Jesus, I Have Promised" as you had asked. Father said that when they sang, "I shall not fear the battle, if Thou art by my side," he thought the roof of the church would come off. They sang it with all their hearts.

I think I'll stop for now.

Thinking of you both.

With much love,

Emmy x

Saturday 29th March 1941

Dearest Bunty,

Your granny said that you are feeling a little better. I can't tell you how pleased we all are.

Thelma said she meant to send you peppermint creams as their Stanley used all this month's sugar on making some for you. But after he'd tasted one he became worried the rest might get squashed in the post. So to avoid disappointment he's hanging on to them until you are better. He is also worried that if someone doesn't eat them, they may very well go off.

I thought that might make you smile.

With much love,

Emmy x

Tuesday 8th April 1941

Dearest Bunty,

How are you feeling? I'm not sure if you're reading these letters, but I say to myself that you are and it makes it seem as if I am chatting with you.

Kathleen asked after you today. I told her you are doing tremendously well. She asked me to send you this shawl. She's been off with her tonsils again and knitted it while she was in bed. It's for when they let you out into the open air. She hopes you like it.

With much love,

Emmy x

PS: I asked Father and he says it's all right, you can't catch tonsillitis from wool.

Monday 14th April 1941

Dearest Bunty,

Your granny said you are leaving the hospital? I am so thrilled, really so very pleased.

It will be lovely for you to be back in the countryside and everyone will be terrifically glad to see you. London will be strange without you. I know we haven't seen each other, but it has been nice to think you are near.

Mr. Collins asks how are you? I said absolutely tremendously well.

Safe journey.

With much love,

Emmy x

PS: I am planning to come home the weekend after next for Mother's birthday, just in case you need anything brought down from the flat.

I continued to write every day. Bunty didn't reply.

Chapter 24

DEAR MRS. BIRD, PLEASE MIGHT YOU HELP?

While I tried to put things into the letters to Bunty that she might find interesting, or sometimes that might even make her smile, I gave little mention to what I was doing. Anything jolly would have looked as if I was having fun while she was on the ropes. Anything dreary would look as if I was moaning.

None of it was satisfactory, but I tried my best.

I wrote to Charles too—letters about nothing very much that tried to be entertaining. I talked about mundane, everyday things, which he said he liked as it was Normal Life. He had been terribly sorry to hear about William, of course, and ever so worried about us all. I had begun to receive regular letters from him, which should have been lovely, but I felt like a fraud for giving him updates about how marvellously well Bunty was doing, when I hadn't seen her for weeks. Nearly a month after the bomb, I couldn't bear it any longer. Even though I knew it was likely he would want to pack me in once he knew, I wrote to tell him the truth.

Dearest Charles,

Thank you so much for your latest letters—two came together yesterday, which was lovely.

I'm sorry I haven't written this week. I have been putting it off as there is something I must tell you about the Café de Paris. I should have told you weeks ago, after it happened, but I have been a coward.

You see, just before that night, William and I rowed—a horrible argument where I was very stupid and accused him of taking too many risks at work. It's all too rotten to go into, but I said some entirely unfair things and never managed to apologise properly. When I visited Bunty in hospital she told me that Bill was terribly concerned about it and when I was late for the dance, he went to look for me to patch things up. And that's when he was killed. There's more to it than that, but the fact is, it's my fault.

Bunty is terribly upset and I don't blame her. When I tell you she is doing well, it's really just what I have heard from her granny.

Charles, I've been a wretched friend to her and have no excuse. I am so sorry to write with such a horrible tale, but I can't lie to you anymore. If you don't want to write to me again, of course I will entirely understand.

You will take the most enormous care of yourself, won't you?

Your own,

Emmy xx

PS: I haven't told anyone at work about this, but if you feel you should tell your brother, I will understand of course.

I posted it with the heaviest heart and didn't expect to hear back. When his next letter arrived I could hardly bring myself to open it.

My Darling Emmy,

I am writing in haste as we are moving camp again tonight, but I had to write back to you straightaway. I have just read your letter and I wish more than anything I was there with you. I should like to put my arms around you and tell you that I think you have been terrifically brave about what happened at the Café de Paris. I am also going to be rather hard on you now and make you promise me something—you must not *blame yourself. Not for one moment. Are you listening, my darling?*

We may not have known each other very long, but I feel I know you would never do anything to hurt William or Bunty. I know you care for them both very much. I hope it is not out of turn for me to say that I thought William a very decent and fine man and I am sure as such he would understand that you only meant well.

It must be terrible for you to be so worried about Bunty. She will come round in time, I am sure.

Keep going, Darling—write to me when you can—your letters do cheer me up—but tell me if you are sad or worried and I won't mind, I promise.

Yours with love,
Charles xxx

PS: I won't mention this to Guy. x

He had never written With Love before. I read the letter dozens of times. It was such a relief and he had been nicer than I could possibly have hoped. It was a tiny shaft of light and kept me going on the worst of days, even if I didn't think he was right about Bunty coming round in the end.

I still kept writing to her, though. Every time I posted a letter it was always with my fingers crossed that she would write back, but it didn't do any good. Mrs. Tavistock kept Mother and Father updated, and in turn, they would call me with any news. There was always Lots Of Progress but always tempered with But Bunty Is Awfully Tired and The Doctors Say She Really Must Rest. Even Father didn't have any news now because Mrs. Tavistock had hired a private nurse to look after her and some fancy doctor who was apparently Terrifically Good.

I missed my best friend like anything. And I missed my friend William too. Even though everyone at the fire station put on their best and bravest faces, we all knew he had left a huge hole. I still struggled to accept we wouldn't see him again.

After Bunty was moved out of London to the country, the chance of seeing her was less likely than ever, but I had to admit a part of me was glad she would be further from harm's way. Having failed so far, Hitler decided to have a really good crack at finishing us off, and as the weather cheered up, so did the Luftwaffe. The raids, although intermittent, had become heavier again. It was almost worse than when it was every night. You never quite knew if it would be us in London or the turn of Bristol or Sunderland or Cardiff. There wasn't much relief to be had when you knew that someone, somewhere was having the worst of it. It wouldn't get Hitler anywhere of course, but even Joan, who enjoyed near gladiatorial resilience, gloomily asked if That Evil Bugger was ever going to stop having a go?

Extra shifts at the fire station and longer hours at *Woman's Friend* had certainly kept me busy and I was grateful for it too. I hated being on my own but didn't have the heart to go out with the girls, although they kept trying and sometimes made me join in.

It was nearly two months since the Café de Paris and despite the cheer of an early May sun, sometimes it felt as if I had become a sort of automaton, forging on with everything with an amount of vim which wasn't genuine. Still, I knew that sort of defeatism wasn't the right spirit, and on a bright morning where spring appeared to be telling summer to get a move on and turn up for work, I marched through the foyer on my way up to *Woman's Friend*, waving a hello to the receptionist.

I got into the lift, wondering if I could have a quick nap during the ride up three floors. Two journalists from *The Evening Chronicle* were discussing a big story they thought would break, but without mentioning any names. A few months ago I would have eavesdropped like mad, hoping to get a hint of an exclusive. Now I closed my eyes and willed the lift to get stuck so I could sit on the floor and nod off.

"Morning, Kath," I called as I pushed open the doors into the long dark corridor of *Woman's Friend* and poked my head round Kathleen's door on my way down to the larger office I had now almost permanently made home. She was usually as keen as me to have a chat, but today her chair was empty and there was no coat on the stand.

Instead, Mrs. Bird loomed out of her office with a thunderous face and the news that Kathleen's mother had telephoned to say she had a rotten bout of tonsillitis and would have to have them taken out War On Or Not. It was a display of dazzling weakness as far as Mrs. Bird was concerned.

"Should have been done as a child," she said. "Miss Lake, you will have to muck in. Mr. Collins will have to manage without you."

With that, I was installed back in Kath's room and given a heap of typing to do before being sent on an errand to North London which involved some sharp words and a parcel smelling strongly of farms.

Within the day I had a newfound respect for Kathleen. For someone who wasn't in the office very much, Mrs. Bird generated an enormous amount of work. It wasn't what you could call relaxing. Copy checking all the patterns, which took Kathleen about ten minutes, took me hours. Kath always knew where everything was, had the magazine contributors' phone numbers and addresses in her head, and, without making the slightest fuss, always managed to find a way to sort everything. I was sent on no end of missions too, invariably to deliver Important Parcels to Mrs. Bird's Good Works or to queue up for Vital Supplies that she couldn't manage without.

By the end of that week, it was safe to say our small team couldn't wait to have Kathleen back. I tried hard but often failed to understand Mrs. Bird's shouted, coded instructions, Mr. Collins had to step up and start doing most of his own admin, and Mr. Newton from Advertising had to come in more often. Mrs. Bird permanently complained that everything was a bother. No one had the heart to disagree.

It also meant I'd had very little time to sift through the readers' letters, so the following Monday I arrived early to catch up on the post. It was quite a chipper little pile of correspondence, starting with a letter to Mr. Collins' film column asking for a signed photograph, which cheered me up. I couldn't wait to see the look on Mr. Collins' face when he saw that. It might give him some sort of attack.

I carried on, opening an envelope addressed to Henrietta Helps. The letter was from a reader who at forty-five was struggling with A Difficult Chin. It was exactly the sort of letter Mrs. Bird enjoyed, although I felt sorry for Difficult Chin, who was likely to be told off for appalling amounts of vanity At Her Age.

The next one was rather odd, however. Typed rather than handwritten and with no stamp or return address, it was written to Mrs. Bird, and signed Anxious.

I turned to the beginning and started to read.

Dear Mrs. Bird,

Please might you be able to help?

I feel ashamed to write to you but I don't know what else to do. You see, I am letting everyone down. Earlier this year I was caught up in an air raid and was injured, and now I think I have lost my nerve. Whenever I hear guns or even loud noises, I jump out of my skin. I don't like going outside or leaving the house and I am worried that I will never be my old self again.

I stopped for a moment. I had read letters like this one before. Readers who had been through an absolute time of it, really dreadful, but who now felt embarrassed as they thought they were no longer pulling their weight.

They shouldn't have to feel this way, of course. No one should be expected to just buck up after being through something awful. I realised that more than ever now. Even before the bomb at the Café de Paris I had felt tremendously sorry for the women who wrote in about feeling scared or suddenly finding themselves afraid of bangs and crashes or even just the dark when they never had been before. I had written to several trying to be kindly and had petitioned Mrs. Bird to answer one in the magazine, but she had given no quarter.

"Spines, Miss Lake," she said. "That's what these women need. Nerviness will not win us the war. They should pull themselves together and crack on."

It was Mrs. Bird at her worst, rejecting anything she saw as weak. She expected everyone to be limitlessly resilient, relentlessly tough. No wonder people felt dreadful if that's what they were up against.

As far as I was concerned, it was perfectly reasonable to be scared of someone dropping a bomb on you. No one in their right mind would become blasé about that. It didn't mean you were weak or didn't want to soldier on.

I chewed my bottom lip. Perhaps I was just biased.

But no, I wasn't. This reader—and all the others who had written to Mrs. Bird; in fact *any* of us, come to that—had decent reason to feel wobbly. I was absolutely sure that what they needed was some friendly support, not a lecture on spinelessness.

I returned to the letter.

I promise I am absolutely not giving up. I am going to go back to work as soon as they will let me and I can move a bit more. But I am worried as I know I will be nervy, which is unpatriotic and wrong, and I feel such a coward for being so low.

I lost my fiancé recently, and since he was killed I don't think I will ever want to love anyone again.

I bent closer to the words.

I don't even want to speak to people, not even my best friends.

Could this possibly be from Bunty?

I miss him dreadfully, I can't even tell you how much, but I know that there are lots of people far worse off than me and I should buck up. There are hundreds of girls of my age doing war work, looking after their families, and pulling their weight, and I am ashamed to admit I get scared, especially when I hear the siren or planes.

I expect by now you think me very weak, but I worry that awful things will happen again. In your magazine you write about what we must do for the war effort. What should I do when all I feel is useless and alone?

Yours sincerely,

Anxious

I put the letter down on my desk, sat back in my chair, and looked around the office, as if the answer might be sitting there looking at me.

Then I tutted in frustration and looked at the envelope. The postmark said Cheltenham. That was nowhere near Bunty and I knew for a fact she didn't know anyone there. But still.

It had been a wild moment when I'd thought it might have been from her. Silliness itself. If Bunty wanted to speak, she would have written to me, not Mrs. Bird of all people. I let out a big sigh, feeling horribly flat.

Poor Anxious. I read through her letter again and felt awful for this girl at her lowest ebb. What if Bunty was feeling like that as well? Just so very down and not even able to confide in her best friend?

I should write to Bunty about it. I should write to her about this other girl. Perhaps it would help her or even turn things around?

Dear Bunty,

There was this girl who wrote in to Mrs. Bird who was frightened and feeling dreadful and couldn't face anyone and was embarrassed that she was scared.

And it made me think of you . . .

Oh yes, that was exactly the sort of letter you'd want to receive after being squashed half to bits and losing your fiancé because of the woman who was now writing to tell you how wretched and ashamed you must be.

I shook off thoughts of my friend. It didn't actually matter that it wasn't from Bunty; it was still enormously sad. A reader who had lost almost everything but was desperate to get back up and do more, to respond to the call to pitch in.

I realised I didn't just feel sorry for this girl. I felt proud of her. Enormously proud that she was brave enough to admit she was scared.

After all, could any of us truly say we had not felt like this once in a while? Secretly? Just to ourselves so that we wouldn't let anyone else down?

I remembered watching William and the boys trying to get the children out of that bombed-out house. I had stood on the pavement scared out of my wits, feeling useless, terrified that one or all of them would get crushed to death. I had been scared as I ran toward Coventry Street, dreading what I might find as the bombs fell on the Café de Paris. And how many times had I jumped when the phone rang too early in the morning, or very late at night, in case it was bad news?

But I never told anyone, because that's not what one did. The papers and radio and even magazines like ours went on about pluck and bravery and spirit. They talked about battles fought, advances made. They talked about everyone stepping up to the mark, keeping homes going, keeping things the same for when the men came home because that's what they were fighting for. Making sure you still looked nice, what hair to have, how you mustn't let yourself go because that would show Hitler he would never get us down. And on top of keeping the home front going after six months of bombing, we expected our readers to keep a pretty blouse and the last of the rouge ready for special dates and romance when their men came home on leave.

How often did we say well done to our readers? How often did anyone ever tell women they were doing a good job? That they didn't have to be made of steel all the time? That it was all right to feel a bit down?

I knew how Anxious was feeling; I knew she needed a friend.

It had been weeks since I last wrote to a reader, sticking like glue to my promise not to get into trouble or let Bunty down. No more letters, no sneaking things into the magazine. Just ignoring them, no matter how much I thought I could have helped.

But this was different. This one I had to write back to and try to help. I opened the top drawer of my desk, pulled out a fresh piece of paper, and fed it into my typewriter.

Dear Anxious,

Thank you very much for your letter. I am so sorry to hear you have had such a time of it. We all hope you will get well very soon and we send our most sincere condolences for the loss of your fiancé.

Without thinking about it, I clicked into the big-sister style I had always tried to use for readers' letters. I tried to sound like the sort of person you could trust, who understood and was your friend when things were awful.

Now then. You may find this a surprise, but I want to say Well Done You for writing your letter to me. I am going to be very clear with you here and you must listen and take my advice. You are not a coward, you are not letting anyone down, and in fact you should be very proud of yourself for doing your best when things are at their worst.

You have been injured and lost someone you loved very much. Don't for a moment think that feeling low or scared is cowardly or wrong. I am sure our other readers will not mind my saying that many of us understand exactly how you feel.

We are all doing our absolute best to ensure that we win this war, and because of girls like you, win it we shall. Feeling low when something awful has happened shows that you are a normal and very decent person. Anyone in their right mind would feel down if they'd lost someone they love.

That right mind is exactly what we are fighting for and why a certain madman will never win.

I paused for a moment. I *knew* I was right, and I wanted Anxious to know too. I typed more quickly, the typewriter clattering away, the keys nearly jamming as I went as fast as I could.

All over the civilised world, women like you are caring deeply about their loved ones and pushing on with things in very difficult times, just as you are trying to do. If Hitler had his way, no one would ever care about anyone or anything other than him and his appalling ideas.

Well, my dear, you must know that that is fascism and Hitler is a fool.

The day we stop caring or showing we are human is the day we might just as well give in. So don't you worry about feeling watery at present. You may not realise it, but you have probably been trying just a little too hard to be brave. Don't be shy to chat to your friends about it. It isn't unpatriotic to share a worry with a close pal, and perhaps you'll find you may be able to help each other along.

I hesitated before trying to write the last part of my letter. Was there anything I could say that might help?

Finally, I'm afraid there isn't an easy answer about ever loving again. Give yourself time. You'll never have to forget your lost love and you don't have to find a new one right away. I wish I could wave a magic wand for you—sadly I can't. But always know that you are not alone.

Everyone here at Woman's Friend *knows that you and so many of our readers are making the most tremendous effort and being quite extraordinarily brave.*

We are inordinately proud to stand with you all.

And then I stopped. Usually I would sign off with "Yours sincerely, Mrs. H. Bird" and start to write out the envelope, but then I remembered this one had no return address.

I released the clamp and pulled the paper out of the typewriter, placing it on my desk before leaning on my elbows and putting my fingers into my hair.

Mrs. Bird would never consider answering this letter in the magazine. Even if I threw caution to the wind and tried to sneak it into Henrietta Helps, it was far too long to squeeze in with the other letters and hope no one would notice. It would take up most of the Problem Page on its own. There was nothing for it but to throw both the letter and my reply into the wastepaper bin.

A sharp gust of wind blew through the open window, making the papers flutter on my desk. I slapped my hand on top of them protectively.

It just wouldn't do. I didn't want this letter to be lost. This girl deserved better than being ignored. Our readers deserved better. Bunty deserved better.

I got up from my desk and went over to shut the window. Then I paced to the other end of the room and back again. Any minute now Mrs. Bird would be in, shouting orders before exiting the office on one of her Good Works and leaving the rest of us to push on. We really were missing Kathleen. There had been more hoo-has since she went on sick leave than I had seen in all my other weeks at *Woman's Friend.*

Who, after all, had time to check Henrietta Helps? With Kathleen away, who would even spot if the Problem Page looked a bit different than usual? Who would notice if it consisted of just one letter and just one reply?

It was a crazy idea.

As my heart thundered like mad in my chest, I put the letter along with my reply into a large buff envelope and handwrote Mrs. Mahoney "HENRIETTA HELPS SPECIAL—TO BE TYPESET" on the front.

A familiar voice boomed out from somewhere in the corridor.

"MISS LAKE? IS ANYBODY THERE?"

As ever, it sounded like someone was using a foghorn at a séance.

"Coming, Mrs. Bird," I called, getting up and bracing myself for more shouts.

"NO NEED TO SHOUT," she replied.

Putting the envelope for Mrs. Mahoney into the out-tray on my desk and telling myself that everything would be fine, I hurried off to answer her call.

Chapter 25

MY NAME IS MRS. EILEEN TREDMORE

The buff envelope went to Mrs. Mahoney and the typesetters. If I had second thoughts about it, which in the dead of night, *every* night, I did, it was too late. The letter from Anxious and my reply were going to be in the magazine. And they were going to take up almost the entire half page of Henrietta Helps. I had never done anything as risky as this.

I tried to put it out of my mind and concentrate on other things. And soon it was a case of Break Out The Flags for us all when a week later Kathleen returned. I was on my way to her office with stationery supplies when her smiley face poked through the main doors to the *Woman's Friend* office. She waved enthusiastically with both hands in a jazzy way while whispering a Hello. Her throat was still sore but she was here.

"Oh, Kath, it's so wonderful to see you," I said, giving her a big hug. I was thrilled to have my friend back, and it wasn't because she would take on the full weight of Mrs. Bird. The office had been a far drearier place without her.

"Mrs. Bird has been like a bear with a sore head while you've been away," I said. "And she's been saying nice things about you."

I'd meant this as a compliment but Kathleen looked alarmed.

"No, that's good," I said quickly. "She says you know what's what, which is more than can be said for the rest of us."

"Crikey," rasped Kathleen. We both knew that was about as good as it got.

"She'll be pleased you're back," I said, knowing full well Mrs. Bird would rather launch herself under a bus than admit it.

Kathleen looked delighted, which was the main thing. She jolly well deserved it too. It was lovely to have her back in the office and my spirits were higher than they had been in weeks.

Standing in the corridor, despite the fact she wasn't supposed to be making a sound, Kath and I fell into easy conversation. I'd been sent out on another Mrs. Bird Mission the day before, which had involved going to Fortnum & Mason to look for butter that came in a tin. It was a far cry from my early dreams of being a War Correspondent and I turned it into a funny story so that Kath would think everything was absolutely fine.

I was just acting out a spectacular part of the anecdote where I played the role of two sales assistants, a man with a parakeet, and myself when Mr. Collins arrived, relatively on time for once, and Kath insisted I start the whole story again. I hammed it up even more and for the first time in ages the corridor was filled with the noise of laughter. Waving a stapler in the air for effect, I got to the punchline of the story.

"And he said, 'I don't think so, do you, Gladys?' " I finished, with a flourish, and my colleagues laughed even more.

It was at that moment Mrs. Bird arrived.

As soon as I saw her, I knew that something was very wrong.

For once Mrs. Bird was silent. She had glided into the corridor, almost as if she were on wheels, with no bustling or loud announcements. Her face was set, not just unsmiling, which I was used to, but with a look of absolute venom.

Kathleen and Mr. Collins had their backs to her, but as my smile had disappeared, they both looked round and quickly moved to the side of the corridor in case she wanted to pass through. Mrs. Bird ignored them. She didn't take her eyes off me.

Mr. Collins glanced first at her and then at me.

"Good morning, Mrs. Bird," he said, entirely properly.

Mrs. Bird did not answer.

"Good morning, Mrs. Bird," echoed Kathleen and I together.

Mrs. Bird continued to stare. I had never seen anyone look so icy. None of us moved. Then, still without looking away, Mrs. Bird reached into her enormous black bag and pulled out a piece of paper.

"This," she said in an ominous voice, "is a letter."

If I had ever found her shouting on the scary side, it was nothing compared to this. Her face was white and she looked as if she might explode.

"This is a letter that was sent to me," she said through her teeth. "Which, in the absence of staff support, I opened myself yesterday. Miss Lake, would you like to know what it says?"

I managed to nod.

Still glaring at me, Mrs. Bird handed the piece of paper to Mr. Collins. "Mr. Collins. If you would be so kind."

Mr. Collins took it from her without speaking. I hoped, rather than expected, that he might make a comment, say something to lighten the mood, which sometimes he was able to do. Now, however, he just did as he was told.

" 'Dear Mrs. Bird,' " he began. " 'My name is Mrs. Eileen Tredmore. I believe you are in personal contact with my daughter, who you will know as Mrs. Mieczslaw Wardynski.' "

Mr. Collins looked up at Mrs. Bird and then over to me. I must have gone even whiter than Mrs. Bird. So much blood had rushed out of my face that I had to catch my breath to make sure I didn't pass out. As soon as I heard the name, I knew I had finally been caught.

"Do read on, Mr. Collins," said Mrs. Bird.

Mr. Collins cleared his throat tentatively and continued.

" 'Mrs. Wardynski is my daughter. Her name is Dolly Tredmore and she is seventeen years old. Until last month she lived with my husband and me at our home in Uxbridge, Middlesex.' "

I swallowed. My throat felt desert dry. Seventeen was terribly young to get married, even during a war. I hadn't thought that Dolly might have been quite so young. She must have needed her parents' permission to marry. *I had been worried about Mother*, she had written, *but you helped me be brave . . .*

I had assumed she had been able to talk her parents around.

"'You should know,'" read Mr. Collins, "'that some weeks ago my daughter eloped to Scotland with a twenty-one-year-old man she thinks she is in love with. Against our wishes, without our consent, and—as I have recently found out—based on your advice.'"

He stopped reading and, running his free hand through his hair, turned to Mrs. Bird. "I do apologise, Mrs. Bird, but I don't quite understand."

Mrs. Bird at last dragged her steely glare away from me.

"I think you will find, Mr. Collins," she said, "that Miss Lake has been playing a little game."

I started thinking like mad. How on earth had Mrs. Bird decided it was from me, and more to the point, what could I possibly say in my defence?

"I . . ."

"Forged my signature. Badly," spat Mrs. Bird, who was holding on to her temper by a thread. "Mrs. Tredmore was good enough to include the letter her daughter had received, on *Woman's Friend*–headed paper, signed in blue-black ink by a Mrs. Henrietta Bird. An appalling communication I most certainly did not write, with a signature in a colour I never use. Although, I believe, one which is favoured by Miss Lake. Not to mention the fact that you, Miss Lake, are the only person who has access to my readers' correspondence."

She loomed towards me.

"Really, Miss Lake," said Mrs. Bird. "It is hardly a case worthy of Agatha Christie, do you not think? Unless you are going to suggest that someone else is involved?"

There was no alternative but to come clean.

"I'm sorry," I said in the smallest voice ever. "It was me. I wanted to help."

If I had believed confessing was a good idea, I was entirely wrong. Mr. Collins and Kathleen whirled round to look at me, mouths open in surprise. Kathleen's horror was bad enough, but far worse was Mr. Collins, who looked absolutely appalled.

"I really am very sorry, Mrs. Bird," I said again. "I didn't mean to pretend I was you."

As the words came out, they sounded more and more feeble. How does one write an entire letter, sign it in another name, address it, send it, and *still* not mean to pretend to be someone else?

I had become too used to doing it. While I had written in Mrs. Bird's name, the concern and words of advice were my own. It had made perfect sense to me. Mrs. Bird wouldn't even look at these letters and I was just stepping in to help out.

Now it sounded ridiculous.

I was still clutching the stapler that five minutes ago I had been waving around, showing off to make people laugh. My hands were now sweating so much I could hardly keep hold of it. I had often wondered what would happen if I was found out, but I had never properly imagined the effect it would have on my friends.

To her enduring credit and going far beyond the call of duty, Kathleen spoke up.

"Perhaps, Mrs. Bird," she whispered, "it was a silly mistake? I'm sure Emmeline didn't mean any—"

I couldn't let Kathleen go down in flames for me. It was already a dead cert I was going to get the sack. It would be even worse if I dragged my friend down into the bargain.

"It's all right, Kathleen," I butted in across her. "Thank you, but it's all right. This is entirely my fault. I really am terribly sorry, Mrs. Bird. I'll go and get my things now."

I moved towards the office to pick up my coat and hat. I really wasn't sure if she was about to call the security guards or throw me out into the street by herself.

But Mrs. Bird was having none of it.

"Exactly WHAT do you think you're doing?" she cried, finally losing her rag. "You don't honestly think you can walk out of here just like that? Miss Lake, are you deranged?"

Her face was now a furious purple.

"How many?" she hissed. "How many of these have you done?"

Kathleen looked at me in desperation, clearly willing me to say Just The One.

"I'm not sure," I said, which was the truth. I did some sums in my head. It was actually quite a lot when you added them all up. "Um. About. Possibly . . . thirty? Or a few more?"

I felt myself blush. If the others thought it was because I felt guilty, they were wrong. It was because I had lost count.

I didn't dare even think about the letters I had sneaked into the magazine. If Mrs. Bird found out about those, I dreaded to think what she would do.

"Thirty?" Kathleen gasped, eyes like soup plates. Even Mrs. Bird was taken aback.

"Jesus Christ, Emmy," said Mr. Collins under his breath, and Mrs. Bird shot him a withering look.

I could hardly look at him. He had bowed his head and wouldn't look at me. He just kept his eyes fixed on the floor.

I had to admit, thirty sounded an enormous amount. You couldn't explain this away as a well-meaning mistake. I had gone behind everyone's back on a huge scale.

Mrs. Bird was just managing to keep hold of herself. "I see," she said. "All of them, all written in my name?"

I nodded miserably. I wanted to say they were all to people who I hoped I, we, *Woman's Friend*, had helped. That quite a few had written back to say thank you, including readers who had read the two problems I had put into the magazine and felt bolstered by the reply. And that actually, whatever her mother might think, Dolly Wardynski had married the man she loved and was now wonderfully happy. But I didn't say any of this. Because in the very cold light of the *Woman's*

Friend corridor, writing letters as somebody else, whatever the reason, was just plain wrong.

"Miss Lake," said Mrs. Bird. "Do you realise how serious this is? I barely know where to begin. Fraud, libel, defamation of character . . . The police will take this very seriously indeed."

"The police?" It came out of my mouth in a squeak.

"Of course."

Mrs. Bird paused, and before she could speak further, Mr. Collins leapt in.

"Now let's hold hard, everyone. Let's just all remain very, very calm," he said as Mrs. Bird turned an enraged face to him. "Henriet . . . Mrs. Bird, please." He fought for the right thing to say. "Miss Lake has been a very stupid young woman." He gave me a look almost as angry as hers. "But I am sure we can handle this difficult matter without the need for the police."

I could tell he was thinking fast on his feet. "After all, there might be, er, Publicity. Yes. Which could be even *more* damaging for Launceston Press."

It was an inspired argument and I wanted to hurl myself at him and thank him a hundred thousand times.

"I am sure," he finished, "that this can be handled in the appropriate way within Launceston's own walls."

"I have already informed Lord Overton," said Mrs. Bird.

Lord Overton. Now I did feel sick. The man who was in charge of everything. The man I would have given anything to impress.

The chips were well and truly down. But Mr. Collins did not give up.

"And rightly so," he said, heroically managing to combine respect, charm, and concern all at the same time. "Lord Overton will know entirely the best thing to do. In full consultation with yourself, of course."

Mrs. Bird pursed her lips and thought for a very long moment indeed. She may have been beside herself with anger and two steps away from calling the police, but she was also enormously loyal to Launceston and the Overton name.

"Hmm," she said. "I will see." And then she straightened herself up to her full formidable height and, as if having to address me was the most distasteful task of her life, said simply, "Miss Lake, you have misrepresented me, my magazine, your employers, and your colleagues, who perhaps thought of you as a friend. If you are lucky enough for me not to press charges—and there is no guarantee of that—be aware that the termination of your job and the reference I shall write will mean any career you might have followed is over. You are suspended without pay, with immediate effect. Mr. Collins, the boardroom."

And with that, she turned on her heels and swept out of the door.

There was the most awful silence. Kathleen looked as if she would rather be anywhere else on earth and Mr. Collins looked as if he was having a battle with himself as he struggled for something to say.

Mrs. Bird was right. I had let my friends down terribly.

The look on their faces was awful.

"Kathleen, Mr. Collins," I started. "I am so, *so* very sorry. I was trying to help. I didn't think it would—"

Mr. Collins held up his hand to stop me.

"Emmy," he said, looking at me at last. "What the hell have you done?"

Kathleen looked even more distraught than before. If Mr. Collins was at a loss, what hope was there?

I opened my mouth to try to apologise again, but Mr. Collins cut me off.

"No," he said. "I really don't want to know. Just wait here until I get back. And for God's sake, try not to wreck anything else in the meantime."

And then he left.

For a moment Kathleen and I stood still. I had no idea what she was thinking, but I was frantically trying to find something to say that would convince her I had only meant well. It mattered enormously to me what she thought.

Finally, she spoke. She still looked terribly upset and you could tell she was thinking about every word.

"It's all right," she said slowly. "Mr. Collins will sort it out. It will all be all right."

Dear Kathleen. Dear, good-hearted Kathleen, who always looked for the bright side of things.

"I don't think so, Kath," I said. "I've really done it this time."

At that moment, the *Woman's Friend* doors opened once again and I jumped three feet into the air, expecting to see Mrs. Bird flanked by the police. But to my unbounded relief it was Clarence, holding a bundle of this week's new issue.

"Good morning," he said with some uncertainty. It was clear something was going on. "I have your house copies."

"Thank you, Clarence," said Kathleen, and for once Clarence didn't go red or panic at her voice. He handed the bundle to me as if it were an unexploded bomb and rushed out of the doors as fast as he could.

"Well," said Kath, mustering a brave smile, "at least we have something to read while we wait."

I didn't have it in me to smile back as I followed her into the tiny office.

"You will let me explain, won't you, Kath?" I said.

"Of course," she replied, her voice hoarse. "I'm not supposed to be speaking anyway."

She began to take her hat and coat off, leaning over to hang them on the stand in the corner of the room.

I put the package down on her desk. As usual the printers had wrapped the copies in a bigger, uncut section of the magazine. The familiar heading of the Henrietta Helps page stared out at me.

There it was. As clear as day. The letter from Anxious I had put into the magazine.

Chapter 26

ABSOLUTELY NOTHING TO LOSE

As soon as Mr. Collins came back from the boardroom, I told him about putting the letter into the magazine. In print, the letter and my answer had taken up most of the page. As reality finally struck, even I wondered what must I have been thinking.

I'd assumed Mr. Collins would go into a fury. Instead, after a moment's disbelief, he looked utterly defeated, which was actually far worse. After saying Jesus Christ (twice), he went very quiet before finally giving his response.

"I'm very sorry, Emmy," he said. "But I don't know how I'm going to be able to fix this."

And then I was sent home.

I didn't know what to do.

I walked back to the flat in a daze, barely noticing my surroundings and taking far longer than the hour it normally should. Usually if I walked, I played my favourite guessing game as I left *Woman's Friend* and headed along Fleet Street. Who was a journalist? Who was hurrying back to their office with a scoop of the highest order? Just a few months ago I had thought I might count myself among them. Today, I kept my head down. I had nothing to do with journalism now.

I half-heartedly looked for a bus, but I didn't want to sit or be still. If I sat down on the bus, I might just put my head in my hands and howl. Instead, I desperately tried to pull round. What a dismal article I was.

It was a normal working morning to everyone else and as I walked along Victoria Embankment I wondered if anyone could tell that I was well and truly done for. Everyone else seemed to have somewhere to go, something important to do. Post boys running past with packages, important looking civil servant types on their way to the Ministry of Supply, women from the suburbs blinking in the May sunshine as they made their way around the sandbags and out of the Underground.

I wanted to run away or hide or just not exist for a while. How could I possibly set things right?

I had no idea how long it would be until I heard from Mr. Collins or Mrs. Bird. The thought of waiting at the flat in the quiet, surrounded by memories of Bunty and Bill, was too much. I supposed I could go home to my parents but the thought of telling them covered me with shame.

I walked the long way home, lingering along Millbank and staring into the Thames. Tonight I would have to turn up for my shift at the fire station with a bright smile and look them all in the eye. What would Thelma think of me? Of our secret, thoughtful chats about the readers? Would she now think I had just been using her for advice?

And as for telling Charles. I let out a groan and a lady pushing a pram looked at me in alarm.

Would Mr. Collins tell him? I wouldn't blame him if he wrote immediately to inform his brother what kind of a girl he had nearly got himself involved with. I couldn't bear to think of it. Charles had been so lovely in his letters, so concerned after the Café de Paris. He was always optimistic and tried to make things at his end sound all right, and he had been quite extraordinarily decent when I wrote to him about William. But I was sure this would be a step too far. Whether he found out from his brother or me, I shouldn't think he would ever want to hear from me again once he was aware of the truth.

With every step things felt worse. I had let so many people down. Most of all, though, I would have to explain myself to my best friend.

Dear, lovely Bunty. Now, more than ever, I wished we were still friends. Bunty would know what to do. Of course, I wouldn't blame her if she flew into a rage at me for messing everything up so dreadfully at work. But I knew she would have stuck by me.

As I finally arrived back at the flat, I had made up my mind. I had absolutely nothing to lose.

Before it became official and all my family and friends discovered the truth, I would have one more go at speaking to Bunty. One last try to tell her in person how sorry I was.

The phone was in the hallway on the ground floor. It was jade green, which was both unusual and enormously showy, and Bunty had persuaded Mrs. Tavistock to buy it the year before last. Mrs. Tavistock loathed it and said it was the sort of thing actors and mistresses would have, but she'd got it all the same.

It brought a sad smile to my face as I sat down by the rosewood console table and, before I could change my mind, dialled the operator to make the trunk call.

"Hello, Mrs. Vincent," I said to Mrs. Tavistock's housekeeper when I was put through. "This is Emmeline Lake speaking. May I speak with Mrs. Tavistock, please?"

Mrs. Vincent hesitated and then said she would see if Bunty's granny was at home. I waited, getting to my feet with fidgety nerves and twisting the green cord of the telephone around my fingers. After several minutes I heard the receiver being picked up.

"Emmeline. How nice," said Bunty's granny. "Are you well?"

"Yes, thank you, Mrs. Tavistock," I lied. "I hope you are very well too?"

Mrs. Tavistock confirmed that she was and asked about the weather in London. I confirmed that it was fine and asked after the weather in Little Whitfield, which, it turned out, was fine as well.

Everything, it appeared, was equally first-rate.

Finally, after enduring a torturously pleasant conversation about the late-spring flowers in Mrs. Tavistock's gardens, I plucked up the courage.

"Mrs. Tavistock," I launched in. "Would it be possible to speak with Bunty, please? That is, if she is feeling strong enough for me to say a hello?"

It was the first time I had dared to ask since the hospital. I was still twisting the phone cord, which was now in danger of being pulled so tight it might break.

I held my breath. Even with everything else so utterly awful and hopeless, if I could just say hello, if Bunty would just let me ask how she was, then none of the rest of it would matter.

Mrs. Tavistock didn't reply straightaway. Then she cleared her throat and spoke very gently.

"I'm sorry, Emmeline," she said. "Bunty isn't feeling well enough to speak on the telephone."

There was a short silence as I searched for a reply. I had a Plan B up my sleeve which perhaps would catch Mrs. Tavistock off guard.

"Righto," I said, trying to sound upbeat. "Then perhaps I could pop in and see her instead? Only for a minute. She wouldn't have to get up to come to the phone or do anything tiring really. Just sit there. Just for a minute."

But Mrs. Tavistock was not easily swayed.

"I'm so sorry, Emmeline," she said. "But Bunty isn't seeing anyone. You see, she has gone away. I'm sorry, Emmy," she said again. "Bunty does not want to speak."

Chapter 27

LORD OVERTON HIMSELF

Mrs. Tavistock couldn't give me details of where Bunty was but said she would pass on my very best regards. After that I lost hope. I spent the next days going for long walks by the river and trying not to think of the future. Or of anything much at all.

A week later, it was almost a relief to get called to Launceston House, even if it was to face Lord Overton himself. As far as Mrs. Bird was concerned, sacking me on the spot was an easy way out. With Anxious's letter now printed in the magazine, it seemed almost inevitable that she would carry out her threat to press charges. I had no idea what I would do then.

At half past twelve on the day I was to face one of the most influential men in the whole of publishing at a disciplinary hearing, Mr. Collins was nowhere to be seen. I had thought he would be there, but I was alone. I couldn't blame him for bailing out. I wondered if I would ever see him, or his brother, again.

I had never actually seen the owner and Chairman of Launceston Press until now, but as I stood in Lord Overton's office wearing my very best suit and wondering just how angry he would be, I recognised him immediately. The life-size portrait that dominated the marbled entrance hall was a good likeness, and even if it hadn't been, every floor in the building featured a large photograph of him looking statesmanlike and severe. Now here he was, a towering figure with huge white eyebrows, sitting behind a gigantic teak desk, just the sort I had once imagined the Acting Editress of *Woman's Friend* would have.

To the side of his desk sat a granite-faced Mrs. Bird, rigid with latent fury in her enormous black feathered coat.

"So, Miss Lake," said Lord Overton, looking through half-moon spectacles at what I assumed was a document listing my offences. "Am I to understand that you *purposely gave advice to the* Woman's Friend *readers using Mrs. Bird's name*?"

It seemed even worse when he put it like that.

Lord Overton sounded as if he were speaking to someone entirely beyond reason.

"Yes, sir," I said. "I'm afraid I did. Although not exactly on purpose," I added, which made Mrs. Bird nearly fall off her chair.

"I object!" she cried, turning to Lord Overton and looking apoplectic.

The Chairman raised an eyebrow.

"Lord Overton," said Mrs. Bird, rustling in her chair. "Not only using my name but *abusing* my name and that of *Woman's Friend* and Launceston Press, with the most ill-informed, dangerous rubbish. I shudder to think what she has told other readers. And in addition," she continued as Lord Overton looked as if he might try to speak, "she has behaved with an entire lack of morality, worming her way in with senior staff in order to further her career. It really does beggar belief."

Lord Overton stared at me over his glasses, said Hmm, and glanced at the report again.

"Miss Lake," he said. "This reads as a quite extraordinary catalogue of deceit. *Extraordinary*. Do you have anything to say in your defence?"

Mrs. Bird was always so angry about everything that I had almost become used to it. Today she was outraged, but I had expected that and was anything but shocked. Lord Overton, however, was different. Just a few months ago, I had been so thrilled at the thought of getting a job in his company that I hadn't even listened at my interview. I cared desperately what he thought, but all he knew about me was written on the damning report in his hand. *A catalogue of deceit.* No wonder he looked at me as if I were a dreadful idiot, a slur on his publishing empire.

I couldn't let him think so badly of me. I couldn't deny the accusations, but I could try to put up a fight as I went down.

Lord Overton was waiting for an answer. I took a deep breath.

"Sir," I said, "I would like to say how tremendously sorry I am for all the trouble I have caused. I have apologised to Mrs. Bird unconditionally and I realise my actions are indefensible."

I carried on without drawing breath in case he thought that was it.

"But, Lord Overton, I really wasn't trying to *be* Mrs. Bird or do anything that would give her a bad name. I only wrote back to the readers as Mrs. Bird said she wouldn't answer them because their problems were Unacceptable—there's a very long list of things you have to ignore." I threw this in as an aside. "Anyway, lots of them sounded so sad and worried and miserable. They'd written in as a last resort in some cases. And some of their problems are just terrible. They're all trying so hard with everything and their husbands are away or they don't have their children with them. Or they do, but they feel dreadful about that too, in case they get bombed, which some of them actually have. And they're tired and . . . and *lonely* sometimes, and then when that happens, sometimes they fall in love with the wrong man and—"

"MISS LAKE."

Mrs. Bird shouted at the top of her voice. She had leapt to her feet with some agility and to all the world looked as if she might thump me.

"REALLY. THIS IS UNACCEPTABLE."

I had nothing left to lose.

"No, Mrs. Bird," I said, raising my voice. "You're not being fair."

Mrs. Bird's hand flew to her chest as her mouth dropped open.

"I'm really very, very sorry," I said quickly to Lord Overton, lowering my voice again and trying desperately to look like a sensible grown-up rather than a petulant child. "But honestly, sir, I just wanted to help. I might not know much, but I know what it's like to be young and a bit at sea, and I know what all the other magazines say and do for their readers," I said, almost pleading. "They answer modern problems. They sell lots of copies too," I added.

I ran out of steam and finished in a despondent heap. I had practised what I had hoped was a well-thought-out and dignified defence and I'd used none of it. This had to be the end.

There was a sharp knock on the door, which was flung open even before Lord Overton had a chance to snap Come, and Mr. Collins hurried into the room. He looked more dishevelled than usual, his hair unwashed and his tie at half-mast. It wasn't at all the way to attend a hearing like this but I didn't care. I was immensely pleased to see him.

"Good afternoon," he said. "Lord Overton, Mrs. Bird. I do apologise for being so late."

Mrs. Bird had What Kind Of A State Are You? written all over her face, but she glowered silently as Lord Overton greeted Mr. Collins and cordially accepted the apology. I noted that they appeared to be on familiar, if not exactly equal, terms.

"Well, Collins," the Chairman said. "This is something of a mess, don't you think? A pretty grim show. Mrs. Bird informs me that Miss Lake was originally employed by you?"

"That is correct, sir," Mr. Collins answered.

"Without consulting me," interrupted Mrs. Bird.

"I believe, Mrs. Bird," said Mr. Collins politely, "you were out of the office and otherwise engaged for much of the period."

"Important War Work," snapped Mrs. Bird, grabbing the opportunity to direct the discussion. "Lord Overton, I must raise that Mr. Collins is unable to speak without personal bias in this case. I am afraid he has Personal Relations with the accused."

Lord Overton's eyebrows shot into his hair.

"Good God," he said. "Really?"

I looked at the ground, not knowing what to be more embarrassed about: being referred to as The Accused, which made me sound like a murderer, or the fact that Mrs. Bird had just made rather a wild suggestion.

"I believe Mrs. Bird is referring to my younger brother," said Mr. Collins coolly. "Miss Lake has met Charles and is writing to him while he is away serving in the army. That's no secret. I think it's rather a decent thing actually. It's damn hard out there. Sorry, sir . . . er, *rather* hard."

Even Mr. Collins knew that today it was preferable not to swear.

"Fair's fair. I'm sure he's doing a fine job," said Lord Overton. "Not relevant to this discussion." Mrs. Bird humphed and was ignored. "So," Lord Overton said, directly at me. "Miss Lake, while I commend the passion with which you speak of our readers . . ."

My heart jumped. Mrs. Bird started to interrupt, but Lord Overton held his hand up for silence as my hopes momentarily soared, and then quickly plummeted.

"The fact remains that you took it upon yourself, without permission, to correspond in Mrs. Bird's name. You must understand that this is entirely unacceptable. However well-meaning your intentions, you have damaged the reputation of both your Acting Editress and *Woman's Friend*. I really can't—"

"Please don't sack me, Lord Overton," I said in desperation.

"Sir, might I just interrupt?" said Mr. Collins at the same time.

"What?" said Lord Overton, his patience wearing thin. "I do have another meeting. Oh, go on then, Collins, but please keep to the point."

"Thank you, sir. I will." Mr. Collins nodded. "I've just come from the Advertising Department. I have some information I think you might like to hear." He pulled his journalist's notebook from his pocket and flipped it open near the back, continuing to talk as he looked for the right page. "You see, it would appear that *Woman's Friend* is having something of a new lease of life."

Lord Overton said Hmm and Go On.

"According to Mr. Newton—he's our revenue man—subscriptions have increased quite markedly in the last two months and readers have given the thumbs up to a number of items Miss Lake has been directly involved in. Several new features of mine have been entirely her idea, and she's made me up my game on the fiction front too. I won't bore you with that," he added hastily as Lord Overton raised his hand for quiet again. "And also—"

"All right, Collins, that'll do," said Lord Overton.

"THIS IS OUTRAGEOUS," bellowed Mrs. Bird, making everyone jump. "Mr. Collins is entirely biased. Must I remind you of the appalling, unpatriotic letter printed behind my back last week? A nervy reader given almost an entire page of sympathy? It made it look as if we are working for Hitler. Lord Overton, don't listen to him."

"That went in by mistake," lied Mr. Collins evenly. "Advertising revenue is up nineteen per cent," he continued.

"Really?" said Lord Overton, looking interested. "Over what period?"

"Last four weeks," said Mr. Collins airily. "We might need to go up a sheet if we can get the paper supplies. Mr. Newton thinks we've got a good chance to turn things around."

"Lord Overton, I really must—"

"THANK YOU, Henrietta," Lord Overton snapped back. "Really, I can hear quite well. Now then. Unpatriotic. I don't think I'd go quite that far. I showed the letter in question to my wife and she thought the response extremely kind. I rather liked the part where it called Hitler a fool."

"POLI-tics, Lord Overton," snapped Mrs. Bird, remembering halfway through not to shout. "In *Woman's Friend*. Where will it end? Bolshevism, that's where."

"Bad news for What's In The Hot Pot?" said Mr. Collins under his breath. "Cabbage mostly, I'd say."

"Hardly Bolshevism," said Lord Overton, beginning to sound bored. "I thought it rather put the lunatic in his place. Now could everyone please keep quiet?"

Mrs. Bird looked as if she might die on the spot.

We all kept quiet while Lord Overton made a clicking noise with his tongue as he mulled things over. Finally, he spoke again.

"I'm sorry," he said. "But the fact remains, Miss Lake . . . oh, for God's sake. Is that my secretary? What is it now?"

We all looked towards the door. Outside we could hear Lord Overton's assistant firmly telling someone they could not see him now.

"Absolutely not," we heard her state.

"I'm terribly sorry," came a female voice. "But we really must . . ."

The door to the office flew open.

"Who the devil is this?" said Lord Overton, now at his limit.

"Wait!" I heard myself cry out. And then in a far quieter voice, "Wait."

There, in the doorway, struggling manfully to keep the door open while trying not to drop a huge, overstuffed postbag, was Clarence.

And with him, pale, skinny as anything, with a livid scar on her forehead and leaning heavily on a walking stick, was Bunty.

Mr. Collins strode across the floor and offered his arm to her. Bunty took it and walked slowly with him into the room.

Bunty was here.

I let out a half sob, half laugh, unrecognizable mad-person noise.

I couldn't for the life of me understand why she was here, but it didn't matter. It didn't matter that I was about to get the sack and everything else was a disaster. Bunty was better, or at least on her way to being better, and she was here, and I would get to speak to her.

All of a sudden, I was scared. I had so much to explain. I couldn't just run over and say how sorry I was. What if she was here for a reason I hadn't thought of and not to see me anyway? What if she still hated me?

"Hello, Em," said Bunty as the bravest smile in the world lit up her thin face.

Ignoring the fact she looked so tremendously fragile, I pushed past Lord Overton and gave her an enormous hug.

"I'm so sorry," I said. I could feel she was skin and bones under her coat. "I'm so very sorry."

"It's all right," said Bunty. "Honestly. It really is."

"Would someone please tell me what is going on?"

Bunty pulled away from me and, with her most charming smile, introduced herself.

"Lord Overton, I am sorry to barge in. My name is Marigold Tavistock and I wrote the letter that was printed in last week's magazine. The one that Emmeline answered. And this is Clarence, who I met downstairs."

Lord Overton was wearing an expression which clearly said I Haven't A Clue Who Any Of These People Are.

I stared at Bunty, my mouth open, as she continued.

"Clarence had just delivered this. It's full of letters, sir. To *Woman's Friend*. People liked what Emmy wrote. They, um, liked my letter too."

"Sir," said Clarence, which took everyone by surprise, including Clarence himself as it came out in the most magnificent baritone and made him sound as if he were in a Welsh male-voice choir. Astonished, he left it at that and concentrated on staring into middle distance and looking noble to go with his new voice.

Lord Overton now had the look of someone who had wandered into a modern art exhibition and couldn't be bothered to pretend any of it made any sense. He narrowed his eyes and looked suspicious. Mrs. Bird had been rendered momentarily speechless but had now gone quite terrifically red and was fidgeting and looking as if she were about to lay a great big egg under her feathery coat.

"How," said Lord Overton, "have so many people seen it? *Woman's Friend* has the circulation of an ant. Yes, yes, I know the subs have been going up, but to this extent?"

Mr. Collins shifted uneasily.

"I, er, well."

"What is it, Collins? What have you done now?"

"Well, sir, I mentioned Miss Tavistock's letter to a journalist friend at the Press Association," Mr. Collins said. "They thought it rather an interesting angle about young women on the home front and wired the story out—honesty and pluck and all that. It's had quite some coverage. Actually, we came out of it pretty well."

"Lord Overton, sir, I thought you might like to see some of the letters," said Bunty. "So I made Clarence bring them all up."

I had no idea how Bunty knew about this. I was nearly as bewildered as Lord Overton.

"There will be more to come, I should think," said Bunty. "Oh, Lord Overton, please don't sack Emmeline or call the police. She's been a perfect fool, but she didn't mean it, and honestly, she won't ever do it again."

Bunty looked up at the Chairman and gave him such a sad little smile that I very nearly laughed. I jumped in too, assuring him I would do everything anyone said from now on.

"I'm afraid, ladies," said Lord Overton, unmoved, "that this is about business, not doe eyes and sad faces, affecting though they are. However, no one will be calling the police. Now, Henrietta, before you say anything, I understand exactly how you feel and I don't blame you. The whole business is a disgrace. But I won't have my organization a laughing stock." He glanced at an ornate mantel clock and looked impatient. "Arresting a Junior would give the competition a field day. And as for the tabloids—"

"Lord Overton," interrupted a strangled voice beside me. "I must protest. This is an outrage. I shall have to resign. The whole affair," said Mrs. Bird, gathering momentum, "is a nonsense. I shall take legal advice."

Lord Overton took a deep breath.

"Henrietta," he said to her, almost in an aside, "you've been threatening to resign on a weekly basis since you came back."

"I may sue," said Mrs. Bird.

"Please don't," said Lord Overton mildly. "It's so very nouveau."

For a dreadful moment I thought Mr. Collins was going to laugh, but he managed to turn it into a cough. Lord Overton could not have been more inflammatory if he had set fire to Mrs. Bird's coat.

"I see," she said, mustering dignity from every fibre of her body. "In that case."

With one final, majestic rustle of feathers and crepe, Mrs. Bird swept past us all and out of the room.

Lord Overton sighed again, not uncheerfully this time.

"Well then," he said as the door slammed. "Much as this has been a diverting episode and I haven't had as much fun since my grandfather made me do a week in the post room in 1889, yes, you may well stare, young man"—Clarence forgot to be noble and nearly passed out—"this has taken up far too much of my time. Miss Lake, I am not taking this lightly. Mrs. Bird is absolutely correct. Your behaviour has been intolerable. Not a complete disaster by the look of the post, but that's hardly the point. You cannot go around making up your own rules."

"No, Lord Overton," I said, jumping to attention. "Never."

"You need clear guidance and someone to watch you like a hawk."

"Yes, sir."

"But you do seem to have some sort of understanding of the young people."

He looked at me thoughtfully.

"And if this response is anything to go by, you could be on to something. *Woman's Friend* has been with the family for decades, although, I will admit, perhaps somewhat neglected. I'd rather it didn't keel over and die. I will discuss this further with Mr. Collins. Now please get out of my office, Miss Lake, and take your friends with you."

I didn't move. Mr. Collins rolled his eyes at me theatrically.

"You Are Not Losing Your Job Just Yet," said Lord Overton, spelling it out as I looked blank. "Don't come back until Monday."

Then he turned to Mr. Collins.

"Collins," said the Chairman, "you're going to have to take her in hand. And to prove she will knuckle down, I want the circulation doubled in the next three months. Manage that between you, and I might allow Miss Lake to stay."

"In the bag, sir," said Mr. Collins with a spring in his step.

Lord Overton looked at me again and lowered his eyebrows.

"Young lady, you are damn lucky. Damn lucky. Now go away and leave me alone." He paused and I was sure I saw him try not to smile. "And for God's sake, don't tell Henrietta I said *damn*."

Chapter 28

YOU NEVER GAVE UP

I began to thank Lord Overton profusely, but he had already turned his back and was making his way to a tray of crystal decanters. Mr. Collins motioned at me to get out before the Chairman could change his mind, and as Clarence heaved the postbag back outside and hot-footed it downstairs, Bunty and I followed carefully behind.

With the door closed behind us, I guided her to a large Chesterfield chair in the waiting area outside Lord Overton's office. She looked drained and quite horribly frail.

Lord Overton's assistant, Miss Jackson, glanced over from where she had returned to sentry duty at her desk. I assumed she was about to tell us to move on, but I was wrong.

"That's all right," she said, getting up. "You can have a sit-down. We don't want anyone passing out and making the place untidy." She smiled at Bunty. "I've just read your letter to *Woman's Friend.* Don't you go worrying. You've been very brave. Well done you."

Bunty looked surprised but pleased.

"Now," added Miss Jackson, "you can have five minutes here while I make tea for Lord Overton."

"I think His Lordship may have gone onto something harder than that," I suggested.

Miss Jackson looked at me. "Hmm. You did make an impression, didn't you?" she said, and then turned to Bunty again. "I shall bring you a cup too. Sit there and if you feel as bad as you look, put your head between your knees. No offence meant."

And then she left Bunty and me on our own.

For a moment neither of us said anything. So much had happened, and now, with today's drama over, Bunty was clearly exhausted. I struggled to know where to begin.

"You've definitely driven Lord Overton to drink," said Bunty, looking up at me with a small grin. Then she ran out of steam and stared at her shoes.

Encouraged by the fact that this was exactly the sort of thing the old Bunty would say, I tried to begin.

"Thank you, for, um, coming today." I hesitated. "How did you know?"

"I saw my letter," Bunty answered. "In *Woman's Friend.* And your answer. I knew you must have written it, but I couldn't believe it was in there. From what you'd said, I was sure that Mrs. Bird wouldn't have allowed it. So I managed to get hold of Mr. Collins and he told me everything. He said he was trying to help sort things out but it looked a bit steep." She paused. "I couldn't help feeling it was all my fault. After all, if I hadn't sent the letter, you wouldn't have answered it in the magazine. I wrote it from where they sent me to a specialist, hoping you might guess it was me."

She petered out as a wave of distress washed over her face and she tried again.

"I know that was stupid," she said. "I should have just written to you. But I didn't think I could. After all these weeks of not answering." Then she looked dreadfully sad. "I'm so sorry, Em. I should have spoken to you. I've been awful."

I stared back in amazement.

"*You've* been awful?" I said, sitting down on a matching chair. "But, Bunts, it's all my fault."

I had practised in my head a million times what I would say if I had the chance, but now she was here, in Lord Overton's office of all places, it was hard to find the right words. I was still scared as anything to actually talk about what had happened.

"I messed everything up," I said finally. "Not about *Woman's Friend*, although I know I was an idiot to write to the readers. But that doesn't matter."

I took a deep breath.

"I messed it up with Bill," I said. "You were right. It's my fault he died."

Bunty began to say something, but I shook my head and she let me go on.

"We had these stupid fights. It was none of my business and I should have backed off." I felt my voice crack. "I shouldn't have been late to the . . ." I didn't want to even name the place. "To the Café de Paris. It was all my fault. I am so sorry, Bunty. I am, really."

Bunty grabbed my hand and held on to it hard.

"No, Em," she said. "It wasn't your fault. It wasn't anyone's." She bit her lip, concentrating on what she wanted to say. "I mean it. Bill told me about the rows. He said you'd tried to make things right but he hadn't let you."

She looked me straight in the eyes. "Emmy, it wasn't because of you. You must never think that. If he hadn't gone to look for you and I hadn't gone to find the telephones to call you, we would have both gone back to our seats."

Her voice wavered, but she didn't look away.

"Em," she whispered. "*All* the people in that section died. They all died."

She swallowed hard.

"I blamed you, Em, and it wasn't your fault. I was so angry about losing him. I think I just wanted to hurt someone. I'm the one who should say sorry. And actually, do you know the worst bit?"

I shook my head. Bunty's eyes brimmed with tears.

"It was the thought of losing you too. It was bad enough that he died. But without you, it was like there was no one left. I don't know what I thought I was doing."

"I can't imagine it," I said.

"I haven't coped very well," said Bunty. "And I meant what I said in that letter. I feel such a dud. Look at you, marching on. You wouldn't give up."

"I would," I said quickly. "Crikey, if it had been me, I'd have been all over the shop. And anyway, look at the hash I've made of things here. I've been pretty bloody useless myself."

Bunty wiped her eyes again and managed a smile. "Does everyone swear in journalism?" she said.

I grinned back. "They do seem to. Not that I'm really in journalism. And I was very nearly not in it at all until just now. You turning up with Clarence and all that post saved the day. You and Mr. Collins and his revenue talk."

"No," said Bunty. "Your letters did, Em. They saved me every day. I read every one you sent me. Even when I didn't know how to write back, you never gave up. And however bad things got, however desperate things felt, I always knew a letter would come. *You never gave up on me.* So in the end I knew I would have to not give up too."

I didn't know what to say. There was a fairly decent chance I would burst into tears just as Miss Jackson was likely to come back. I tried to focus on today, rather than the past.

"I still can't believe you came to the office, Bunts," I said. "And barged in on Lord Overton. It was like something out of a film. Ever so heroic."

"I didn't mean to," said Bunty, looking surprised at herself. "I'm only supposed to be in London to see how I feel about going back to the flat. Granny's a bit worried about that. She's waiting for me there now. Actually," she continued, "I'm a bit worried about it too. Just, um, you know, seeing all the wedding things."

"Mother and I tidied up a bit," I said gently. "We were ever so careful."

Bunty looked grateful but concerned. "Did you really? Thank you."

"It's all still there, of course. For when you want to look at it all."

Bunty bit her lip again. I ploughed on.

"So," I ventured. "Are you planning to come back?"

Bunty nodded. "Unless you've found yourself a new flatmate?" she managed.

"Well, Clarence is too young," I said.

"And Mr. Collins too old," said Bunty on purpose, adding as I looked mortified, "What a shame he doesn't have a younger brother."

We both laughed.

"You never mentioned Charles in your letters," Bunty continued. "Is everything all right?"

I nodded. "I hope so. I didn't think you'd want to know."

"You idiot, of course I want to know," said Bunty. "I want to know everything that has been happening. I've missed you like anything, Em."

From behind the heavy oak door to Lord Overton's office, a deep bellow of laughter broke out.

Bunty and I looked at each other.

"That's a good sign," whispered Bunty.

"Fingers crossed," I said. "You will come back to London, won't you, Bunts?"

She nodded. "If you don't mind me clumping around after you with this," she said, looking at her stick and giving the floor a dull thump with the end.

"Don't be silly," I said. "And anyway, you'll be whizzing around soon."

"It's going to take me forever to get up to the flat," said Bunty. "I've asked Granny if she wouldn't mind letting us use some of the other rooms. She's not thrilled with me coming back in the first place, to be honest, but she said if we wanted to, it was all right."

Bunty didn't need to spell it out. I knew it wasn't about managing the stairs. The flat held too many memories now.

"We could get a lodger," I suggested brightly.

"Can you imagine Granny's face if we did?" laughed Bunty. "She'd go mad."

"Someone she'd approve of," I suggested, laughing too. "A distressed gentleperson. Or someone from the Women's Institute."

"Or from work?" joined in Bunty, looking properly interested. "The War Office has tons of people who need rooms."

"Top secret people," I said. "Or even . . ."

"SPIES!" we shouted at the same time.

"We could let out the basement as well," I added.

"Oh yes," said Bunty, warming to a new plan. "That would be terrific. Mrs. Harewood next door knows lots of Interesting Types. Displaced Europeans, Free French . . ."

"All bound to be undercover," I interrupted, looking knowledgeable. "Our side, of course."

"Of course," said Bunty. "Honestly, Em, I think this is a super idea. We could have all sorts of exciting people to stay." My best friend's thin little face lit up. "Oh, Emmy," she said. "I'm so pleased to be back."

"Me too," I said, grinning. "Come on, Bunts." I took her arm as she leant heavily on her stick to get up. "Let's go home and start a new plan."

AUTHOR'S NOTE

The idea for *Dear Mrs. Bird* began when I came across a 1939 copy of a women's magazine. It was a wonderful find—a glimpse into an era and world where I could read about everything from recipes for lamb's brain stew to how to knit your own swimwear.

But the thing I loved the most was the Problem Page. Among the hundreds of letters I went on to read while researching the novel, there have been many that made me smile—such as asking what to do about freckles, or trouble with people who pushed into queues. Most of all, though, I was struck by the huge number of letters in which women faced unimaginably difficult situations in the very toughest of times.

Readers were sometimes lonely, hadn't seen their loved ones for years, or knew that now they never would. Others had turned to the wrong man or "lost their heads" and found themselves in trouble with no one to help. Some faced problems any of us might relate to, but of course in circumstances I hope we never will. Many wrote in for advice about decisions they knew would impact their lives forever.

It was clear that wartime women's magazines provided even more to their readers than making do, getting the most out of rations, or knitting and sewing—important and necessary though these all were.

The replies from the agony aunts surprised me, too. They weren't just clichéd Keep Calm and Carry On responses. More often than not they were sympathetic, supportive, and suggesting practical help.

Slowly the magazines became a bridge into a world I wanted to write about, an inspiration for characters that wanted to speak and the adventures they wanted to have.

Whenever I show some of my collection of magazines to people as we talk about *Dear Mrs. Bird*, I love seeing how it is only ever a matter of seconds before they are drawn into the lives of women in wartime Britain. Digital age or not, magazines are something lots of us still know, read, and love—reading old copies somehow transports us back in time. When I pick up a magazine that is now nearly eighty years old, I always wonder where it was first read: Was the reader sitting in their kitchen like me? Or sneaking a look during her lunch break, or sitting on a bus engrossed in a story while it drove past bombed-out buildings? Perhaps she was even reading it out loud to friends in a shelter as a diversion during a raid? I'll never know, of course, but in my head sometimes I raise my mug of tea to her and hope everything turned out all right.

Many of the readers' letters in *Dear Mrs. Bird* were inspired by the letters and advice, articles and features printed in those wartime magazines. I found them thought-provoking, moving, and inspirational, and my admiration for the women of that time never stops growing. Our mothers, grandmothers, great-grandmothers, and friends, some of whom I hope may even read and enjoy Emmy and Bunty's story. It is a privilege to look into their world and remember what incredible women and girls they all were.

AJ Pearce

ACKNOWLEDGEMENTS

I am so grateful to the best people ever, who have helped, supported, and cheered *Dear Mrs. Bird* on its way to becoming a book. Without you I'd still be sitting in an office looking out the window and wondering if I could ever write a book of my own.

When writing the novel, I read widely—books and papers, of course, and hundreds of magazines from the period. But most of all I would like to thank everyone who listened to my questions about living through the war, especially my parents, who had endless visits, phone calls, and emails quizzing them about their childhood, and Mrs. Brenda Evans, who graciously let me ambush her when she could have been enjoying family events. My special thanks to Mrs. Joyce Powell, who, with her daughter Jane James, so kindly answered my questions about working for the Auxiliary Fire Service. Mrs. Powell, you inspired the spirit of Emmy, Bunty, and the girls on B Watch in the air-raid scenes. I hope I have done you and your friends justice—and that you will forgive any poetic licence I have taken. If there are any factual errors they are entirely my fault, of course.

Thank you to Jo Unwin, my ace agent, who is kind and clever and fearless and funny, and the ultimate warrior for a worrier. You make this the most brilliant fun. To Saba Ahmed, Isabel Adomakoh Young, and Milly Reilly, thank you for always making me feel like a proper writer.

To the marvellous Deborah Schneider at Gelfman Schneider, who made the dream of having a publisher in the USA a reality, I am so grateful to you and everyone at Scribner, especially Nan Graham, who I still cannot believe I get to say is my publisher. And to Emily Greenwald, Stephanie Evans, Jaya Miceli, Kate Lloyd, and Kara Watson, who puts up with manuscripts arriving stuffed full of eighty-year-old Britishisms with such wonderful grace.

To everyone at Picador and Pan Macmillan, thank you for being so supportive and enthusiastic about *Dear Mrs. Bird* right from the start, especially Paul Baggaley, Anna Bond, Katie Tooke, Kish Widyaratna, Camilla Elworthy, and Nicholas Blake. And of course, special hugest of thanks to Francesca Main for her thoughtfulness, kindness, and sheer editorial amazingness. It really is an honour to work with you all.

To Alexandra McNicoll, Alexander Cochran, and Jake Smith-Bosanquet at C+W for sending Emmy and Bunty around the planet and risking international relationships daily by sending *Dear Mrs. Bird* with them. I still really hope you have a big map and lots of little wooden books being poked across it with a stick!

To all my brilliant friends, especially:

Katie Fforde, Jo Thomas, Penny Parkes, Judy Astley, and Clare Mackintosh, thank you for your encouragement and belief from the start and for telling me to get on with it. Katie, you are my hero and always will be! Julie Cohen, for being the most patient, insightful, and inspiring mentor: a writing Wing Commander of the highest, kindest order. And Shelley Harris, for reading a first scrappy half-draft and having the generosity to make me believe that one day a real live agent might possibly want to read it.

Janice Withey and Inca, who walked hundreds of miles with me as I went on and on about the dream. You let me talk and never once told me to shut up—that deserves a marathon gold! Gail Cheetham for listening and understanding what I care about the most. And Rachel and Chris Bird who lived all of this pretty much from day one and were always there, whatever happened. Mrs. Bird would be proud to share your name, although obviously thoroughly appalled at the thought of wine and snacks being handed over the fence.

And to Brin Greenman, Nicki Pettitt, Mary Ford, Sue Thearle, and Ginetta George. There are a million things for which I owe you, but I absolutely treasure that you all just took it for granted I would be able to write a book. With you as friends I reckon it might just be possible to achieve almost anything.

Finally, to Mum, Dad, Toby, and Lori. For everything. We may be small in number, but there isn't a family in the world that is mightier in heart. Thank you.

DEAR MRS. BIRD

AJ PEARCE

This reading group guide for *Dear Mrs. Bird* includes discussion questions and ideas for enhancing your book club. The suggested questions are intended to help your reading group find new and interesting angles and topics for your discussion. We hope that these ideas will enrich your conversation and increase your enjoyment of the book.

Topics & Questions for Discussion

1. "There's nothing that can't be sorted with common sense and a strong will" (page 36) begins the description of Mrs. Bird's column, Henrietta Helps. In theory, that's not such a bad approach, but how does it fall short of addressing her readers' concerns?
2. Why does the memory of her friend Kitty's experience affect Emmy so strongly? How does it inform her actions?

3. Author AJ Pearce incorporates charmingly old-fashioned expressions to help convey a sense of the time period. What were some of your favorite terms? Did the language help your understanding of the era and the characters' personalities?
4. Mr. Collins advises Emmy, "Find out what you're good at . . . and then get even better. That's the key" (page 54). Is this good advice for Emmy? Does she follow it?
5. Why does Emmy hesitate to tell Bunty about writing to Mrs. Bird's readers? Is she only worried about Bunty's disapproval or is it more than that? How do secrets affect their friendship throughout the novel?
6. Do you think Emmy was right to confront William after he rescued the two children? Was his reaction warranted? Why do you think they took such different views of the event?
7. One of the major themes of the novel is friendship. Discuss Emmy and Bunty's relationship and all the ways they support and encourage each other over the course of the novel.
8. After the bombing at Café de Paris, Bunty is distraught and angry, but is some of her critique of Emmy fair? Does Emmy interfere too much?
9. Whether it's readers writing in to Mrs. Bird, Charles writing to Emmy, or Emmy writing to Bunty, letters are of great importance throughout *Dear Mrs. Bird.* How does letter-writing shape the narrative?
10. The letter from Anxious on page 239 strikes a chord with Emmy. She thinks, "How often did we say well done to our readers? How often did anyone ever tell women they were doing a good job? That they didn't need to be made of steel all the time? That it was all right to feel a bit down?" (page 243). How did the book make you think differently about women's experiences in wartime?

11. Emmy's mother says to her, "Once this silly business is all sorted, you and Bunty and all your friends will be able to get on and achieve whatever you want" (page 86). How much do you think expectations have changed for young women since World War II? What careers do you think Emmy and Bunty would aspire to if they were young now?

12. In the Author's Note (page 277), AJ Pearce describes how reading advice columns in vintage magazines inspired her to write *Dear Mrs. Bird*. She says, "I found them thought-provoking, moving, and inspirational, and my admiration for the women of that time never stops growing. . . . It is a privilege to look into their world and remember what incredible women and girls they all were" (page 278). Discuss how magazines, then and now, provide a unique window into people's lives.

Enhance Your Book Club

1. Discuss advice columns as a group. Do you read them? Which ones? What are some of the group's favorites? Bring some advice columns in and discuss them together. How would you write an advice column?

2. On pages 204 and 205, Emmy describes seeing propaganda posters meant to motivate and boost morale on the British home front during the war. Visit the Imperial War Museum's website to see examples: www.iwm.org.uk/learning/resources/second-world-war-posters.